Destination Unknown

A Tale of Time Travel

Kathleen Ballantine Watson

ARCHWAY
PUBLISHING

Archway Publishing books may be ordered through booksellers or by contacting:

Archway Publishing
1663 Liberty Drive
Bloomington, IN 47403
www.archwaypublishing.com
1 (888) 242-5904

Because of the dynamic nature of the Internet, any web addresses or links contained in this book may have changed since publication and may no longer be valid. The views expressed in this work are solely those of the author and do not necessarily reflect the views of the publisher, and the publisher hereby disclaims any responsibility for them.

Any people depicted in stock imagery provided by Thinkstock are models, and such images are being used for illustrative purposes only. Certain stock imagery © Thinkstock.

ISBN: 978-1-4808-4899-3 (sc)
ISBN: 978-1-4808-4897-9 (hc)
ISBN: 978-1-4808-4898-6 (e)

Library of Congress Control Number: 2017911424

Print information available on the last page.

Archway Publishing rev. date: 01/17/2018

Many thanks to my children, grandchildren,
family and friends who have listened to me tell my story
at one time or another in the last thirteen years.
This book is for *YOU!*

Friday

September 16, 2016

Chapter 1

The song "Easy like Sunday Morning" by Lionel Richie played on Beth's cell phone. She listened to the music through the earphones while eating her ham and cheese sandwich.

She enjoyed the view of Diamond Lake and pondered the name. The sun's rays glistened on the water like millions of dazzling diamonds. She nodded *Yep, it fits.*

A gust of wind brought with it the sweet aroma of jasmine. Beth took in a deep breath. *There can't be a better place than this right now.*

Flipping her long blonde hair over the bench, Beth leaned her head back closing her eyes. She heard birds chirping, children laughing, and rustling of leaves. Embracing the euphoric moment, she was mesmerized by the variety of sounds. It amazed her how the sense of hearing seemed amplified when one took away sight.

What she didn't hear was hidden behind the bushes. Not far from where Beth's erratic thoughts had her captivated, the snapping of a camera slipped by unnoticed. Unheard were the footsteps of a man in the shadows as he disappeared, satisfied with his work.

Beth pushed back a feeling of dread and glanced at her watch. She realized the time had gotten away from her. She jumped up like the rabbit in *Alice in Wonderland* and brushed the crumbs off her slacks. With the other hand, she stuffed the rest of the sandwich in her mouth. She gathered her things and while exiting the park, she picked up her pace.

Nearing the hill bordering the park, she came to a steep, concrete staircase and sprinted up. When reaching the top, the energy switched from positive to negative. Instead of happy people in a serene setting, frustrated, impatient people rushed everywhere.

The scene changed from park benches and swans to skyscrapers and traffic lights.

The noise of jackhammers and honking replaced the sound of birds chirping and squeals of laughter.

The stink of smog took over the aroma of jasmine.

In the midst of the crowd, Beth worked her way to the traffic light. Squeezing through the mass to the edge of the street, a red sports car zoomed by. The deafening racket caused her to stumble back into the mob of pedestrians. The light turned green, but now she couldn't move, she stood and shook like a leaf.

Once her nerves calmed, Beth hustled across the street. She dodged her way down the busy sidewalk to the *Willis Mortgage Company*. Upon entering her workplace, she turned slamming the door as if something was chasing her.

A co-worker rushed up to her. Silvia, a spunky redhead, resembled a wind-up toy that never stopped. The other co-workers didn't like her bossy manner. But as a friend, she had your back.

One of the company's underwriters, she and Beth worked closely together. During work they acted professional, but after hours they morphed into the nonsensical ones. Friday nights they spent dancing and partying at the local club - although, not much lately.

"Beth Nielson, where've you been? Get in here." Silvia grabbed her arm. "There's been another murder." She pulled

Beth into the large break room where their co-workers stood in front of the television.

Channel elevens news announcer reported on the Minneapolis serial killer. "In the last eleven months, six women's lives ended in their homes. Each had been stabbed twice in the chest and their faces slashed beyond recognition."

He continued with their description, "All identical with long blonde hair, blue eyes, and a slim frame of five foot, six."

"Beth," Tony said, "That's you in a nutshell."

Beth loved Tony like a brother. They'd worked together four years, but he had a lot of drama. The handsome twenty-six-year-old wore a neatly trimmed goatee, and with his mussed up dishwater-blonde hair, he could turn a girl's head.

However, he was gay. That made him as much fun as Beth's female counterparts, if not more. Tony had been the class clown throughout his years in school and claimed, "Laughter's the mask of masculinity."

"Tony, that description fits a lot of women." Beth rolled her eyes as she walked out of the room. *All I need now is a serial killer after me. I already have an ex-boyfriend stalking me.*

Beth dragged her feet to her piled-high desk and stared at it. Rather than digging in, she turned on her heel and headed for the bathroom where she locked everyone out. Sauntering to the padded bench across from the vanity, she plopped down and bent over. Putting her head in her hands, she thought, *my life is the complete opposite of 'Easy like Sunday Morning.'*

Silvia knocked on the door. "Can I come in?"

"Is there nowhere to hide?" Beth mumbled. She stood, shuffled to the door and swung it open.

Silvia, along with Tony, slipped in.

She returned to the bench and plunked down.

Silvia and Tony followed and sat on each side of her. There

wasn't room for all of them, but they squeezed in anyway. It actually made Beth giggle a little.

Inseparable, the three were the center of the party wherever they went - but not so much anymore.

Silvia tapped Beth's hand. "We're worried about you keeping to yourself all the time. Talk to us."

Tony, being facetious, said, "You don't even go to the club with us anymore. I can't be the center of attention *all* the time."

"Oh, p-l-eez." Silvia rolled her eyes.

"Girlfriend," Tony pointed at Beth. "You need a night out. A bunch of us are going to the club tonight. Come with us. What do you say?"

Beth's lips quivered as she answered, "Not this evening Tony." Pausing long enough to wipe a single tear away, she cried, "I hate my life. I'm twenty-five years old, and I've got no control of my destiny. I want kids, but you have to meet a decent guy first, right?"

Silvia placed her hand over Beth's. "I think there's more to your depression. Let's see if we can figure it out. Stop me if I'm wrong. A psychotic ex-boyfriend's stalking you. You work for one of the busiest mortgage brokers in the area with the meanest boss. Worse, you're her assistant and the one she kicks around the most. Does that about cover it?"

Beth crossed her legs. With an elbow on her knee, she rested her chin in her palm and let out a sigh. "You forgot to mention I'm homeless. I should never have given up my apartment to move in with that knucklehead."

Silvia threw her hands up in the air. "I told you to stay with me until you get your place."

"You have a studio, Silvia. Thanks anyway, but the motel's temporary. Next week my apartment will be ready. Besides, it's not just that. It's everything. My job used to be great, but with all the changes, it sucks."

Tony crossed one leg over the other. Wiggling his foot he

stated, "Well, we no longer have Mr. Willis. He held this place together."

Silvia smiled, "He reminded me of Mr. Grant from the *Mary Tyler Moore Show*. Beth, you're the Mary replica, only with blonde hair." Silvia laughed and gave her friend a playful nudge.

Tony, still shaking his foot, said, "He never put us beneath his feet like what's going on now. The place had real camaraderie back then. Bummer you had to be the one to find him, Beth."

Six months ago, Beth discovered their former administrator passed out in his office chair. He never regained consciousness. He died at the hospital that night from a massive heart attack. At sixty-four, he'd looked forward to retiring in a year. His death devastated the entire staff. The place hadn't been the same since the owners brought in the new administrator. Mrs. Steinhart, a stout fifty-six-year-old towering woman, filled Mr. Willis' position. Since then, there has been nothing but stress and hurry, hurry, hurry.

"I think Steinhart is miserable because she's in the wrong business. She should be a prison warden," chuckled Tony.

Silvia chortled, "Oh my God, Tony, it's funny you say that. Last night, I watched the TV series, *Wentworth*. I thought Ferguson, the warden of the prison, looked and acted like Steinhart. The prisoners call her *The Freak*. What a hoot."

Another knock on the door, it was Cheryl this time. This attractive brunette, shorter in stature than the rest, was a little on the chunky side. Regardless, she always looked well put together with her fashionable attire. She was also the calm one of the group with her soft-spoken demeanor and was the one to go to when sharing confidences.

Cheryl talked through the closed door, "Beth, Mrs. Steinhart's on her way. She wants to see you in her office the minute she arrives."

Beth, Silvia, and Tony all stood at the same time and frowned at each other.

"Great," Silvia rolled her eyes. "Back to prison, *The Freak* is coming."

Beth gathered a deep breath, opened the door and came out with Silvia and Tony following.

Cheryl shot a sly look at the lone male, "Really, Tony? I thought this was the woman's bathroom?"

Tony strutted past her, raised his brow and shook his finger saying, "And don't you forget it, girlfriend."

Cheryl gave him a high five. "It's a good thing everybody loves you, Tony. Now get back to work."

Employed by the Company for six years, Cheryl was the office secretary. The woman reminded Beth of a female version of Radar from the series *Mash*. Cheryl had an uncanny way of knowing things before they happened. She would take the words right out of Steinhart's mouth. It was quite comical to watch. Dumbfounded and speechless, Steinhart never knew how to react. When it happened during the board meetings, the office manager, Lori, wouldn't dare look Beth's way. Keeping a straight face would be impossible. At times the two had to excuse themselves because they couldn't keep from laughing out loud.

Cheryl took Beth aside. "Listen, that rumor going around," she pursed her lips and paused, "it's not a rumor, Beth."

"Which rumor?"

"The company plans to stop home mortgages. They're going to focus on large business loans." Cheryl placed her hand on Beth's arm. "There will be changes around here, more than we thought."

"Will the company send me for training?"

"That's what I need to tell you. Mrs. Steinhart's bringing her assistant from her last job. Claims this woman is qualified and won't need any training."

"What will happen to my job? She won't need two assistants."

"I'm sorry, but she plans on moving you to one of their offices in Illinois. You'll educate the new employees on home mortgages. She told them you'd be perfect and wouldn't require training. Sound familiar? Guess she uses the same line every time."

"But I don't want to move to Illinois. What if I say no?"

"She'll offer you compensation pay and unemployment and will justify it by saying your position no longer exists."

"But my brother Russ lives here. He's the only family I have. What can I do? Now's not a good time to make big changes."

"I wanted to give you a heads up. With Mr. Willis gone, the owners are doing what they've always wanted to do. Heck, we may all wind up leaving."

Tony came from around the corner and pointed toward the entrance door. "Ferguson alert."

Beth wanted to run and hide. Before she could put off the inevitable, Steinhart spotted her and motioned for her to come. So hanging her head like a whipped puppy, Beth obeyed.

Steinhart got settled in her office and turned to Beth. "Sit down. We've something important to discuss."

Rumors floated around the office like feathers from a down pillow. Nobody knew which were real and which ones were false, except Cheryl and sometimes, Lori, the office manager. The companies' petite office manager was Beth's age and another one of the weekend partiers. But she took her job seriously and if anybody knew anything about the company, she did. Tony, in his spare time, hung out in her office. His co-workers would send him in there to get the truth, or at the least, the latest gossip. The copy machine sat in the corner so Tony often brought in unnecessary paperwork to make it appear he had a legitimate reason for being in there.

Lori sat at her desk going through a stack of documents when Tony came in. Setting the papers on the copy machine,

Tony plopped himself onto the overstuffed chair meant for clients.

"Lori, I'm worried about Beth. Her plate's piled high, and now her asshole ex is giving her a hard time."

"Yeah, I know. Beth told me he's stalking her. Creepy." Lori continued working.

"You got that right. Did she tell you she filed a restraining order against him?"

"Yes, she did. I never trusted that guy. Ever since I met him, creepy Gary went overboard to impress everyone. He's always buying stuff like a boat or something big. Then we have to listen to him brag about it. It got sickening. I couldn't stand to be in the same room with him."

"That won't be happening anytime soon. Have you heard the latest? He got busted for pedophilia."

Lori stopped working and stared at Tony. She had not heard this. "Did he get arrested?"

"Not by a cop. Gary got busted by a guy pretending to be a fifteen-year-old girl on a chat line. Anybody can go to the website and read the conversation between him and who he thought was a teenager."

"What?" Lori got up and shut the door. She swung around and asked, "Are you sure about this Tony?"

No sooner had Lori closed the door when Cheryl opened it a crack. "Hello? Is this door closed for a reason?"

Lori pulled Cheryl into the office, closed the door and pointed to her. "Does she know?"

Tony nodded.

"I'm the office manager, the one everybody tells everything to. So why is it I haven't heard this? Poor Beth." Lori's hand went to her forehead as she walked around in small circles.

"Listen, guys," Cheryl said, trying to keep them calm. "Things are going to hit the fan around here. Beth needs all the support we can give her so let's keep this under our hats, okay?" She glanced at her watch. Beth had been in Steinhart's office for fifteen minutes and Cheryl was getting more nervous with every passing minute.

Tony, jumping to his feet, asked, "What do you mean craps going to hit the fan? What are you talking about?"

"Change comes with new bosses. Not always the kind we want."

The door opened and Beth came in. Cheryl's eyes widened as she gave Beth a "What happened?" look.

Beth made her way to where Tony had been sitting and eased into the chair. Moments passed before she said anything.

Tony and Lori gave Cheryl a "What's going on?" look.

Beth finally spoke, "I guess Mrs. Steinhart's leaving Monday to go out of town for a week. She wanted to go over everything I need to do while she's gone."

Cheryl gave a sigh of relief, pulled out a chair and plopped down. She had been expecting, a - not so good scene.

Beth leaned over to Cheryl and said in a low voice, "Guess I dodged a bullet for another week."

Silvia poked her head in the door and warned the rest saying, "Mrs. Steinhart's on her way, so break it up in here."

Tony gathered his papers and reminded Beth, "Honey, don't forget, next Friday we're having your twenty-sixth birthday party. No park that day, okay? Now I'm getting the hell out of dodge before the warden arrives. I advise you all to do the same."

Beth and Cheryl followed suit.

At a safe distance, Cheryl pulled Beth aside. "Let's meet after work tonight for a drink. You can vent, cry on my shoulders if you want."

"I can't, Cheryl. I have all my stuff in the car. I'm going straight to Russ'."

"Come on Beth, its Friday! Your brother only lives an hour away. You've gone to his place every weekend for a month. I miss you."

"Russ needs me and I need him during these weird times. Give me a little more time to work things out. I don't think I'd be much fun for anybody tonight. How about we plan to go out next Friday for my birthday?"

"Promise?"

Beth put two fingers up. "Scouts honor."

Chapter 2

Russ Nielson stood at the kitchen stove with a wooden spoon sampling his spaghetti sauce. A red droplet fell from the utensil onto his shirt. Grabbing a towel he hurried to the sink. After soaking a corner with cold water, he dabbed at the stain. *Damn, I shouldn't have put this on yet.*

Russ tossed the towel over his shoulder. He turned the burner down to a simmer and headed for the dining room mirror. After examining the shirt in his reflection, he decided it was good enough. Leaning closer, he rubbed his fingers over his chin. He's one of those handsome men who looked great with a five o'clock shadow, but tonight he was cleanly shaven. He ran his fingers through his dark brown hair. His pompadour style haircut with the sides cut short accentuated his strong-jaw-line.

Turning around Russ inspected the dinner setting. Normally, they had TV dinners, or some pre-made dinner served on paper plates. He had no time for cooking and cleaning. But since Beth had been going through such a rough spell lately, Russ wanted to do something special for her. Plus, he had something of importance to tell her.

The setting consisted of his mother's delicate china which complemented the cherry wood Victorian table. In the center sat two tapered candles ready to be lit. Beth's favorite wine,

Cabernet Sauvignon was chilling in the ice bucket ready to be uncorked.

This event is the first time Russ used the formal dining room since the fatal car accident. The misfortune claimed the lives of their parents nine years ago. Russ just turned twenty-one, Beth was seventeen.

They cared for one another after the horrific tragedy. Still, Beth experienced a severe depression while Russ' pain proved to be productive. It drove him further into his passion.

As an inventor, he never remembered a time when he wasn't making some gadget or another. At fourteen his parents turned over the 500 square foot basement room for him to use as a laboratory. After clearing out the storage, Russ and his father hung sheetrock and cleaned the unused fireplace. Beth and her mother painted the walls and set up a quaint sitting area around the hearth. His dad set up two long tables for his son's drawings and blueprints. Shelves and drawers lined the walls. The budding inventor had more storage than needed for organizing his inventory, which back then consisted of small appliances and electronics, or whatever his father's work buddies donated for him to dismantle.

Russ lived on the outskirts of Forest Lake, a quaint town twenty-seven miles north of Minneapolis, Minnesota. Beth leased an apartment in the metropolitan area. Commuting over an hour in horrendous traffic was too stressful for her. But lately, because of all the adverse events, she drove back and forth every weekend.

Satisfied with the table setting, Russ headed back to the kitchen and prepared the garlic bread. Afterward, he set it aside and glanced at his watch. There was time to spare. He took off the apron, hung it on the hook and headed for the lab.

In the basement, he shuffled down the long hallway and stopped halfway to the door on the right. This room, where ideas come into existence, is where Russ spent most of his waking hours, and it was kept locked at all times.

Pulling the keys out of his pocket, Russ unlocked the door and stepped in. His face lit up as his eyes narrowed in to his most incredible invention ever.

Russ named it "The Scorpion." In the dim lit room, the thing appeared to be a monstrous scorpion ready to strike. On the tip of the tail, a curved strip of lighting bent backward, forming a stinger. The thing cast an eerie shadow resembling an arachnid.

Russ turned on the light, and the Scorpion revealed itself. It wasn't huge. The cockpit, made from a small electric car frame, stood not much bigger than a large motorbike. Russ cut each piece to his preferred shape and coated them with multi-layers of stabilized zirconium-reinforced with titanium hardware.

The machine sat two passengers, one in the front and one behind, like a small plane.

Located on the control panel was the starter switch and a green return button - which brought the machine back within seconds of the original time. In the center were two levers for controlling past and future speed.

The blue cobalt tail of the machine contained the complex mechanism which powered the vehicle. It embodied five separate hulls scooping upward from the cockpit. The casings went from big to small, which made the device appear as a tail.

It took Russ ten years to build his dream and now, he was ready to become one with it.

Chapter 3

Beth worked until 6:30 p.m. to finish the tasks given by the *Freak* as Silvia so titled Steinhart. She bid goodbye to the ones still working and headed for the almost empty, dimly lit parking lot. Thinking about the disturbing news on the television earlier, she picked up her pace. The announcer reported the women died in their homes - not parking lots. That brought a minuscule amount of relief.

She scurried to her vehicle, scrambled in, locked it and took a deep breath. After starting the car she turned, and that's when she spotted the black sedan. It sat four spots away on the opposite side. She recognized it by the broken left headlight and the dent on the passenger side.

Somebody has been stalking her for over a week now, but she had ditched the car before getting to the motel. It was always after dusk so it was difficult to see the person driving. Beth heard her ex-boyfriend bought a different car, and she suspected it was his.

After backing up, she left the parking lot. She turned onto the busy three-lane street and took a right at the corner - so did the black sedan. As she headed toward the interstate, she made some unnecessary turns to lose the stalker. The sedan kept up with her in the late hour traffic but kept a distance of two car lengths.

When hitting the red light- the longest one on the route - she dialed Gary's phone. If the person answered, she'd be sure it was him. She used star six-seven so her number wouldn't be revealed. The phone rang once.

"Hello?" Gary bellowed.

It stunned her when he answered so quickly. She glanced in the rearview mirror - the individual did not have a phone to their ear.

"Hello?" Gary shouted again.

The background was noisy, probably a bar during Happy Hour she figure. Someone called his name, and he hung up.

Beth sat dumbfounded. Her eyes strained to identify the dark figure through her mirror. Irate now, she muttered, "Who in the *hell* are you?"

Chapter 4

Did she spot me? The stalker wasn't sure but couldn't take any chances. So when Beth made a right, he continued straight and drove home.

After parking the car, the man shoved his keys into his pocket. Old rundown three-story brick structures lined the street and the only street lamps working were the ones flickering. He trudged his way through the shadows and down the cracked filled sidewalk to his apartment. Taking hold of the railing, he pulled himself up the steps to the entryway of the decrepit building. He threw the door open and tramped inside, disgusted at himself for being so careless. *I shouldn't have gotten that close!*

The bent-over man limped up to the second floor and hobbled down the long, dingy hallway. The stained, ripped carpet stunk of bad mildew. He heard a baby crying in one apartment and the brawling of a man and a woman in another.

When getting to his residence, the pursuer pulled the keys out of his pocket and unlocked three locks. He made his way through the filthy studio that smelled like cigar smoke - to another secured door. Once unlocked, he entered a tiny room which comprised a twin bed and a small nightstand. The area was to serve as closet space but now it was a provision for his deviant needs.

The man reached into his pocket, pulled out a switchblade and tossed it onto the unmade bed. A cockroach scurried up the wall attempting to remain unseen. The nasty bug darted behind a picture. It wasn't an ordinary wall hanging like you'd expect to see in the homes of normal people. Instead, it proved to be the one of many that revealed the core of this man's sick and perverted life.

Photographs of blood-splattered faces covered the wall. Pictures of his victims posed like statues. Some images, all different, were before their horrifying deaths, but the after pictures were similar. All had blood smeared blonde hair and blue eyes still propped open.

Theodore James Collins was born 1985 to Edward and Grace Collins in Mason City, Iowa. He came out screaming like an ordinary newborn but wasn't by any means normal. Born with a spinal deformity causing a heinous hunch back, the baby was also cursed with a cleft palate and had a hair lip clear up to his nose making it look like a constant sneer. The moment his parents laid eyes on the infant they found him loathsome and repulsive.

Once home, his parents left the disfigured baby alone in the crib. Cuddling wasn't an option. Many times he wore the same diaper for hours on end. Through his toddler years and beyond, the boy never bonded with one human.

Four years later, Theodore's mother gave birth to another baby. A beautiful girl, who grew up to be her daddy's princess and her mother's pride and joy. After the birth of his sister, Theodore's parents moved him to the basement. His new scrounge room contained a mattress on the floor while his sister's room looked like a beautiful kingdom, fit for a princess.

His toilet sat in the spider-filled corner. The young boy would spend his days searching for bugs. He would put them in jars and took pleasure in pulling them apart torturing them a little at a time until they died. He imagined the insects were his parents, who in the meantime went about their lives as if they had no son.

The flawless daughter grew to be a gorgeous child with thick blonde hair and baby blue eyes that sparkled like topaz gemstones. At the young age of ten, she had already won numerous beauty contests.

Her beauty on the inside wasn't so appealing though. Spoiled beyond rotten wasn't enough to describe the girl. His sister was no better than the ones who gave birth to him. She treated Theodore with abominable contempt even refusing to be in the same room with him.

The sixteenth year of Theodore's miserable life, he murdered his family while they slept. He stabbed his parents three times in the chest but took extra time with his sister by slashing her face beyond the point of recognition.

Theodore spent the next twenty years in a mental asylum. Because of good behavior, an appeal was requested. It was approved as long as a rehabilitation program was completed. He followed through with flying colors, and the courts released him back to the public. It proved to be a horrible mistake because it wasn't long before he began killing women who looked just like his sister.

A year later, Theodore moved to Minnesota with a former patient, George Wilcox. George took over his deceased uncle's old black sedan along with a little cash. Like Theodore, he now had no family. George talked him into going on this trip, which didn't take much convincing. Halfway to Minneapolis, Theodore murdered George and took over his car and identity.

Now he's a dishwasher in a busy restaurant in Minneapolis. His alias is George Wilcox, and nobody gives him the time of day. He's left alone, and that's how he likes it.

Six women are now dead in Minneapolis, and his focus is on the unsuspecting Beth. He's been watching her for over a month. However, his plan to kill her became complicated.

Now she's staying at a motel. He prefers to kill women in their homes, as he did his family, but he could wait.

Theodore shuffled to the wall covered canvas of raw images and narrowed in on a picture of Beth, sitting at the park. He ran his fingers over her face and hissed, "Soon, very soon."

Chapter 5

After exiting the hectic interstate, Beth needed to stop at the little country store that was located in the middle of nowhere for eggs. It seemed Russ had her picking up one thing or another every time she went to his place.

Beth pulled into the parking lot and before unlocking her door, she made a visual sweep. Still not confident she wasn't being followed, she raced to the store. Once inside, she slowed down to a stroll. Beth paid for the eggs and once outside, zipped to the car.

The six blocks to her brother's home were void of street lights which made the drive creepier yet. Since she left the city, she saw no signs of being followed, but she couldn't shake the eerie vibes.

Beth pulled into the long driveway and parked close to the house. She still had a twenty-foot walk to the entryway. Grabbing her overnight bag she unlocked the car door. With keys in hand, she dashed to the house still looking over her shoulder. She unlocked the door and scurried inside and wasted no time turning to lock it. But the latch wouldn't catch. After a few frustrating tries, the bolt finally worked.

Taking a deep breath of relief, Beth dropped the overnight bag and set her purse on the entryway table. She threw her keys into the bowl completing the ritual and went in search for Russ. Hearing him in the kitchen, she headed that way. It surprised her to find him cooking.

"Well, well, look who's making a meal."

No sooner did she say that when Russ handed her a plate of spaghetti. He grabbed the garlic bread and led Beth to the dining room.

Beth gasped when they entered. The leisure ambiance setting cried out, *relaxation*. She spotted the table setting and tears came to her eyes. "Oh my God, you're using Mom's China." Beth sauntered over to the table and ran a finger around the rim of a plate. Before getting any more emotional, she glanced at Russ and teased, "What's going on? Is this my birthday party?"

"Your birthday isn't until next week. Sorry. But I do have something important to tell you tonight." He pulled out a chair for her, poured them a glass of wine and took his seat. "You first, tell me about your day."

Beth told him about the sedan following her and the situation at work. She paused long enough to take a sip of wine and asked, "By the way, what's wrong with your door? It took forever to lock."

"That started giving me problems yesterday. It needs to be replaced. About that sedan following you, why don't you stay here until your apartment is ready?"

"I've been contemplating it. Not real crazy about the motel. I'll get my stuff from there on Monday. Beth chatted the entire time they ate. She washed down the last bite with a gulp of Cabernet and reclined with her hand on her belly. "I'm so full. So, Russ, what's up?"

Russ set his fork down, picked up his napkin and wiped the corner of his mouth. Leaning forward, he put his forearms on the table and said with a grin, "It's ready."

Beth's heart skipped a beat. She didn't want to hear what she knew was coming. "Are you talking about the time machine?"

The question sounded silly, but she kind of hoped it was about a car or something.

"Yes, of course, I'm talking about the Scorpion."

Beth sat straight up, set down her wine glass and cried, "Are you sure? I thought you had more glitches to work out?"

"Well... I can't fix glitches I don't know exist. Come on, let's go downstairs. Grab your wine."

Not only did she take her glass, but she also snatched the bottle.

Russ unlocked the door to the lab, and they entered. The large room had changed little since he was fourteen. A futon in front of the fireplace replaced the conventional couch. It served as a bed when needed, which is where Russ slept most of his nights. Also in front of the hearth sat a recliner and an end table. A beautiful antique mirror hung above the mantle.

The daunting Scorpion, on the opposite side of the room, took up most of the space.

Russ watched Beth grimace every time she glanced at it. "Don't worry sis. I won't change the past or the future."

"But you can't be sure. Every time you travel, you'll come across possible paradoxes. What if you go to the past and die? Would you exist now?"

"Probably not." Russ chuckled, but noting Beth wasn't in laughing mode he said, "Quit being such a worry wart. This machine is for observing and learning. I won't be mingling with the past or future dwellers."

"I can't process this in my mind. How can something go to another time?"

Russ stood next to the Scorpion and pointed up to the hulls. "This is where the laser electromagnetic propulsion generator is. The mechanism contains, suspends, and drives the helium superfluid at an absolute pressure. Remember when I explained this to you?"

"Yes, and everything bounced off my head then too."

Russ ignored her and continued, "Now, it's imperative the plasma rotates for the Scorpion to move through time. Between these first two hulls, the superfluid moves counterclockwise and between the next two it moves clockwise. They also contain the magnets and the lasers. Are you with me so far?"

"Not really."

"Okay, moving right along." Russ pointed to the top of the tail. "The laser's job is to circulate a beam of light which jump-starts the magnet effect. Space and time then get twisted together."

"I understand nothing you're saying, so there's no sense in explaining any further." Beth walked to the recliner, plopped down in the recliner and gulped her wine.

Russ went to the file cabinet and removed a photograph of his father and himself when he was fourteen. In the image, they were standing in the basement room before it was a lab. The photo was dated *May 16, 1968.* Handing the picture to Beth, he said, "This the year I will attempt to travel to. At least I won't end up in a pile of storage. But, if something's in the way, the hovercraft will keep the machine from tipping." Russ paused a moment and chuckled, "At least, that's what supposed to happen."

"I don't think this is a laughing matter. What if something happens and you don't come back?"

"I'll be back." Russ opened the door and pointed inside. "The two levers are for going to the past and the other to the future. The further you push them the faster you go. Hit the *return* button and the Scorpion will appear within seconds to the original time."

"I told you, Russ, I won't be the one using your contraption, so there's no need to go into depth." Beth, being positive she would not talk him out of it, asked, "When do you plan on doing this?"

"Tomorrow morning after breakfast, I wouldn't want to travel on an empty stomach." Russ chuckled.

"Enough with the jokes. Let's go back upstairs. I need to take all this in."

They retired to the library where Beth plunked down onto the sofa in front of the fireplace. She filled their glasses and set the wine bottle on the coffee table.

Russ strolled over to the stone hearth and stoked the fire. When the orange and red embers blazed and crackled, he sauntered over and settled in next to Beth. As they finished their wine, they went over everything one more time. When confident with the plan, they sat in silence gazing into the dying ashes that were now, a warm glow.

As Beth set her empty glass down she noticed the 155-year-old encyclopedia that had been with the family for generations. Nobody - not even their parents - knew how it got in the library. Beth picked up the book flipping through the pages. "I love this book. Why's it off the shelf?"

"I'm keeping it here for now. It'll come in handy if we travel to those years."

"You make it sound like we're planning a cruise or something. When you say *we*, do you mean you and the mouse in your pocket? I've no intentions of going anywhere in that contraption."

Beth yawned and set the ancient book on the table. The antique grandfather clock chimed midnight, and they stood as if on cue. Beth gave her brother a long hug fearing the embrace may be their last.

Russ made a beeline to the lab. He turned off the lights except for the one over the machine. Before laying his head down, he whispered, "Good night Scorpion, tomorrow we shall travel."

Chapter 6

Beth woke to the aroma of black coffee wafting under her door. She glanced at her clock. 6:45 a.m. She threw the covers off, sat up and brushed back a feeling of dread. *Russ plans to travel to the past today. Maybe if I stay in bed all day, he won't do it.*

The smell of sizzling bacon filled the entire house and staying in bed wasn't an option. Beth slid into her slippers and shuffled to the door. She threw on her robe and proceeded to the kitchen. Russ stood at the counter whistling while cracking an egg into pancake batter.

"Good morning sunshine," Russ said, with a big grin.

Beth didn't answer. She put on her sad puppy look and strolled over to the counter where a cup awaited her. She filled it with coffee and took it to the booth, refusing to help. She was the one who prepared the meals, but since he proved by last night's dinner he could cook, she let him wait on her for a change. It drove her nuts when her brother continued to whistle as he flipped the pancakes. *He acts like there's no lurking danger.*

Beth blew the steam from her coffee and stared out the window. The unkempt backyard made her mouth droop. She began a mental list of chores that would need to be done in case Russ doesn't return. *What would I tell everybody? Nobody would believe me. Someone might accuse me of murdering him. But since there wouldn't be a body I guess there'd be no case. Oh brother, why am I thinking like this?*

Russ set the bacon and pancakes in front of Beth snapping her out of her daydreaming. He sat on the opposite side of the booth and dug into his breakfast. His appetite couldn't be better.

Beth's upset stomach would accept nothing but coffee.

After breakfast, Beth dressed in a white sweatshirt and jeans and prepared herself for the worse. She entered the lab and observed Russ. He sat with his feet stretched out while writing down his notes. *He looks too damn calm.* She glanced at the clock on the wall. 7:58 a.m. *Remember this time.* Strolling over to the fire, Beth picked up the poker and stoked the dying embers. Her bottom lip quivered.

Russ, noting her anxiety, led his sister to the futon and sat her down and said, "Look at me. Look into my eyes."

Beth's locked eyes with him wiping away a tear.

"I will be back before you can count to thirty. Stay here on the couch and don't come near the machine once it's activated. Remember. Do *not* call 911 if something happens. If this machine gets into the wrong hands, it would be devastating."

"You don't have to tell me again. We've been through this." She brushed away another unwanted tear. "I love you, Russ."

"Save it for when I get back, okay?" He patted her hand and went to the Scorpion and slipped in. Placing his finger on the switch, he told himself, "This is why I built the Scorpion. Now, let's see what's out there." Russ wasted no more time flipping the switch.

In the mirror, a brilliant flash bounced off exposing the entire room as if it were in the middle of a terrific lightning storm.

Beth sprang up and turned toward the machine yelling, "No, please don't do it!" The glare blinded her. She shielded her eyes, and when taking her arm away, the platform was empty.

She felt as though her world had fallen out from beneath her. She dropped to her knees and sobbed.

Another brilliant flash - only lasting a few seconds - filled the room. The machine re-appeared, the door flung open, and Russ fell out in a heap. His crumpled body shook for a few moments and stopped as suddenly as it started.

In a flash, Beth was at his side. *How can this be happening? I walked into this room only two minutes ago and already I have to revive him!* Patting his face, Beth screamed out her brother's name.

He moaned and slurred something indiscernible.

Beth took his pulse - it was slow. While assisting him to stand, she realized he had no coordination. With all the strength she could muster, she dragged him to the couch.

"I...I... I'm so cold," he breathed out.

It occurred to her he had hypothermia. Beth grabbed the throw blanket on the futon and wrapped him like a cocoon. Throwing two logs into the fire, she grabbed the poker and stirred until the flames caught hold. She then sprinted upstairs and pulled off the down comforters from the beds. Rushing to the thermostat she turned the dial to ninety degrees and ran back to the lab. She piled bedding on her brother swaddling him tight.

In the worst way, Beth wanted to call 911, despite Russ' warning. If he were to die, she'd never forgive herself. Somehow, she restrained herself from doing so and pushed the recliner closer and waited.

After a few hours passed she couldn't take the heat any longer. She also needed to relieve herself and nature called big time now. She scurried down the basement hallway to the bathroom off the laundry room. After doing her business, she rummaged through the clothes in the dryer, found a tee shirt and jogging shorts and changed into them.

Russ' shaking slowed down around 2 p.m. so Beth made a trip to the kitchen. She grabbed an apple and three bottles of water out of the refrigerator and a banana off the counter. She drank an entire bottle and tried to wake her brother again. After failing, she curled up on the chair and closed her heavy eyelids. It didn't take long before she drifted into a restless sleep. In her nightmare, someone chased her down a deserted alley. The stalker knew her. He called her name over and over again.

"Beth... Beth, wake up."

Beth woke up flinging her arms until she realized she'd been dreaming. Then realizing Russ was conscious, she cried, "Oh my God, you're awake. Are you okay?" She turned on the lamp and noted it was 8:10 in the evening. Grabbing the water, she knelt by his side lifting his head and put the bottle to his lips, "Try to drink, you've been in and out for twelve hours."

Russ swallowed a sip and pushed her away. "I have to sit up."

"Not yet. Take your time and drink more."

"Why am I so warm?"

Beth pulled the two comforters off but left the throw blanket wrapped around him. "I'll be right back. Don't move." Running upstairs to the thermostat, she turned it down to seventy-seven degrees. She then went to the bathroom medicine cabinet and got the thermometer. When she returned to her brother, he wasn't moving - and for a moment - she worried he was unconscious... or worse. She was reassured when he shivered once again. She grabbed a blanket and re-wrapped him. "Russ, can you hear me?"

He nodded.

Beth articulated every word, "Good, I need to take your temperature. I'm putting the thermometer under your tongue. Do you understand?"

Russ nodded and opened his mouth a crack.

Beth inserted the thermometer and waited for the beep.

"What's it say?" whispered Russ.

"Ninety-three point five."

Russ grinned, *"Now,* I have a glitch to work out."

Morning came around fast. Beth's night in the recliner was full of nightmares, while her brother slept like a baby.

After waking, Russ needed to use the bathroom. He tried on his own but woke his sister when stumbling into her chair. "Sorry... I'm trying to make it to the boy's room."

"Let me help you." Beth jumped up and put her arm through his and helped him to his feet. She got him to the toilet and waited outside.

The return trip didn't exert him as much. He walked on his own with his sister by his side.

Beth's headache was back. She dragged herself to the kitchen for coffee and made him hot chocolate. Back down in the lab, she handed her brother his mug and asked, "So, what was traveling through time like?"

Russ' hands shook as he blew on his heated milk. His brows furrowed as the remembrance came to him. He took a sip from the cup, set it down and began, "As soon as I pushed the lever it looked like I was in a tube. Streaks of light moved all around me. It reminded me of silly string. They started out luminous, and the next moment they were dark. As I slowed down the strands formed into shapes." Russ pointed to a window. "For instance, the brightest ones ended up being the sunlight. Figuring out when to shut it down was like focusing binoculars. I stopped when the blurry room came into complete focus."

He paused and struggled to recollect what happened next. After a moment, he continued, "I had this sensation of being out of my body, and after I shut the machine down, I noticed my hands were a blur. I knew something was wrong. So I hit the *return* button, and that's all I remember."

"Maybe you were in another dimension. Or you could've died. That would explain why you felt out of your body."

He didn't like the way his sister observed him, doubting him. "No, I was in this room. I've no doubt about it. I'll figure out how to fix this glitch and will try again. Don't worry though. It won't be for a while. The Scorpion needs some fine-tuning."

Later that evening, Russ sat at the table in his bathrobe. He went over his blueprints exploring possibilities of solving the defects.

Beth, in her robe also, relaxed on the other side with a cup of tea. "Do you want me to call in tomorrow? I'll stay home if you need me."

"No, I have to concentrate on this. No offense, but I think I can accomplish more alone."

"Okay, but I'll be home late. I have to collect my stuff from the motel. In fact, every night I'll be late since Steinhart has given me two weeks of work I have to finish in one."

Setting down his pen, he looked at Beth and said, "That's fine. I'm glad you're staying here until your place is ready. Call me when you're on your way. I'm going to a gun show in Minneapolis on Friday. Why don't you go with me and we'll pick out a couple guns? We could meet somewhere."

"Sorry, I already made plans. I'm sure my co-workers have a big thing planned for my birthday. If I dodge them anymore, they'll kill me."

Beth's headache was worse than ever. She wanted nothing, but a good night sleep, and an uneventful week. She headed or bed and fell asleep as soon as her head hit the pillow and the horrible nightmares began again. Only in this dream, it was Gary chasing her with a butcher knife.

Chapter 7

Beth couldn't believe it was Thursday afternoon already. So far, this week proved to be much more bearable than the past four. It appeared nobody was following her anymore. That took a big load off her shoulders. Now that Russ was better, Beth could concentrate once again. The bonus was Steinhart gone for the week. The workplace had its camaraderie back.

Since Beth committed to leaving early on Friday to go to the club, she skipped going to the park every day. Steinhart's tasks were the first to get done and with those out of the way, she was ahead of the game. Beth got a cup of coffee and headed to Lori's office. It'd been a while since they've had girl talk.

Beth came into the room, and as usual, Tony was perched in the overstuffed chair. He rambled on while Lori worked. He jumped up and made a gesture for Beth to sit, and she took him up on it. After taking a sip of her coffee she mentioned, "There's a fresh pot of coffee in the break room if you guys are interested."

Tony meandered over to the copy machine like he planned to use it. "No more coffee for me - but I'll tell you what I *do* want - a humongous margarita. I can't wait for your party tomorrow night. Everybody's bringing a used gift and have I got a surprise for you."

Lori snapped at Tony, "I thought that was supposed to be a surprise."

He slapped his mouth, "Oops, never got the memo. Sorry about that. We're excited to get you out again girlfriend. We miss you."

"Hey Tony, can you get me a cup of coffee?" asked Lori. "I'm expecting a phone call and can't leave my desk."

"Can't you tell I'm busy here?" Tony pointed to the pile of papers.

Lori gave him a look of scorn.

Tony, rolling his eyes, mumbled, "Okay, okay, I'm on my way."

As soon as he was out the door, Lori turned to her friend, "Beth, has Gary been leaving you alone? I heard about the online bust he got from chatting with a guy who claimed to be a teenage girl. Is that right?"

Beth drew in a deep breath and sighed, "Yes, I wanted to tell you myself, but the last few weeks have been insane.

"How did you find out?" Lori got up and moved to the chair on the other side of the desk.

"Last month someone delivered an envelope here at work. The guy pretending to be the fifteen-year-old girl sent it. I guess his teenage daughter got molested by an older man and now it's his mission, as a dad, to expose creeps. I received an envelope containing the printout of the whole conversation. It continued for days between Gary and the supposed girl. He planned on meeting her at a motel. He even promised to take her shopping for whatever she wanted."

"Unbelievable. Did he admit to it?"

"He didn't have to, I had all the evidence. That night I packed a bag, and he tried to stop me. Remember I told you about how he yanked my hair and about broke my neck. He scared the hell out of me."

"Yeah, I remember that. What a pathetic loser. You're wise for getting a restraining order on him."

"I'm still constantly looking behind my back. The first two

weeks after we split up that knucklehead wouldn't quit stalking me. He showed up everywhere and would try to talk me back. So, I got the restraint and changed my phone number.

Tony returned carrying the coffee with his bottom lip sticking out. He was pouting because he didn't like being excluded from serious discussions.

Lori stood up, took the coffee from him and returned to her chair behind the desk. "Thanks, Tony."

Beth stood and gave Tony a hug. "Tony, I can't wait to find out what you have for me."

"It will be a hoot," he promised.

Beth left work and headed straight for Forest Lake. This time, Russ had her stop at the country store for milk. Turning on the blinker, she prepared to turn. Her eyes about popped out of her head when spotting the black sedan. Parked on the far side of the dim-lit parking lot was the familiar broken headlight.

Half a dozen questions went through her head. *Why's it here? I've only seen it in Minneapolis. Has he followed me somehow without me seeing? Maybe he got Russ' address on the Internet?*

Beth didn't turn into the parking lot. Instead, she sped up. *Russ can get his own damn milk.*

Beth drove the remaining six blocks peering in her rearview mirror. She saw nothing but blackness. *What if he has his lights off?*

Beth called Russ and asked him to meet her at the door. Pulling into the driveway a minute later, she parked and spotted her brother on the porch. She rushed past him into the house and plopped herself down on the entryway bench. Leaning over, she put her head in her hands and breathed a sigh of relief.

"Was somebody following you again?"

She explained what happened and put her head back in her hands rubbing her temples.

"Tomorrow night I'll be at the gun show until nine. It's only a mile from the club. Why don't we meet up? I'll follow you home."

Beth sat straight up and asked, "Will you have a gun then? Do you plan on buying one at the show? I need one in my car."

"I'll buy two guns. It'll still be a few days before I get them. When I do, we'll get carrying licenses. Don't worry. Nobody will hurt you. Not on my watch."

Chapter 8

Beth woke up feeling like she'd been run over by a Mack truck. Moaning, she crawled out of bed and shuffled to the closet. Since Friday's dress down day, she picked jeans along with a sky-color cashmere sweater - which made her blue eyes pop. She dressed it up with a silver necklace and the sapphire earrings her mother gave Beth on her 17th birthday.

Since Silvia lived close to the club, Beth decided to spend the night at her place. After giving her friend a quick call, she proceeded to the kitchen.

Russ sat at the table drinking his coffee, engrossed in his notes. He didn't bother to acknowledge her.

"Good morning, Russ. I spoke with Silvia. I'm sleeping at her place, so you won't need to meet me tonight."

After several seconds of ignoring her, he looked up briefly mumbling, "Leave me a text when you get there." His gaze returned to his notes and without looking back up he said, "I've been trying to figure out what caused the hypothermia. I need to raise the molecular activity to stabilize for shifting time space. The coldness slowed me down to the point of inactivity. I'm sure it made it safer to transfer into a new period. It might have saved me. The machine's door could use a tighter seal too. It couldn't handle the pressure."

Beth replied through clenched teeth, "I wish you'd forget about that thing."

Russ snapped, "That's not going to happen. I can do this with or without your help."

"Hey, don't yell at me. You couldn't do it without me yesterday. I had to save your life."

He didn't reply. He continued studying his notes.

Beth poured a cup of coffee, took it to her room, and packed an overnight bag. When she returned downstairs, Russ had gone down to the lab. She left the house without saying goodbye.

Upon arriving at her job, Cheryl informed Beth Mrs. Steinhart still planned on bringing in her new assistant the following week.

Beth's shoulder's drooped *how can this day get any worse?*

At 3:30 p.m. some of her co-workers were leaving to go home to change for the club. Beth organized her desk in case she's asked to remove her belongings. *This isn't a good day.*

Silvia asked if Beth would like to ride with the others to the club and she declined. They would stay into the wee hours and she was positive she wouldn't make it that long.

Beth arrived at the dance hall at 4:45 p.m. the same time the carpool did. The staff assisted in pushing together tables to sit fifteen and a separate table for the gifts. The group got situated, and the waiter took their drink orders.

Beth wished she could be excited about her party, but that wasn't happening.

One by one her colleagues arrived and soon the party would be in full gear. Margaritas and mixed drinks were going down fast by all, except for Beth's which was almost untouched.

Beth could felt Silvia's eyes on her the whole time so finally, she told her she wasn't spending the night because of being sick.

It didn't come as a surprise to Silvia because Beth looked as if death warmed over. On behalf of her friend, Silvia took charge. She stood and announced the time has come for Beth to open her presents. "Come on girlfriend." Silvia clasped Beth's hand and led her to the gift table.

Beth plopped down in the chair and gave her a "Thank you for looking after me" look.

Tony grabbed what he brought and handed it to Beth and gleefully said, "Open mine first."

She took the present and thanked him. Slowly pulling the tape from the wrapping, she took care not to rip the paper. The room became silent as her co-workers waited in anticipation, wishing she would speed it up.

Tony, like the kid at the party who has to get their hands in there, grabbed the package out of Beth's hands. He ripped most the wrapping off and handed it back. "Now that's how it's done. Nobody's saving wrapping paper around here, am I right?"

"Hell no, rip those presents open," Cheryl blurted out, causing a stir of laughter. She's usually the quiet one of the group.

Beth ripped the rest of the paper off, crumpled it, and whipped it to the floor. "There, is that better?"

They all applauded.

Tony's surprise was a Polaroid camera he had come upon in his closet. "Oh, this is great." Beth laughed, "Who needs a camera on your phone when you can have one of these?"

Tony interjected, "Also included are two packages of film and batteries."

"That's too funny," Beth giggled as she reached for another present. After reading the card, she announced, "This is from Cheryl. Oh look, it's a portable disk player with an Adele disc and headphones. Oh, and more batteries."

Cheryl chuckled, "Sorry, I couldn't find the AC adapter."

Silvia handed Beth her gift and Beth, now experienced in opening gifts, tore into it. She held the object up for everyone to see. "It's a battery run hand fan with batteries."

Beth also got a butane-filled lighter with a new can of fluid, a baseball cap that had *I'm older than the Internet* written on the front and a bag of lollipops. Tom, another underwriter, gave her a small hand-held video camera.

"This recorder looks expensive," Beth remarked.

Tom shrugged his shoulders, "I have another one at home, but I never use them. I mean, why would I? All that we need is on our phones now, right? Sorry, no batteries included."

"That's okay, Tom. I have enough batteries to last me a lifetime."

When the gift table was empty, Lori handed Beth a bag, "You'll need this."

Beth reached in and pulled out a rhinestone handbag. "Oh my God, Lori, I thought you loved this purse."

"You love it more. Besides, now you have something to put your presents in."

Silvia and Tony got busy stuffing the presents into the Rhinestone bag - all except one.

Tony turned to the group holding up the Polaroid camera and shouted, "Group picture, everybody, squeeze together."

A waiter offered to take the picture, so the group huddled together and made goofy faces.

Beth forced a smile but her upset belly caused her to cringe.

Silvia, noticing her friend was about to lose her lunch, stood and announced Beth was sick. Trying to be comical - and yet being serious - she told them they needed to get her the hell out because she's contagious.

The staff ushered out a beautiful cake lit with twenty-six candles. Beth's loopy co-workers sang Happy Birthday, all in different keys. Worse yet, it was so slow it sounded more like a funeral procession. They cracked up laughing and after many cheers, they yelled, "Make a wish."

Beth waved her arms and groaned, "I won't spread my sick germs on this cake. Someone else blow them out."

As if on cue, Lori, Silvia, and Tony jumped up and blew hard. All but one candle went out.

Tom held up his index finger. "Doesn't that mean she has a boyfriend?

Without due process, Beth bent over and puffed out the remaining candle. "For the record, I have no boyfriends. Now if you'll excuse me, I'm off to the lady's room."

Chapter 9

Since her trip to the toilet, Beth's upset stomach was much better. Plus the drive home wasn't as unpleasant as she feared. Maybe because the thought of her bed awaiting her, took precedence in her mind.

She exited the interstate and headed for the country roads. The clouds rolled in covering the moon. If it weren't for her headlights, it would be total darkness.

The little store came up and Beth slowed down as she passed. Only one automobile sat in the parking lot and to her relief; it wasn't the dreaded sedan.

Six more blocks to go.

Before leaving the club, Beth sent Russ a text saying she was leaving early. She wished he was home now, but he wouldn't be on his way for over an hour. She regretted not telling him goodbye that morning.

Two more blocks.

Beth spotted something ahead. She leaned in close to the windshield and squinted. The black sedan all of a sudden appeared out of the darkness! It was parked on the side of the road. She had no choice but to pass by it. Stepping on the gas, she sped up - so did the black car.

"Shit!"

One block.

Almost in tears now, Beth reached to the passenger seat

for her phone. *Damn, it's in my backpack.* She turned onto the driveway and the car came to a screech.

With her bag over her shoulder, she whipped the door open and sprinted to the house.

Beth fumbled with the keys as she unlocked the entry door - she remembered - *the lock never got fixed.*

The sedan squealed into the drive. She didn't take any extra time to look back.

Once inside, Beth raced for the basement. She would escape to the lab where she could lock him out. Breathing heavily, she scrambled down the stairs and whisked through the hallway.

"Damn." she cried, fumbling with the keys. After unlocking the lab door, she turned and saw the stalker blazing down the steps.

There's no time to lock the door. Her eyes darted, *there's no place to hide!* She turned and faced the Scorpion.

Beth felt like she had been punched in the gut. With no other choice, she bolted to the machine. Whipping the door open, she slid in just as the madman burst into the room.

His body halted in mid-motion when he saw his trapped victim. He revealed a distorted mouth full of crooked teeth as he grinned. He pulled the switchblade from his pocket and tossed it from one hand to another, teasing his prey.

Beth let out a scream when he lurched toward her. She slammed the door and without hesitating, she flipped the switch and pushed the lever into full throttle.

Theodore stopped dead in his tracks when the flash exploded. He covered his eyes and when bringing his arm down, the girl and the Scorpion were gone.

Tuesday

September 4, 1860

Chapter 10

Daniel was in need of a little silence. He threw his jacket over his shoulder and headed out into the crisp night air. His tired body leaned against the broken-down rails of the small porch. The tiny house had two rooms - that is if you don't include the loft. A straw-filled mattress that slept two children took up that area. The ladder to the garret had been falling apart for some time and was now missing a rung.

Only an hour ago the warm sun had taken its rest behind the horizon. It left a deep cadmium yellow with multiple shades of amber that dry-brushed the entire heavens. The vast golden rows of corn husks in the field appeared as if they were incandescent. They blended with the streaks of orange and crimson that graced the heavens.

The black sky was now void of color. The night brought with it a brisk chilling breeze. Daniel slid into his jacket as he peered into the darkness. The moon hid behind the clouds which made the barn in the distance almost invisible. If it hadn't been for the white billowy clouds that still attracted the retired sun's reflection, there would've been no light at all.

After concluding all was well on the farm, Daniel perched himself on a rickety chair. He ran his hand through his short, sun-bleached hair and let out a long sigh. Daniel's weathered beaten face looked older than it should, although he was still a handsome man at thirty-one. He felt as though his torso was as worn out as his old house. However, the back-breaking tasks of running a farm kept his muscular body lean and hard.

Daniel reclined and took in a deep breath as he gazed at the clear lucent moon. Only minutes ago the clouds had covered it. He took note the moon would be in its full lunar cycle in five days. That meant something different to his family than the other farmers who lived in the Township of Forest Lake.

Every month, Daniel set apart for his three children the first night of the full moon. This one time their father let them speak of their deceased mother. He didn't think he could handle more than that. His wife, Kristine, died at twenty-eight giving birth to their one-year-old son, Toby. Daniel never got over it, and as a result, his children suffered.

Anna, at eleven, had the responsibility of caring for Toby and Sara, their eight-year-old sister. With Anna's bossy demeanor, she had no difficulty in raising the young ones. Her authoritative commands made even the farm animals obey. Her high-hand temperament had taken over the household in its entirety relieving her pa to the run the farm. Sara, Toby, and the animals never seemed to mind her pushiness though, because Anna made up for it with kisses and cuddles.

The "Full Moon Fun-Night" is what they called it. It became a tradition long ago while his wife still lived. Together the family would build a bonfire in the backyard pit.

Sara, in her too tight and scuffed up shoes, would run around like a chicken with its head cut off. She would search high and low for little branches to use for kindling. Once the fire going strong, the search for the perfect length stick she poked the fire with would begin. In her younger years, she'd run around near the woods demanding, "I need a 'Play in the Fire Stick.'" The name became catchy, so the family designated it and it's called that to this day.

It took a lot to keep Sara's attention being that she was such an active child. It presented quite a challenge for Anna.

Unlike Anna's blonde, long and straight managed hair, Sara's russet brown shoulder-length hair was always in a tangled, matted mess. Her potato sack dresses were hand-me-downs, passed on by Anna. By the end of each day, Sara's attire's crumpled and soiled. Her pockets are full of rocks she collected throughout the day. Unbeknown to Sara, Anna would throw most of them back outside in the evening.

No matter how unruly Sara appeared, she possessed a most excellent quality. This girl had the sweetest disposition that exceeded all others. She seldom was without a grin which lit up her oval face. Her mother used to tell her that her smile was a gift from God.

Once the Fun-Night took off in full gear, the family would sit around the crackling fire, and the two sisters reminisced about their ma.

Toby never knew his mother, but his sister's stories made him think he did. The blonde curly locks falling around his face were in dire need of trimming. His eyes, big and round, twinkled like aquamarine gemstones.

The toddler learned to walk at eight and a half months old and achieved potty training at fourteen months. He was a happy kid despite the lack of affection he received from his father.

Also on Fun-Night, they get the treat of gingersnaps. That is if they have molasses. They got that from Mrs. Knutson, a woman who lived a few miles away. The woman also owned and operated the only store around. Daniel had known her for a long time, in fact, he knew all the farmers in the community. The group of immigrants traveled together from the Wisconsin territory to southeastern Minnesota. Daniel and one other farmer grew corn. The rest harvested wheat.

At Mrs. Knutson's business, Daniel traded corn for grain, corn for cloth material, corn for beef, and in this situation, molasses, which meant cookies during the bonfire.

The most important thing about the Fun Night for the kids was it brought their father's affection. The children soaked up as much loving as possible because they knew it would be another month before their pa showed any emotion.

Daniel sat on the porch wondering where he'd get the strength to carry on when something snapped him out of his thoughts. He turned and saw Anna standing in the doorway. He raised his brows giving her a "What do you want?" look.

"Toby and Sara are ready for bed, Pa. Do you want to read them their book tonight?"

"No, you read to them. Your mother didn't teach you reading for nothing."

Anna's body drooped. As she turned to go back into the house, her eye caught an intense blaze lightning up the barn.

Daniel, seeing it too, feared it was on fire. He pushed Anna aside, reached inside the door and grabbed the kerosene lamp off the small entry table. He also took the broom.

"Anna, get in the house and stay with the kids," he ordered, darting toward the building.

When Daniel reached the barn, he threw up the wooden latch, spread his feet, and after getting a good grip, he pushed the sliding barn door open. Two terrified cats ran out beneath his legs along with several frightened chickens clucking up a storm.

Peering into the dark, Daniel saw nothing. He sniffed for a trace of burning hay but only smelled the familiar animal odor that permeated the shadows.

Daniel grabbed a larger kerosene lamp hanging on the inside planking. He set the broom aside, knelt down and lit it putting the wick up high. He carried the lantern with one hand and grabbed the broom with the other. More chickens ran past him cackling, and then it got quiet, almost too quiet.

As the lamp directed Daniel's steps, his eyes darted back and forth searching for the fire. They settled on a light coming from the far end of the barn. The moon's rays nestled in between the wooden slats of the boarded window. The beams acted like spotlights aiming at something that wasn't there earlier. Daniel followed the moonbeams down to the mysterious object. He took a few steps closer, straining his eyes as he focused in on the thing. The monstrosity that hid in the shadows came into view. It appeared to be a humongous Scorpion! Shocked by what he saw, Daniel stumbled backward almost falling.

"What in tarnation is that?" Daniel threw down the broom and grabbed the pitchfork. Never taking his eyes off the thing, Daniel edged closer. He stood about fifteen-feet away now holding the pitchfork high in front of him ready to strike.

Daniel's eyes adjusted to the dark, and he saw the machine clearly. He knew now it wasn't a giant bug.

How did that get in here? Daniel gazed the ceiling. It was intact. His concentration went back to the machine. He froze when he heard moaning. Daniel turned his ear toward the noise. It came again from the opposite side.

Walking like you don't want to wake a sleeping grizzly is how Daniel tiptoed at that moment. His heart pounded in his chest. He worked his way closer, far enough to peek around the corner. He saw what looked to be a hand. It wasn't moving. Daniel approached it and saw a curled up body. He wasn't sure if the thing was dead or alive, but protecting his family took top priority. Without another thought, Daniel held the pitchfork high in the air. As he prepared to thrust it, someone screamed.

"No Pa, it's a girl. Don't hurt her!"

Daniel swung his head around, and there stood Sara. Anna, holding Toby, was a few feet further back. All three children, mouths gaping, stared at the girl.

Chapter 11

The brilliant flash left Theodore stunned, and for a few moments, he saw nothing but white spots. The man shook his head, rubbed his eyes and stared at the empty place where the machine disappeared. He concentrated on the platform almost like he expected the contraption to reappear.

"What the fuck! Where are you, bitch?"

Turning on the light he scanned the entire lab. The perpetrator shuffled to the left to the long tables and flashed his beady eyes underneath. Bewildered when there was nothing, he stood eyeing the rest of the lab and spotted a closet. He hobbled over and whipped the door open - only shelves took up space.

The confused man jutted his body around and limped over to the sitting area. He stopped and did a full turn. There was nowhere big enough for her to hide. He scratched the bald spot on top of his head and brushed the remaining straggled hairs away from his round, sweaty face, not sure what to do.

"What the hell?" The baffled man hobbled back over to the tables and examined the blueprints. They made no sense to him so he moved to the desk where the notepad and calendar lay open.

Theodore spotted a photograph of the time machine with Russ standing next to it. He picked up the picture and brought it closer. He read the writing on the bottom, "The Scorpion."

Curious, he cocked his head and glanced back at the empty platform. "Well, well, well. Wada ya know, this guy's an inventor."

Theodore glimpsed at his Rolex watch - a keepsake from one of his victim's homes - 8:30 p.m. He put the picture down and picked up the day planner. He noted what Russ jotted down for today. "Gun show 7 p.m. Meet Beth 10 p.m."

As he stood holding the calendar, his brows scrunched as he stared trance-like. His mind raced. He was getting ideas. According to the notes, Russ would not get home until after ten. Theodore's been casing the house for a week, ever since Beth moved out of the motel. He learned while staking out the place, Russ was habitual. Theodore knew when he would leave and when he would come home. Now the madman needed future access to the inventor's calendar planner.

He set his plan into action. Theodore searched for a window that had something sturdy under it. On the far wall, under a curtain-covered window, was a hope chest. *How convenient.* Shuffling to the piece of furniture, he stood on top making sure it would hold his weight.

After determining the box would work, he pushed the curtains aside and unlocked and opened the window as wide as possible. *Now for the tricky part.* He needed to boost himself up and out. It surprised him how easy it was. Now he was standing in the backyard scanning the area noting all details. Once satisfied, he climbed back in. *Piece of cake.*

Next, Theodore needed to rig the lock so he'd have access to this room when Russ was gone. He rummaged through boxes on the shelves and found a small, flat, pliable piece of tin. He returned, stood on the chest and maneuvered the metal making the window appear secure.

Once satisfied with his task, he returned to the desk and picked up the calendar. He made a mental note of Russ' future errands. Theodore's suspicions of Russ being habitual proved to be correct. Russ scheduled tasks at the same time on the same days. Theodore hoped nothing would change once he finds his precious Scorpion gone.

Theodore's plans were to stake out the future notes and calendar of events. He hopes Russ will build another machine and begin the search for his sister. Once he does, he'll bring her back, and Theodore will be in the shadows waiting. When the time is right, he'll kill them while they sleep.

The room had to appear no one had been there. He bolted the door lock from the inside and returned to the tampered window and boosted himself out. Reaching in, he snuggled the tin piece between the latches and straightened the curtain.

Scurrying around to the front, he found the door stood open from the chase. He released the bolt and shut the door. It didn't lock, so he tried again. Now, impatience was setting in as he tried lining it up with the frame and shut it again. It took two frustrating minutes getting the door secured.

On his way home, Theodore smirked and critiqued his plan in his sick mind. *Next time, I'll take detailed pictures of the blueprints. If the bitch never comes back at least I can get rich off the machine.*

Chapter 12

"**G**et back in the house!" Daniel ordered.

"But Pa, it's a girl," screamed Sara. "Don't hurt her."

Anna shouted to her sister, "Sara, get over here."

Sara stopped dead in her tracks and with big sad eyes she pleaded, "Please, don't stab her."

Daniel turned to the curled up figure, picked up his lamp and inspected it. It could be a girl but the trousers threw him off. He gave the torso a little nudge with his foot. When it didn't move, he leaned the pitchfork against the wall and knelt on one knee. His hands shook as he reached to touch her hand. It stunned him when the being's body suddenly convulsed causing Daniel to jump back. Losing his footing, he fell back into a pile of hay. He sprang up grabbing the pitchfork again.

"No Pa, look at her. She won't hurt us." cried Anna.

"She's freezing." cried Sara, "We should bring her in the house."

"No, we don't know if the thing is safe." Daniel set the tool aside again, bent over and realized it may be a girl. He took hold of both arms, dragged her away from the machine and laid her on the hay. Her skin felt cool and clammy. He straightened the body out and looked around for something to cover her.

"Anna, give Toby to your sister and bring me a blanket. Get the one off my bed."

She handed over her brother and raced to the house.

Daniel bent over the female and brushed the hair out of her face and remarked, "This isn't a girl. This is a woman."

Anna returned in a flash carrying a down-filled covering along with jackets for Toby and Sara. Daniel took the comforter and covered her. The woman's tremors got worse.

Anna couldn't stand watching the lady shake. "Pa, it's not working, she's still shivering. We can put her by the fireplace."

"You need to listen. We're not bringing her in. Bring the children to the house. I'll stay here."

They wouldn't budge.

He figured the girls didn't trust him so he kept quiet. Another fifteen minutes went by, and now the September's damp air caused them all to shiver.

"Anna, put more wood in the fireplace." Daniel removed the blanket from the woman and handed it to Sara. "Place this on the floor by the hearth." Scooping up the lady, he carried her to the house and laid her on the blanket. He instructed Sara to get more coverings.

Anna threw three logs into the fire and stirred it making the flames shoot blazing crimson sparks into the air. Once the fire was under control, she closed the door and window shutters to keep the heat within.

In the meantime, Sara climbed the ladder to the loft and pulled two blankets off of the mattress. She threw them over the rail, came back down and helped her father wrap the woman up.

After she was taken care of, Daniel said, "We need to have a family meeting - now - at the table."

Anna sat down at her spot with Toby on her lap. Sara perched herself across from her sister and Daniel settled in the wooden chair at the end of the long table. The children sat silently while they waited for him to speak.

Daniel slipped off his jacket and hung it on the chair next

to him. He leaned over and put his forearms on the table and folded his hands. He drew in a deep breath. "We've done all we can for her tonight. You understand that, right?"

He stared at Anna and Sara with raised brows while waiting for a response. They glanced at the woman, then back at him and nodded. Toby, observing everything, mimicked them and nodded his head too.

"Okay, you children sleep in my room. It'll be too warm up in the loft."

"But Pa," Sara wouldn't stop. "Did that thing bring her here?"

"I don't know. But when she wakes up, she's returning to where ever she came from.

Once the children were in their bedclothes, Anna tucked Toby under the covers while Sara slipped in the other side. Anna crawled next to Toby and cuddled him.

When the kids got settled, Daniel came in to put out the lamp.

"Toby's trying to take off his shirt off, he's hot," whined Sara.

Daniel ignored her. "Keep this door closed so you won't get too warm. Now go to sleep, all of you."

He settled in the rocking chair and wiped the sweat off his forehead. The room was sweltering, but the lady continued to shake. After observing her, he doubted she'd make it until sunup. *What'll I do with the body? And that contraption, that'll be tough getting rid of.*

It didn't take long before his thoughts drifted together into one and he fell into a dreamless sleep.

Chapter 13

At 9:50 p.m. Russ arrived home. He pulled into the driveway, parked behind Beth's car and strolled up the porch steps with keys in hand. The inside looked dark which made him think Beth must've gone to bed. Russ hoped she'd still be up. She hadn't said goodbye that morning and knew it was his fault. He'd been short with her. He looked forward to relaxing tonight and hoped they could have a glass of wine together.

Russ unlocked the door and struggled with locking it back up. He cursed himself for not fixing it yet. The new one sat on the foyer table.

After throwing his keys into the bowl, he did a double take noticing Beth's keys weren't there. Russ proceeded down the hallway to the kitchen. Beth wasn't in there.

Figuring she had gone to bed, Russ took out an opened bottle of Merlot out of the refrigerator. He poured himself a glass and skipped down to the lab. After unlocking the door, he stepped inside and flipped on the light. Turning toward the Scorpion, Russ froze. He stood and stared at the empty platform.

"What the hell?" He glanced around the room. Everything looked as it should. Russ searched the top of the tables for anything out of place or a note from Beth. *Why would Beth take the machine? She hates it.*

Russ set his glass down and raced up the stairs to the second floor. Beth's bedroom door stood open. Her bed sat untouched and her purse wasn't on the dresser.

Russ darted from room to room yelling her name. He bolted down the stairs and scanned every room again. He felt sick to his stomach.

Hurrying back to the lab, he stood again staring at the empty spot. *She came home. Her car's here. Maybe she dropped it off and rode with someone?* Russ didn't think it was likely but made two phone calls. He tried Beth's number but got no answer. He hung up and called Silvia.

"Hey Russ, what's up?" Russ' name showed up on Silvia's ID which puzzled her. He never called unless it had something to do with Beth.

"Hi Silvia, hey, is Beth with you by any chance?" Noise filled the background. He figured she was still at the club.

"Hold on Russ," Silvia moved into the ladies room. "I can hear you now. What'd you say?"

"Beth's not here, is she with you?"

"No, she left a little after seven. She wasn't feeling well. She's not home?"

"No, her car's here, but she isn't." He didn't want to get Silvia anymore worked up, so he lied, "She must be in bed. I didn't check her bedroom.

"You'll call me if she's not home, right?"

Russ had already hung up. He concluded that, for some odd reason, Beth must've taken the machine. *But why would she take it?*

Russ sat at the desk and slumped with elbows on his knees and stared again at the empty platform. After a few moments, he stood and paced the floor. *Should I call the police? Should I wait to see if she comes back? Why? Why would she go in it?*

The recollection of the sedan following her came to him - he made his decision.

While Russ waited for the police to come, he folded his blueprints and put away all evidence of the time machine.

When the doorbell rang, he opened it, introduced himself and led two officers into the living room.

A short pudgy cop introduced them, "I'm Officer O'Leary, and this is my partner Officer Murray." He sat on one end of the sofa and Murray followed suit on the other. O'Leary pulled a small notebook from his shirt pocket along with a pen. "What seems to be the problem, Mr. Nielson?"

Russ explained the situation, leaving out the part of the time machine.

"Let me see if I got this straight." O'Leary read his notes. "Your sister left the club in Minneapolis at 7 p.m. You know she made it home because her car's in the driveway. You've already confirmed she's not with her friends. Is this correct so far?"

Russ nodded.

"Mind if we look around?" O'Leary asked.

"Not at all, let's go."

Russ led them from room to room leaving the lights on behind them. He brought them down to the basement - the laundry room - the workshop - and down the long hallway.

"What's in this room?" Murray asked, pointing to the locked door.

"It's my laboratory." Russ pulled out his keys and unlocked the door.

"What do you do in here?" O'Leary asked.

"I invent things. Little things, it's just a hobby."

O'Leary walked around the room while Murray - a large man and at least six inches taller than his partner - stood next to Russ with his hands folded behind his back. When O'Leary felt satisfied with his findings, he suggested they return to the living room.

Once upstairs, they took their original places. O'Leary took his book out of his pocket again and jotted down the final notes.

Putting the book away, he said, "A report usually isn't done on a missing person for twenty-four hours unless it's a child. Somebody must have met up with your sister since her purse isn't here. Correct?"

"Wait a minute," Russ cried out. "I forgot to tell you. Beth said someone in a black sedan was following her, it happened a few times." Russ shook his head *how could I forget to tell them that?*

O'Leary frowned, "And you didn't think to tell us this earlier?" he removed the notebook once again, "Okay, this black sedan, did she give you any more details?"

"Yeah, it had a left side broken headlight, and the passenger door had a dent."

"Did she get the make of the car, or the year, license plate number, anything?"

"No."

"Did she see the person driving?"

"Beth said the windows were tinted, and the car was too far away."

"Too far away? Why did she think it was following her?"

Russ told them how she saw the sedan several times in Minneapolis. He also explained how she'd seen the same car at the country store.

"Did it follow her here?" O'Leary asked.

"Beth said it didn't."

"Do you have a recent picture of your sister?"

Russ took a picture off the fireplace mantle and handed it to him. "This was taken three weeks ago."

"Long blonde hair, blue eyes, how tall would you say she is?"

"She's five foot, six."

O'Leary showed the picture to Murray and Murray glanced at his partner and said in a low voice, "You thinking what I'm thinking?" Murray leaned over to O'Leary and whispered, "I doubt she ever made it into the house."

"You mind if we take this picture?" O'Leary asked.

"Let me take it out of the frame for you."

O'Leary handed the picture to Russ and continued, "We'll write this up, so I need a little more information."

"Why the sudden change?"

O'Leary, not wanting to alarm Russ, assured him, "Not a big deal, I figure since we're here we might as well write it up."

Russ didn't like the look they gave each other, and he didn't appreciate Murray whispering. Now O'Leary was vague on answering Russ' question.

"What's going on? Do you know something I don't?"

The two officers looked at each other and O'Leary said, "Your sister matches the victim's description of the Minneapolis serial killer."

Russ was appalled *why didn't I know about that?*

O'Leary cleared his throat and asked, "Mr. Nielson was your door locked when you got home?"

"Yes, it was."

O'Leary stood and handed Russ a card, "Here's the phone number to call if she comes home or if anything changes. Give them the case number I wrote on the back. If we get any information, we'll notify you."

Back in the car, O'Leary instructed Murray to drive as he slipped into the passenger side. He called a detective friend who headed up the serial killer case.

Detective Tom Watson relaxed in front of the television when his private cell phone rang. He saw on the ID it was his friend, so he answered it.

"Hello Bob, what's up?"

"Hey Tom, you got a minute?"

"For you I do."

"The Minneapolis serial killer case, was a black sedan involved?

"Yes, it was the fourth victim, Janis. Her friend reported Janis had seen someone following her for two weeks. It was a black sedan with a dent on the passenger side."

"Did she mention anything about a broken headlight?"

"Yes, what's going on?"

O'Leary told him about the case which interested the detective. They were running on few leads, so every little piece of information was welcomed.

"I'll put out an APB on the black sedan for Forest Lake area down to Minneapolis."

"Yeah and keep this quiet. I don't want this getting to the press."

"You got it. I'll keep in touch."

"Hey, thanks for calling."

Chapter 14

The message came in loud and clear on Theodore's police radio. He relaxed on his foul-smelling ripped up recliner puffing a cigar, blowing smoke rings into the air.

So they know about the black sedan. It didn't take him by surprise. He figured it would happen which is why he had plan B already in action. He needed a different car and next week he'd have one.

Jimmy Grey worked as a dishwasher at the same restaurant as Theodore. The young man knew him as the alias, George Wilcox.

Jimmy, like Theodore and George, had no family or friends, nobody who cared if they lived or died.

Grey was tall and skinny and about the homeliest nerd Theodore ever laid eyes on. His eyeglasses were thick as pop bottles, making him appear cross-eyed. He also stuttered worse than Theodore heard in his entire life.

The young man was a loner until Theodore took him under his wing. He lied to build up Jimmy's ego. He needed Grey to trust him for his plan to go right.

During their breaks, they would sit in the alley out back. Theodore put ideas into Jimmy's head telling him he should get out and see the countryside. He suggested the two of them save up, quit this joint, and travel. At first, Jimmy would laugh and play along. Over the months, he became convinced and began to put away money. He said he had thirty-one hundred dollars saved. Theodore lied and said he did too and it'd be plenty for them to start their journey.

After much discussion the plan took form. Jimmy's 2001 white Ford Focus was in tip-top shape. They decided that would be the vehicle they'd use. Jimmy used the car on rare occasions. It was cheaper and less stress taking the bus. None of Jimmy's co-workers had any knowledge he had a car.

Theodore convinced Jimmy the time had come. He told him to give a two-week notice and pack only what fits in the trunk.

"Keep this under your hat," Theodore told him. "If someone gets a whiff of this, they'll rob us."

They planned to go north and make a pit-stop at Theodore's uncle's place, which was a half hour off the interstate. He said his uncle was giving him more cash. Of course, Theodore had no uncle.

The black sedan had come in handy, but this week would be the last time it would be used. Theodore planned to leave it in a secluded area outside the suburbs. He found the spot when he'd first moved to Minnesota. A while back, he buried a woman's body there who'd been hitchhiking. The murder was out of the ordinary, but it got him by between his chosen victims. He'd hoped to bury more bodies in there, but now the place had a new purpose.

Friday's their final day at work. Three crushed sleeping tablets will be ready to put into Grey's drink. They'll stop at a convenience store to fill the car with gas. While Jimmy fills the tank, Theodore will get their coffee and will spike the unsuspecting man's mug. Once Jimmy gets too tired to drive, Theodore will take over. By the time they arrive at the deserted sedan, Grey will be out cold. Theodore plans to move him from the Ford into the driver's spot in the black sedan.

He'll cut Jimmy's wrists. The razor - which came from Jimmy's bathroom - will be in Grey's hand. Theodore will wait around long enough to watch as he bleeds out and takes his last breath. He'll take his money leaving a small amount, so it doesn't look like a robbery. Next, he'll slip into Grey's wallet, a photo of each of Theodore's Minneapolis victims, including the one of Beth at the park. After all is done, he'll take the white Focus and head north.

Once in Forest Lake, Theodore will have no problem finding a room to rent and a job as a dishwasher. He'll go back to his birth name, Theodore James Collins. This time he'll use James.

The best thing about this plan is, it'll return him to plan A. He'll only be ten minutes away from Russ' domain.

When the police find Grey in the black sedan with pictures of the dead women, the serial killer case will close.

When the news comes out the killer is dead, the weight on Theodore's shoulders will lift. It'll give him the freedom to come and go in his new Ford to complete plan A.

He's hoping when Russ thinks the killer is dead, he won't be looking over his shoulders anymore. Instead, he'll put his attention on building a new machine. When Russ finds Beth, he'll bring her back, and Theodore will be waiting.

Theodore reclined in his chair with one arm folded behind his head lost in thought. *Once everything goes through without a hitch, and that bitch and her brother are dead, I'll make a mint on the Scorpion.*

Taking a puff of his cigar, he shaped his disfigured mouth and blew out smoke circles. *How do I research the black market for the highest bid for a time machine?*

Chapter 15

"Pa, wake up."

Daniel woke so startled he about fell out of his chair. Three wide-awake children stood staring at him.

"Dang, you scared me. What's going on?"

"We have to pee," whimpered Sara.

"Why didn't you go? Why do you need me?"

Sara pointed toward the barn, "We're afraid of that thing."

Toby rubbed his eyes and sniveled.

"There's no reason to be scaring your brother. You two should know better."

"Know better? We had nothing in our barn before," cried Anna. She was nervous now. The girl wasn't accustomed to speaking to her father in such a stern voice.

Daniel sat straight up and glanced down at the female. Her shaking had subsided. He pulled his pocket-watch. 2:30 a.m.

"I'm sorry girls. Let's go pee. I won't let anything happen to you."

He stood and almost fell. His foot was asleep. He plopped back down, took off his boot and rubbed it.

The woman said something.

Daniel froze, watched her closely and waited. After a few moments, he realized she had mumbled in her sleep. He put his boot back on and told the girls to go to the outhouse. He would wait on the porch with Toby.

As he waited, he kept his eyes on the barn - as if he expected another flash. *Maybe we're being invaded. Did anyone else get something land in their barns?* The two finished their business and tore back to the house as if being chased. Daniel didn't see them until they were almost on the porch. It startled him. Thinking something was after them, he grabbed the broom. The girls zipped by him and to Daniel's relief, they were giggling. *I guess we're all a little spooked,* he thought, shaking his head.

The children got tucked into bed and fell asleep right away. Now he was wide awake. Daniel checked on the woman - no change. He threw two logs into the fire and poked it a few times, fueling the flames. Sauntering outside to the crisp night air, he plunked down on a porch chair. Leaning over he grabbed another chair and pulled it to his feet and reclined. With hands folded on his chest, he turned and stared at the barn through the missing rails. *Why did it have to come here? What am I going to do?* He closed his tired eyelids and the cool September's breeze brushed over soothing him into a deep sleep.

It seemed Daniel barely conked out when something woke him. Still half asleep, he tried to open his eyes. They felt like they weighed a hundred pounds. Somebody was standing in front of him. The sun rising behind the person prevented him from seeing who it was. He saw nothing but a silhouette. He tilted his head back and placed his hand as a shield over his eyes and that's when he saw her.

The woman towered over him!

"Dang!" This time Daniel fell knocking over the chair. He scrambled around and grabbed onto the overturned furniture pulling himself up to his knees. Once he gathered himself, he jumped to his feet and put up his fists preparing to protect himself. For a quick moment, their eyes met and she collapsed. Daniel caught her, lifted her up, and once again carried her inside and laid her on the blanket.

Daniel plunked down on the rocker, slumped over resting his elbows on his knees. He ran his hands through his ruffled hair and when putting them down, he noticed they were shaking like a leaf. *I can't keep this balderdash up much longer. I'll have a damn heart attack.* He sat back and gathered a deep breath and waited for his heart to stop racing. It's strange, but all that came to his mind were those eyes. They were the clearest crystal blue he'd ever seen. They weren't evil or scary, in fact, they were completely non-threatening.

Daniel looked at his pocket-watch, it was already 7:35 a.m. Amazed they'd slept that long, he figured they were more exhausted than he realized.

He pushed himself up, shuffled to the bedroom and opened the door. "Girls, wake up. It's late, time to get up."

All three woke rubbing their eyes. The girls, remembering the woman, bolted up.

"Is she still here?" Sara jumped out of bed and raced past her pa.

Anna, right behind her, left Toby still rubbing his eyes.

Sara stood over the woman. "She isn't shaking anymore, Pa. Is she going to be okay?"

"Everything will be fine. Now, get dressed and do your chores."

Sara pointed to the woman. "But what about her? She might wake up."

He ignored his daughter, "Go get dressed and collect eggs." Turning to Anna he ordered, "You stay in the house today, there're plenty of chores to do inside. When the lady wakes up have your sister fetch me."

They nodded and ran off to get dressed.

All the families' clothes were in their father's room. He built shelves against a wall and each member of the family got their personal shelf.

Anna picked their outfits for the day. She handed Sara a chore dress. "Here, put this on."

"But I don't want to wear that, it has a rip in the pocket."

"You're just doing chores. Now put it on." Anna wasn't used to her sister trying to get her way. Typically, she took whatever Anna gave her.

"No. I'm not wearing that rag."

"What's the matter with you, Sara? Pa will be angry with you for fretting over a dress."

Sara's lips pouted.

"What is it? What's the matter?"

Sara mumbled, "When that girl wakes up I don't want to be wearing a rag. I want a cute chore dress."

Anna understood because she wanted to wear something nice too. "You pick out what you want to wear."

Sara had six dresses to choose from, but she rummaged through them several times. She decided on a faded yellow flowered dress.

"Okay, that's a good one. Would you like me to put some matching ribbons in your hair?"

"Oh yes, please. But let me brush my hair though." Since their mother passed away Sara let nobody near her mussed up tangles.

After dressing and fixing themselves up, Anna got Toby dressed and brushed his soft golden curls away from his face, which didn't stay for long.

Sara ran to the chicken coop and collected eggs while Anna mixed up flapjacks. One thing their mother insisted on bringing was a small cast iron stove equipped with two burners. Anna stuck kindling into the pot belly and brought a wick to the hearth and lit it. She returned and lighted the kindling.

Daniel trudged to the barn to inspect the contraption. Now that it could be seen in the daylight, it didn't seem so scary. He moseyed around the machine and poked it twice with a stick.

He pondered on the concept of it being a space cart of some sort. Daniel sauntered around to the door of the apparatus and glanced inside. It was smaller than it looked. His inspection got interrupted by the cowbell.

Daniel rushed into the house and scanned the room. To his relief, the atmosphere appeared calm.

Anna flipped the last flapjack and Sara set the table. Toby sat in his chair with fork in hand.

Daniel hung his hat on the hook and proceeded to the table. He pulled out his chair and sitting he commented, "Look at you two little women. Don't you look cute in your dresses with matching hair ribbons? I didn't realize today's Sunday, Sara."

"It's not Sunday, and this isn't my church dress."

"Pa's kidding, Sara. He knows it's not Sunday." Anna placed the last of the flapjacks on the table as they all sat down in their usual spots.

"My, my, even little Toby is all fancied up." Daniel eyed his son. "What's the occasion?"

"Pa, we can't be looking like orphans when the lady wakes up." Anna declared, glancing at the woman.

Daniel turned around and checked on the woman and returned his attention back to the girls. "Don't be getting your hopes up on her. The moment she wakes up, she's leaving. Sara, did you feed the hogs?"

"Not yet, Pa, I'll take Toby outside with me after breakfast. We'll feed the chickens and the rest of the animals then."

"That's my girl." Daniel didn't praise his children enough. He thought if he did they'd get soft and couldn't withstand the hard times.

They ate the rest of their meal in silence. When Daniel left to continue his chores, the two girls carried on like hens. They chatted about what they'll say to the mysterious woman when she wakes.

"You'll come and get me the minute she opens her eyes,

okay Anna? Get me before you get pa, He might be mean to her."

"I promise, now take Toby and run along. Don't get Pa any more upset than he already is."

Two hours went by and both girls had their chores done.

Sara was super careful not to dirty her dress and twice she attempted to put a brush through her hair.

Anna cleaned the area better than usual.

Sara perched next to the girl with Toby on her lap waiting for her to wake up.

When finishing her chores, Anna roosted behind them on the rocker.

They weren't expecting it when the girl brought her hand up to her head and moaned. Her movement caught all three off guard.

It surprised Sara so much she almost fell backward.

Toby, alarmed when he sensed his sister's panic, struggled to get off her lap.

Sara held him tight and her eyes stayed fixated on the lady.

Beth's eyes flew open. Three children with big round eyes were staring at her with mouths gaping. She rubbed her pounding forehead and moaned, "Where am I?"

"Sara, go get Pa," Anna commanded in a loud whisper.

Sara, eyes bulging, sat paralyzed. She didn't want her pa to come in yet. Not until she speaks with her first.

"Sara, get Pa now."

This time, Sara handed Toby over to Anna and ran outside.

Daniel was in the barn when he heard Sara calling him. He set down his tool and hurried out.

Sara ran to keep up with him as he rushed to the house. She caught up and ran alongside pleading with him not to be mean to the girl. When they came inside, Anna was holding Toby in the rocker.

Beth attempted to raise herself up, but being too weak, she plopped back down.

"Sara, go get your brother," Daniel ordered.

Sara hustled to the rocker and took Toby.

"Anna, get the lady a cup of water." Daniel walked over to the woman and knelt down on one knee. "You've been out for hours. You should try to drink." Daniel lifted the woman's head and held the cup to her mouth.

Beth pushed it away and groaned, "I have to sit up. Where am I? Who are you?"

"I'll answer your questions when you answer mine. What's *your* name?"

"My name's Beth."

Both grinning, the girls shot looks at each other. Now, they had a name to call her, something other than the woman or the girl.

"So, Beth, where are you from?"

"I...I... I'm from Minneapolis."

"How did you get here from Minneapolis?"

"I don't know how to answer that because I don't know where I am." Beth struggled to sit up. "Can you please help me? I want to get up. I don't need an interrogation while lying on my back."

"First, tell me how you got here."

Beth scanned the area. Since she was lying on her back, all she saw was a bunch of feet. Her brows scrunched *what's happening?* She lifted her head and spotted a fireplace *where am I?* "I don't know how I got here. The last thing I remember I was at my birthd..." *Oh my God, what is happening?* "Help me up, NOW."

"All right, I'll get you in the chair, but I'm warning you, don't try anything."

Don't try anything? What does he think I'll do?

Daniel knelt down, put her arm around his shoulders and

hoisted her up. He sat her in the rocker and stood in front of her with hands on his hips.

Beth looked up at him, got dizzy and slumped over. She hung her head close to her knees *don't faint, don't faint.*

"Maybe you should lie down, I don't want you falling and hurting yourself. I don't have the time or the means to be taking care of one more person."

"No, please... I need to sit up. Give me a moment to adjust. What time is it?"

Daniel took out his pocket-watch, "It's almost noon. Listen, I have work that needs tending to. What am I going to do with you? I don't know you're safe to leave with my children."

Beth's forehead crinkled, *Safe to leave with his...?* She turned her gaze to the children.

Sara sat in the rocker staring at her wearing a wide closed-lip smile.

Anna stood next to Sara holding little bewilder Toby.

Beth turned back to Daniel and snapped, "I would never hurt your children." Her eyes darted back and forth *what is happening? This has to be a nightmare. Oh God, help me."*

Daniel saw he had no choice but to trust her for now. "It's dinner time, we'll take care of this after we eat." Daniel walked to Anna and took Toby from her. "Go finish up in the kitchen. I'm going out to clean up." He turned back to Beth and warned, "You stay put."

As soon as Daniel left, Beth glanced around the room. She guessed it to be about twelve by twenty feet in size. The big stone fireplace she sat in front of filled most of the wall. To the right was the entrance door.

Sara stared at Beth, mesmerized with every move she made. She'd never seen a woman with such perfectly shaped eyebrows. The men's trousers she wore were strange, but they didn't bother her.

Daniel trudged back in, put Toby in his highchair and stood in front of Beth again. "Do you think you can walk?"

"I can try, I need to relieve myself."

Daniel furrowed his brows giving her an odd look.

"I need to go to the bathroom."

"She needs to pee, Pa." Sara spurted out acting like Beth's interpreter.

Beth smiled at Sara and it made the girl feel like she was floating on air.

Daniel helped Beth up. He hoped she could make it to the barn after her stop at the outhouse.

Now that Beth was standing, she got a better look at the rest of the house. Half the area behind her was the kitchen. The room had no refrigerator, microwave or cupboards. All it had was a cast iron stove, and a counter covered with a cloth skirt. An old wash basin and a pitcher sat on top. A small window above the work area had open wooden shutters. Outside the kitchen nook, was a long wooden table. Toby sat next to it in a wood highchair.

Confused by everything she saw, Beth asked, "Am I in your cabin?"

Ignoring her question, Daniel assisted her out onto the porch. He pointed to the outhouse. "There's the crapper. Do you think you can make it?"

Beth frowned, "Don't you have a bathroom?"

Daniel scowled, "What's a bathroom?"

Beth scanned the surroundings. A flock of chickens pecked at the ground and the mooing of a cow was nearby. She cocked her head to the right and noticed a big wagon and to the left of that a chicken coop. A barn, in dire need of paint, sat in the distance. Beth gazed to the left where she spotted a well. Straight out from that was the outhouse sitting in a clump of big oaks. She searched for anything that looked familiar. As her eyes darted around her surroundings, a flashback came to her *I was running from something. But what? I was at Russ's house.* Beth looked at Daniel and her mouth opened to speak, but nothing came out.

"What is it?" He asked.

"I remember being chased."

"Chased? By what?"

"What's today's date?"

"It's Wednesday, Sept. 5th."

"What year is it?" She was afraid to ask.

"It's 1860."

"What?" Beth fainted.

Chapter 16

Beth's eyes rolled back in her head as she collapsed in Daniel's arms.

"Oh great," he muttered, "Not again." Scooping her up, he carried her into the parlor and placed her back on the blanket.

"Pa, what happened?" Sara watched the scenario from the house.

Daniel ignored his daughter and called for Anna to help him.

Anna stopped preparing lunch and moved to her father's side.

He ran his hand through his hair and said, "She fainted again, plus she had an accident. She needs a change of clothes."

Anna, not comprehending, stood with a blank stare.

Sara understood though, and she took charge like a female on a mission. "Pa, I think Ma's clothes will fit her. We still have them under the bed. Shall I get something for her?"

"Yes, Anna, help your sister. I'll take Toby with me. Ring the bell when you finish."

Sara excited and eager about dressing Beth in girl's clothing rushed into the bedroom. She pulled the low box beneath the bed and took off the cover. Picking the perfect dress became her new challenge. She chose a yellow sundress which was her mother's favorite and it was the same color of the dress she wore. She grabbed one of the newer-looking bloomers and pushed the box back under the bed.

In the meantime, Anna placed a small blanket over Beth and

pulled off her jeans. To preserve Beth's dignity was important to the girls. She waited for Sara to come before attempting to remove the top.

"All right, I have everything she needs." Sara came out of the room carrying an arm-full of clothes.

"Maybe we should put the bloomers on her and leave her sweater on." Anna worried they were overstepping their limits.

"Pa told us to change her, and that's what we're going to do." Sara pulled the top over Beth's head and off. The girls made sure she stayed covered as much as possible. They paused long enough to admire her beautiful lace bra. Their mother had nothing like that. They decided that would stay on.

They replaced her soiled undergarment with the bloomers. Anna held the blanket while Sara put the clean ones on and they did it all without looking. When they finished, they stood admiring their masterpiece.

"I should wash her face," said Sara.

"No, you're getting creepy, Sara. Let her wash her own face when she wakes up."

Sara climbed the loft, grabbed her pillow and placed it under Beth's head. "Doesn't she look beautiful?"

The girls stood admiring her when Beth opened her eyes.

"Why is it every time I wake up, I have kids hovering over me?" She raised her hand to her aching head. "You wouldn't happen to have any aspirin would you?"

The girls looked at each other furrowing their brows, saying nothing.

"I didn't think so," she mumbled. While boosting herself up, Beth noticed the dress. "What the heck? What am I wearing? Help me up."

The girls each grabbed an arm and pulled her up into the chair.

Beth looked down at what she wore. She glared at the girls and scowled, "Who put this on me?" She lifted it up and scorned, "Are these bloomers? Where are my clothes?"

Sara, smiling proudly, said, "We dressed you cause you peed your pants, but we didn't peek. That's Ma's favorite dress."

"My name is Anna, and this is my sister Sara. I'll wash your clothes. You can put them back on when they're dry."

"Where's your mother?"

"Ma died giving birth to Toby," answered Anna sadly.

"Oh, I'm sorry. Where's your dad?"

"Pa took Toby outside while we dressed you. We need to tell him he can come inside now," mumbled Sara.

But they weren't in a hurry to get him. They liked having this time with the woman alone.

Beth noticed the dress Sara wore. "Did you pick out my dress Sara? It looks like yours."

"Yes, Ma'am, Anna put ribbons in my hair too. We have more. Would you like some in your hair?"

Beth felt her matted up hair. She was a total mess inside and out.

"I can get you a mirror if you like." Sara offered, sitting down on the edge of the rocker. She spread her dress, smoothed out the wrinkles and folded her hands on her lap smiling the whole time at Beth. She liked this lady and didn't care if she came from space.

"No, but I am a little thirsty."

Anna retrieved the cup Beth used earlier and gave it to her. "I better get Pa now. He'll be cross if he knows you've been awake."

Beth heard Daniel's footsteps on the porch and he came in holding Toby. Giving the boy to Anna, he marched over and stood in front of Beth. He recognized Kristine's dress and it brought a weight of pain to his heart. His brows scrunched as he turned and glared at Sara. He set out to scold her but saw the regret on her face so he backed off.

Daniel turned back to Beth, "How're you doing?"

"I think I can walk."

"Sit a spell. I don't want to be carrying you around again."

Beth remembered nothing about him carrying her. Her eyes squinted trying to recollect the events of that morning. She remembered seeing the barn and the chickens. She recollected the outhouse but didn't recall using it. *I must have fainted. Oh crap, I had an accident. Did he carry me like that?* Just thinking about it made her face turn red with embarrassment.

"I'm sorry… what's your name?"

"My name's Daniel. I see you have water. Can you eat?"

"No, but I'd like to sit at the table if you don't mind." She didn't like facing the fireplace not knowing what was going on behind her.

"That shouldn't be a problem." Daniel offered his hand to help her up. "But we'll wait until lunch is over before we talk further on this matter."

She nodded and with his aid, she walked to the table. Once he got her seated, he disappeared into a room alongside the kitchen.

Beth looked at Toby sitting at the end of the table. "Hello, Toby. How old are you?"

He didn't respond. He just stared at her.

Sara set a plate of pork on the table. "Toby's shy, he can't talk much yet, but he can say, put me down." Sara giggled and skipped off to assist Anna.

Beth glanced around the room. A stone wall stood between the kitchen and the room Daniel entered. The cast iron stove had a sixteen-foot exhaust pipe climbing up the wall and out the roof. On the opposite side of the barrier, was the room Daniel went in to. Above that was a loft.

Her gaze returned to the door - she assumed it was a bedroom.

Daniel came out and he and Beth's eyes locked. He had to

turn away because he hadn't stopped thinking of them since seeing them earlier.

Everybody sat in their assigned seats and Anna fixed Toby his plate while Daniel and Sara helped themselves to sandwiches.

Sara, being the curious one, made the mistake of asking, "How did you get here? Did that thing in the barn bring you?"

Daniel glared at her and snapped, "Sara, eat your lunch and stop talking."

Beth turned to Sara and stuttered, "Ther... There's something in the barn? What kind of thing?"

Beth flung around and glared at Daniel. A sudden surge of energy hit her as the memories started coming. She recollected the horrible man chasing her through the basement. She remembered the time machine and flipping the starter switch. "Is the time machine in the barn?"

Daniel gave Beth a cross look and said, "You need to calm down lady."

"No, I will not calm down. I need to go to the barn!"

Even more firmly, Daniel reiterated, "You'll wait until we finish our meal."

"No, you can all wait. I'm going to the barn." The fog lifted and memories flooded into her head. The recollection of the party, the ride home, and the chase into the machine came back to her. The Scorpion was in the barn. She could go home! Beth pushed her chair back and tried to stand. Her head spun. She plunked down, took a few seconds to regain her composure and tried again, slower this time.

Daniel could tell there was no stopping her, so he got up and assisted her.

Anna eyed her sister and shaking her head, she gave her a "Look what you started this time." glimpse.

"Anna, keep both kids in the house."

Sara crossed her arms over her chest and gave her father an angry, defiant glare, which only made him angrier.

Daniel pointed at her and then at her sandwich and shouted, "That lunch better be gone when I get back." He took Beth's arm and led her to the barn.

Ever since Sara first laid eyes on Beth, she felt like her protector, her guardian angel. The feisty girl got up, dashed to the window and announced, "They're halfway to the barn." She darted back to the table, grabbed her plate and threw the sandwich in the garbage. The gutsy girl bellowed, "There, it's gone." Scurrying out the door, she followed them, staying a safe distance behind.

Chapter 17

They stood, eyes fixated on the hellish apparatus that took over the far corner of the barn. Beth and Daniel hated this contraption more than ever. But now they're counting on it to bring her home. She slid in and examined the controls. There were no working lights. She wished Russ instructed her on what to do in this scenario, but she probably wouldn't have listened.

Flipping and pushing random buttons and switches, seemed the logical place to start. After hitting several of them, nothing happened. She flipped the starter one more time praying it would start, but it did no good. *Oh, my God. Something work. Please.* "Damn it." She acted like a crazy woman yelling at the machine. "Why don't you start?"

Daniel stood feeling helpless. "Do you know what you're doing?"

Beth spun around and screamed, "YES I DO." Tired of his rudeness, she wouldn't take it anymore. "I would appreciate if you'd go to your house and let me fix this in peace." Her lips quivered as she fought back tears. The realization hit her. The Scorpion was unfixable. She slid out, fell to her knees and sobbed.

Daniel took that as a sign things weren't going well, so he kept his mouth shut. He stood there watching her cry her heart out, not sure what to do.

Like a flash out of nowhere, Sara zipped past her father and knelt at Beth's side. She wrapped her tiny arms around Beth and comforted her. Beth gazed into the little girl's face and for a moment, she didn't feel so displaced."

Daniel was relieved Sara came. For once he didn't mind her disobedience. "Listen... I fix all my equipment. Show me how this works and I'll see what I can do."

Beth wiped her tears away and tried to stand. Sara took hold of her arm and Daniel took the other. Once they got her standing, she pushed her hair out of her face, glared at the broken Scorpion and muttered, "Damn. Why didn't I pay closer attention?"

Anna, carrying Toby, came into the barn.

Daniel was passed the point of getting angry at the children for not listening to him. He glanced back at the machine and turned to Beth. "How'd you get that in here?"

Beth took in a deep breath and said, "We should go to the house. I need to sit down. I can explain it there."

Daniel and Sara sat in their usual spots at the table. Beth perched down in the same chair she used earlier which had now become her assigned place. There were still uneaten sandwiches from dinner, but nobody had an appetite anymore. Toby played on the floor with his wooden toys. Anna made coffee.

Daniel leaned over with his elbows on the table and gave Beth his undivided attention.

"Okay, I'm not sure where to start," she said, in a quiet voice.

Daniel and Sara moved their heads closer. Anna stopped what she was doing in the kitchen and also turned an ear.

"That thing out there..." Beth paused, *how do you tell someone you barged into their home in a time machine?*

"It's a vehicle, kind of like your horse and buggy." She looked at Daniel, "You do travel by horse and buggy correct?"

"We use oxen and a wagon."

"Okay... well... My wagon travels too."

You could hear a pin drop as they waited for her to continue. "Did you come from the sky?" Sara broke the silence.

"No, I traveled through space."

They all sat with furrowed brows and vacant faces.

"Let me start from the beginning. My brother, Russ, is an inventor." Beth turned to the girls. "He's about the age of your father."

Now, the whole family sat with elbows on the table leaning in close.

"Russ loved making stuff, even before your age, Sara."

Sara looked up at Beth with a blissful smile. Beth mentioning her name made her melt like warmed butter.

"Russ also traveled to the past but had no problems getting back. He got sick like I did though. He meant to fix the problem, but never got the chance." Beth hesitated. She got emotional talking about her brother. She gathered another deep breath. "When I came home last night a man chased me." Beth paused, *who will believe this?* "This man chased me through my brother's house. My only means of escape was the time machine. I pushed the starter switch, and that's all I remember. Then I woke up in your house. I should've paid more attention when Russ tried to teach me how to use it. I never thought the contraption would work. It's all electronic and computerized and I know nothing about either."

Beth studied the family. They were like posed statues. She could almost see the wheels in their minds spinning. With raised brows, Beth waited for a response. She expected one of them to ask a profound question about time-travel.

Finally, after a few moments, Daniel scrunched his brows and asked, "What's computerized?"

Beth couldn't believe her ears, "Of all the question's you could ask, that's all you can come up with? I'll tell this one more time. I came from the year 2016."

She pointed at the barn and hollered, "I traveled in *that* vehicle and landed in *your* barn. The apparatus took me backward through time. A maniac tried to kill me and I had nowhere to run. My only means of escape was the time machine."

"That's pure nonsense," Daniel argued. He stood and bellowed, "There's got to be someone who can get you."

"What? Do you have a phone I can use?" Beth scowled.

"A phone? I don't have time for this poppycock. I have a farm to run. When you have a better story, send Sara to get me. Now if you'll excuse me, I've got chores to do." Daniel grabbed his hat and stomped out the door.

Toby sat on the floor keeping his eyes down. He'd never heard so much arguing, most of the time his pa was quiet and unemotional.

Sara rested her chin in her palm and smiled, "I believe you."

Beth smiled back, "Thank you."

Anna set a cup of coffee in front of Beth.

Beth looked up at her with a strained smile and thanked her. She ran her hands through her tangled hair and slouched over with her elbows on the table. She groaned and rubbed her temples figuring out her next move. Feeling like crap and sure she looked like it too, Beth faced Sara, "I wouldn't mind that mirror now."

Sara jumped up, got the mirror and handed it to Beth.

Beth took several seconds admiring the beautiful ornate jeweled handle.

"It was our Ma's mirror," Anna volunteered.

Beth looked at her reflection. With the cheval glass being so stained, the reflection was poor. *I wish I had my purse. My makeup bag is in it.* Beth's head shot up. "Wait a minute. I had my purse and my backpack with me." She looked at the girls and said, "We have to go back to the barn."

Chapter 18

The trip to the barn had been worth the exertion for Beth. Anna and Sara assisted her to the out-building and back without their father noticing. Once again, they sat in their spots at the table. Beth's arms wrapped tightly around the Rhinestone bag, it was her only link to the future. She set the large bag on the chair next to her and opened it.

All three children sat with eyes as big as the moon.

Reaching in, she removed her purse and took out the small makeup pouch. Unzipping it, she watched the kids. She paused like waiting for a drum roll. She took out the compact, opened it and put the mirror in front of Sara.

The girl grinned so big you could see all her teeth - except for the two missing ones on the bottom.

Next, Beth put the makeup container in front of Anna.

The girls' mouth dropped open. She moved closer to the mirror and said, "It's so clear. I didn't know I had freckles on my nose."

Toby held his hands out and squirmed. Beth put the mirror in front of him. He pointed and in his babble talk, said, "Baby."

Sara clapped her hands and squealed, "Toby, you can talk." Turning, she put her focus back on Beth. "What's on the other side? Is that rouge for your cheeks?

It amazed Beth that an eight-year-old in 1860 would know what makeup is. "Yes, it's called blush."

"Because it makes you blush?" asked Anna.

Beth giggled, "Something like that."

She pulled out the lipstick next and put a dab on the girl's lips. They giggled taking turns looking at their reflections.

Toby threw a tantrum because he wanted it on his lips too, and he wanted to keep the mirror.

"Stop screaming, Toby. You're a boy silly," giggled Sara.

Beth got an idea that would calm the boy down. She returned the lipstick to the makeup pouch and pushed it aside. Keeping the kids in suspense, she reached into her Rhinestone bag and removed the bag of lollipops.

The children's eyes got as big as golf balls and their mouths formed a perfect shaped O.

Beth picked one, pulled off the wrapper and handed it to Toby. She put the bag in front of the girls and let them choose their choice of color.

Beth dug into her purse and took out her cell phone. It still worked for music and photos stored on the memory card. She chose a picture of her and Russ and showed it to the girls. "This is my brother Russ and me."

Their jaws dropped.

"How'd you get them in there?" Sara's brows rose so high that her bangs about covered her eyes.

"That's too much to explain," Beth chuckled.

Beth and the girls about fell off their chairs when Daniel came barging through the door. He noticed the plates and pots still sat dirty. "Why isn't this mess cleaned up yet?"

They were so wrapped up in the moment they forgot about cleaning. Anna and Sara flew out of their chairs and got to work.

Toby, with sticky face and hands, held up his sucker for his pa to see.

It was enough to set Daniel over the edge. "What in Sam's Hill is going on? What did you give him?"

"If you'll calm down, I'll tell you," said Beth, trying to keep calm herself.

"No, I'll not calm down. I have a broken-down contraption from who knows where in my barn. And now the creature who came in it is feeding stuff to my kids." Things got worse when he noticed the bags. "Where did all this come from?"

"We found her bags in the barn," said Sara, picking up dishes from the table.

Daniel pulled out his chair and sat down hard. He put his forearms on the table and leaned in close to Beth. "Listen, lady, you have one week to get that apparatus fixed. If you can't fix it, you need to leave and go elsewhere."

"But Pa, where will she go?" whined Sara.

Daniel turned to Sara. "I've had enough out of you little lady." He stood up and pointed at her. "You've been turning into a little rebel ever since she got here. I will not stand for it. Anna, get this table cleaned up. Sara, you get outside. I need help."

He turned to Beth and put up his index finger. "One week," he said, stomping out the door.

Embarrassed by the harsh words her father had inflicted upon her, Sara fought back tears. She put down the dishes and followed her father. She turned to Beth shaking her head and whimpered, "Please don't go."

Anna, also embarrassed by her father's rudeness, kept her head down like a dog that got kicked. She gathered up the dishes from the meal that nobody ate.

Toby ate his sucker as fast as his toothless mouth could gum it. He wasn't taking the chance of getting it ripped from his hands.

Beth stuffed everything back into the Rhinestone bag and closed it. She turned to Anna, but the girl wouldn't look at her. So she wrapped her arms around her bag and stood up. As she headed to the barn once again, she swore she'd never enter that house again.

With tears blurring her vision, Beth wiped them away and slipped into Scorpion. It didn't matter what buttons she pushed, it was all to no avail. The Scorpion was going nowhere. Beth banged on the dashboard. *It's no use. I don't know what to do. I can't stay in here forever. How will Russ find me without having a time machine? Even if he did, he wouldn't know what month and year I'm in.*

Tears flowed harder and now her head pounded. Every joint of her body hurt like a toothache. She laid her head on the headrest to rest her tired eyes. Tears ran down her cheeks, but she didn't bother to wipe them away anymore.

Beth didn't expect to fall asleep, but she did. Upon waking, she rotated her head slowly in a half circle trying to loosen her stiff neck. Glancing up at the barn window, she guessed it to be around supper time.

Sliding out of the Scorpion, she peered towards the door and paced the floor. *Is anybody going to come for me? Would I go if they did? That... that man, he is the rudest person I have ever met.*

Beth slid back into the Scorpion. She sat staring into space as another hour went by. It might have been thirty minutes, she had no idea. The chill of the fall evening closed in. Beth wrapped her arms around herself and rubbed her arms. On top of being chilled to the bone, the damp odor of the barn made her nauseated. Being thirsty and dehydrated wasn't helping matters either. She needed a plan and wasn't crazy about the results of staying in the barn. It would mean staying cold and hungry. At least she wouldn't have to deal with Daniel. That man made her boil inside. *Surrendering may be my best choice. At least I would have a hot meal, water, a warm place to sleep. I must learn how to bite my tongue though.*

Beth had a hard time getting past her stubbornness. But she no longer had the vigor to preserve her honor. She made up her mind. With her arms hugging her precious Rhinestone bag, Beth exited the machine. She tromped through the barn and headed back. First, she made a detour to the outhouse and did her business. After that was out of the way, she took long strides and headed to the house. She paused at the steps. *It's not too late to turn around.* Her heart pounded so hard she swore her ears were pulsating. *Will they let me in? What will I say?*

Beth stumbled backward when Daniel suddenly opened the door. She didn't have to worry about what to say because she was tongue-tied.

Daniel stepped out onto the porch with hands on his hips and asked, "Well, are you coming in or not?"

Beth, like a puppy with its tail between its legs, walked up the steps, passed Daniel and entered the house.

Sara and Toby were sitting at the table in their usual spots. Anna was at the stove scooping potatoes into a bowl. The table was set with mismatched dishes and the place smelled like a Thanksgiving feast. Beth's glands released a mouthful of salvia as her stomach let out a loud growl.

Sara gave out a big sigh of relief, "Pa said you'd be back. He told me to put out a setting for you."

Beth glanced at her assigned spot, and sure enough, there was an extra plate.

Daniel held up his index finger and reiterated, "One week."

Beth nodded and asked if she could get freshened up before dinner.

Anna grabbed a pan of water and heading for the stove she said, "I'll heat water for you."

"Thank you, Anna." Beth followed Anna as she carried the heated water outside. She poured it into a big bowl sitting on a tall round wooden table near the well. Anna also placed a small hand rag and a bar of soap on it. "If you need anything just yell," she said, skipping off.

Beth set her shoulder bag on the table and glanced around. *So this is how they clean up.* A big tin tub sat near the well. Knee-high weeds surrounded it. "Don't tell me that's the tub. I won't be doing that here ever," she mumbled, hoping to God Russ would find her soon.

After cleaning up, she dug the mirror out and looked at her reflection. *I look like I've aged years.* At least the smeared eye makeup was no longer there. She cried off that off hours ago. Beth put the makeup pouch back into the bag. Smoothing the wrinkles of her dress she held her chin up high and marched into the house.

Daniel got up and pulled out Beth's chair and she thought, *this man might have manners after all.* She sat down still clutching her Rhinestone bag. Daniel handed her the plate of fried chicken. She looked down at the bird, winked at Sara and asked with a smile, "Is this the unlucky chicken I saw running around earlier?"

The girls giggled and a puff of a chuckle even came out of Daniel.

Beth always liked making people laugh. She was thankful the tension had eased up.

Daniel passed the yams to Beth and asked, "Would you like to set your bag down while you eat?"

Beth passed the sweet potatoes to Sara and without looking Daniel's way she answered, "No, it's not in my way." Taking a bite of chicken, she felt as though she was in heaven. But Daniel had to ruin the mood.

"What's in your bag that's so important you can't set it down at mealtime?"

Can't he just let it be? Beth wanted to tell him it was none of his business. But she didn't want to end up back out in the barn, so she bit her tongue. The tension increased as they ate their meal. *Why does he care if I keep the backpack on my lap? Wait... the proof I need is in my bag.*

She decided to fill her hungry belly before saying anything. As soon she swallowed her last bite, Beth put down the fork. She faced Daniel and stated, "I can prove to you I'm from the future."

"I doubt it," Daniel mumbled.

Beth opened the shoulder bag and dug around in it until she found what she wanted. The three children knowing the bag was full of unique treasures sat captivated.

Beth removed the Polaroid camera. She stood up and took a few steps backward peering through the lens. When she had all four of them in view, she told them, "Smile."

They sat like statues with vacant faces.

"Come on, humor me. Everybody smile." So when they gave fake smile, Beth snapped the button and out came the picture. She sat down and set the picture on the table. The film hadn't focused yet. Turning to Daniel, she handed him the camera, "This is a Polaroid camera. It didn't get invented until the mid-nineteen hundreds."

Daniel turned the gadget every which way examining it. He glanced back at the photo - the picture was blank. His face hardened.

Beth, noting he was ready to blow, said, "It'll take a minute for the image to develop, be patient."

Daniel pushed the chair back and stood to his feet. "What in tarnation are you trying to pull?"

"Give it a moment." The image came into focus. "There it is."

Anna and Sara gasped when they saw the picture come into view.

Daniel sat back down, picked up the photo and inspected it. "How did you do that? This is witchery."

"Oh, P-l-eez." Beth reached into the bag and pulled out her cell phone. Now, I will show you a modern way of taking pictures. It became popular in the next decade. This little thing is called a phone. They're used for talking to other people who also have one."

Beth saw this was going over their heads, so she concentrated on Daniel, "Do you have tin cans? Like bean cans or soup cans?"

Daniel's face contorted. "Cans made from tin?"

Anna turned to her father, "You know, Pa, like the ones at Mrs. Knutson's store."

Daniel grumbled, "Oh yeah, tin cans. We don't trade for them on account they're too expensive."

"Okay, imagine two of those cans. You take the top off of both and make a small hole in the bottoms. After that's done, you put a long string through both holes and knot them."

Beth horned in on Sara, "Sara, you would go out on the porch and Anna would stay in this room. One of you talks into the can and the other puts it to their ear and listens. The string connecting them carries the sound."

Sara looked up at her father with a crinkled forehead, bangs back in her eyes, "Really Pa? Is that right?"

"First time I've heard of it."

"Maybe we can try it, Pa?" Anna always wanted to taste canned beans. "It wouldn't be a waste because we would eat the food first."

Beth saw she had a lot of convincing to do so she continued, "After a time, phones that don't need wires got invented." She figured she better talk fast. Daniel might cut her off at any given minute. Beth held up the phone and pointed to it. "This phone can also take pictures, and it plays music."

More blank looks.

"Let me show you." Beth turned on the phone and hit the gallery icon. She picked a random picture and held it up. "This is a picture of me in 2016 with my friends." It was an image of her, Tony, Silvia, and Lori at the club posing with the band members.

Daniel took the phone after Beth passed it to him. He stared it, "How can this be?" Daniel inspected all sides of the phone. "How'd those people get in here?"

Beth decided taking a selfie might help Daniel get the gist of it. He leaned away as she got close to him. "It's okay, I won't bite." When she got both into view, she snapped the camera.

Daniel's jaw dropped when the picture was immediately there. He expected a paper to come out.

Beth showed him the calendar, the calculator, and the music apps. She opened the music app and played the song, *Bad, Bad, Leroy Brown,* by Jim Croce.

"Wow." Sara sat straight up grinning. "I like that!"

Daniel gave Sara a disproving glance.

Slouching down in her chair, her grin turned into a frown.

Not wanting the phone to go dead, Beth turned it off and put it away. Next, she pulled out the hand fan.

All focused on that now. The wheels in their heads spun as they moved in closer with wide eyes.

Beth put a battery in it, held it in front of Daniel's face and turned it on.

The breeze from the fan slapped Daniel's face, and he about toppled his chair.

Beth laughed putting her hand over her mouth. "I'm sorry. I guess I should have warned you."

Sara giggled and Anna gasped, with her hand flying to her mouth.

After getting his composure, and getting the color back into his face, Daniel told them, "That will be enough entertainment for one day."

Sara moved closer to Beth and beaming up at her, whispered, "I believe you."

Daniel became sullen. His thoughts went to the machine in the barn. *How'd it get in there? The door was latched. There're no holes in the roof.*

Beth broke up his thoughts, saying, "My brother will make another machine, and when he does, he'll find me. If you let me stay on, I can help on your farm. I'll do whatever you need me to do."

Daniel hesitated a moment and asked, "How long will it take him to build another one?"

"Russ has the blueprints. Since he already made one, it shouldn't take him more than a month, maybe less."

"We'll see how things go. Tomorrow you can start by shoveling out the pigsty."

Beth studied Daniel's face to gauge the seriousness and realized he wasn't kidding. He would try to bully her into leaving. But Beth, determined not to be intimidated, said with a grin, "I love pigs."

Chapter 19

Theodore's plan couldn't have gone smoother. Three young men on dirt bikes discovered the body of Jimmy Grey. They spotted the deserted black sedan in the woods with Grey inside, wrists slit.

His wallet contained pictures of the serial killer's seven victims, one being a photo of Beth sitting on a park bench.

A witness of the fourth victim recognized the car. The broken headlight and the dent made it easy to identify.

Grey's landlady disclosed to the police Jimmy's plan of moving. She found it strange Jimmy still had belongings in the apartment. The woman knew nothing of him owning a car.

All evidence pointed to Grey as the Minneapolis serial killer.

The news of the murderer's suicide smothered the media. The assumption concluded, Jimmy, guilt-stricken, ended his life. Case closed.

With everyone thinking the killer was dead, it gave Theodore freedom to come and go. He had no problem finding a room to rent in Forest Lake. Two blocks away from his new residence he scored a job as a dishwasher. His scheme came together like a tee.

Russ ran more errands than usual this week, which also fit into Theodore's strategy. He found a spot a half block away to camouflage his car in the woods while stalking the lab.

Twice, Theodore broke into Russ' house to check the progress of the second machine. Twice, he slid through the lab window to read his calendar and notes.

Theodore displayed no fear. The last time he left the curtain open a tad, just enough to spy on the unsuspecting inventor.

Chapter 20

One week passed since Beth's disappearance. There wasn't a local newspaper that didn't have her picture plastered on the front page.

All the regional news channels competed with one another. Each one scrambled to be first to report the latest details of the horrific event. Consensus linked Beth Nielson as the last victim of the Minneapolis serial killer.

Officer O'Leary worked alongside Detective Tom Watson in solving this problematic case. Watson ordered a ground search on and around Russ' property. The result got them no closer to finding Beth.

Beth's co-workers confirmed she had a black sedan following her. The confiscated car led the police nowhere. A dead man in Ohio owned the vehicle.

The investigation concluded the killer followed Beth to the house. He abducted her in the driveway, murdered her and buried the body elsewhere.

In the beginning, Silvia called Russ non-stop. She and the rest of the co-workers feared the body buried at the crime site might be Beth's. The conclusion proved negative, but still, there was no evidence she was alive.

Russ knew in his gut his sister *did* make it into the house. He wasn't sure if the serial killer chased her into the machine, but he knew she took it for a reason. For days he didn't leave the house. He feared the serial killer might be stalking his home. Three days ago Detective Watson informed him the insane man had committed suicide. Now, confident the killer was no longer a concern, he continued his errands to the big city and began the construction on the second Scorpion.

Russ, relieved he kept precise notes with the first Scorpion, put together the next one faster than expected. He solved the hypothermia issue so now traveling - he hoped - would be safer. Soon he'd be ready to search for her, but he didn't have a clue of what year to start.

Chapter 21

It's been seven days since arriving in 1860. It looks like I'll be staying a while longer. I figured it best I start a journal.

The first day my chores began, I pulled my hair into a ponytail. I put on the cap I got for my birthday. The one that read, "I'm older than the Internet." I dressed in my blue cashmere sweater and my clean jeans.

Daniel came in from outside to fetch me for the job of shoveling out the pig pen. He looked me over and his eyes settled on my cap. After a few awkward seconds, he asked, "What in Sam's Hill is the Internet?" Without waiting for an answer, he told me if I wear those garbs, they'll get ruined before the day's end. His solution was to give me access to Kristine's garments.

Well, I have to say, I wasn't real crazy about that idea. Just days ago when Sara dressed me in his deceased wife's dress it set Daniel into a frenzy. So, I begged the man into letting me wear his pants while doing chores. After putting up a fuss, he lent me a pair of trousers. They were too large for me - to say the least. I solved it by using a rope for a belt, and I rolled up the cuffs. He surprised me with a shirt too. I rolled up the sleeves and tied a knot in the front and was good to go.

Thank God I'd worn my sneakers the last day of work and not my heels. Daniel gave me boots which fit over them. That was a good thing too. By the end of each day, the mud covering the galoshes was enough to make a beaver's dam.

The first week I walked the split rail fence surrounding the acreage. The purpose of the border is to keep the chickens, cows, and oxen from roaming away. Since most of Daniel's cash flow comes from selling the hogs, he prefers to pen his pigs. Even though most of his neighbor's let theirs roam free. So, one of my regular chores became cleaning the nasty pigsty.

Sara, bless her soul, taught me how to milk a cow - on the correct side. I guess these animals are not too high in intelligence and they favor routine. I attempted the chore on Bessie's left side. I got slapped in the face with her tail. Not just once - but twice. Sara, seeing this, led me to the right of the cow which made Bessie happy.

Next, restocking the almost empty woodpile began. Days before, Daniel cut down trees that never got to the ax. The movies make wood chopping look so simple - my muscles feel beat-up.

The frosting that topped the cake - I have to say - was killing, plucking, and gutting a chicken. I had second thoughts about the poultry processing. It grossed me out, but it wasn't a choice as far as Daniel was concerned. So I did it - and afterward - I was proud of my accomplished task, even though it was a slaughter job. It didn't come close to resembling a bird by the time I was through with it. The funniest part of the story is I got teased later at the dinner table when Anna heard it took me forty-five minutes to do what her pa does in seven.

No matter what horrific deeds that man threw at me, I was determined to be a trooper. Not once did I pout or complain.

I got reminded repeatedly, I had one week. But, Daniel hadn't realized how much-backlogged work I could get done. So, despite his better judgment, he gave me two more weeks - lucky me.

In the evenings, I change into my jeans and sweater. I'm careful not to dirty them. Doing laundry outside on the washboard is much more work than it looks in the movies. Every night I wash my underwear and hope they will be dry by morning. Most times they aren't, but I wear them anyway. I won't be caught dead in Kristine's bloomers.

Twice I heard Daniel say under his breath I looked like a damn skinny boy. I'm sure he didn't mean it though. Many times I caught him staring at me - like a guy looks at a woman. I know it will be a cold day in hell before he admits to it.

Now that Daniel gave me more time, something needed to change concerning my sleeping arrangements. The floor comprised split logs and was rough, uneven and cold. Plus, I hadn't one bit of privacy.

Daniel instructed the girls to assist me in making a small straw mattress which we placed in the corner of the parlor. Sara placed the little entry table by my bed to serve as a nightstand. We tacked up a large blanket to use as a privacy wall. This would pose as my sleeping arrangements for my stay. It isn't much, but at least I don't have to wake up with Daniel standing over me anymore.

I offered to help with meals and cleaning, but Anna will have no part of it. She told me the inside is her domain. She let me know - in not such a nice way - she's been doing it on her own for over a year now. No other woman will take her place.

Anna is as stubborn as her father. But, I understand all she wants is her father's approval. It's sad, Daniel doesn't have a clue how Anna longs for his affection. He doesn't even eat dinner with us anymore. Anna fixes a plate for him to eat later. When he does finally come inside, he takes Toby and goes to bed. Anna blames that on me.

Anna brings out her sewing chores every evening. She hopes to draw Sara to her. I encourage the girl to sew with her sister. She told me it used to be her favorite thing to do. But not since I came - one more reason to feel guilty.

Little Sara is a jokester like me. We have this thing with winking - since we're both big kidders - we wink at one another when we joke. She does it all the time now. She cracks me up.

Toby and I had no problem bonding. Actually, I think we bonded when I gave him that first lollipop.

Every night is a repeat of the evening before. As soon as Toby rubs his tired little eyes, Daniel snatches him up and heads for the bedroom without saying goodnight. As if on cue, the girls quit what they're doing and climb the broken ladder to the garret. Anna goes to bed without a

word. Before Sara gets into bed, she pokes her cute little smiling face through the railings and tells me, "Goodnight Miss Beth."
"Goodnight my angel," I answer.

Beth set her journal aside. Every night she fell asleep before her head hit the pillow - not tonight though. She sat leaning against the wall with her legs crisscrossed. Grabbing her bag, she dumped out the contents. Beth picked up her phone, turned it on, and tapped on the gallery icon. One by one she flipped through the pictures of her friends. It was painful knowing she may never see them again. *They must wonder what happened to me.* She turned the phone off and wiped away tears.

Next, she picked up the disk player, loaded it with batteries, and turned it on. She plugged in the earphones and slipped in the disc of Adele.

After stuffing everything else back into her bag, she set it aside and blew out the lamp. She lay on the lumpy mattress and placed her head on the makeshift pillow. Beth slipped the earphones into her ears and closed her eyes. The familiarity of Adele's singing comforted her. She didn't care if she used up two batteries that night. There were lots of them. Russ would be here soon anyway.

Those thoughts were her last as she drifted off into a well-deserved sleep.

Chapter 22

October 9, 2016, Journal of Russ Nielson

I'*ve completed the second Scorpion. I stocked the trunk with a 9mm pistol - flashlight - bottled water - a can opener - and a few cans of prepared food.*

My first trip in the second machine, I traveled to Sept. 23, 1999. At the time I arrived, I didn't know the date. The basement looked empty like it did in the picture.

I tiptoed up the stairs to the kitchen. I opened the door a crack and heard voices. Peeking through the opening, I recognized my parents. They appeared to be the same age Beth and I are now.

Mom sat leaning at the table resting her chin in her palm. Her face lit up with a big smile. Dad leaned against the counter - arms folded at his chest. My father said something, and they laughed.

I noticed a girl's birthday cake on the table. At that moment, a young girl tore into the kitchen - that's when I remembered the date. It was Beth's ninth birthday. I disassembled her video console that day. She blew up and slapped me on the back of my head and ran off squealing to Dad.

Now I had a time and date. I should have left right then, but my curiosity got the best of me.

Beth threw a fit and Dad shouted out my name. At first, it startled me hearing him yell Russ. I was relieved when I realized he was calling the thirteen-year-old.

I heard myself as a boy stomping down the stairs. I waited a few more seconds wanting to observe myself as a young teen.

My dog, back then, Bruno, came sniffing at the door. He barked, and Beth spotted me. She pointed to the door and screamed. Dad told mom to get his gun as he charged towards me.

I turned and ran down the steps, two at a time. I think that's the fastest I ever moved through that house in my entire life.

Dad switched on the light and came after me with Beth close behind.

I ran back into the room and jumped into the Scorpion and got ready to hit the return button. Dad darted into the room. Our eyes locked. Without giving it another thought, I shouted, "Dad, it's me, Russ."

I swear Dad and Beth's eyes got as big as ping pong balls. After closing the door, I pushed the button. Within seconds, I appeared in 2016.

After checking my vitals, I found my blood pressure was high. But no any signs of hypothermia.

After Russ finished writing, he set the pen down. He proceeded to stand when a flashback exploded in his brain. His eyes widened, "I remember that day!"

His hand flew to his mouth as if shutting himself up. He jumped to his feet and walked in circles with his hand on his forehead. *I was thirteen years old. The whole ordeal was over by the time I got down to the basement.*

Russ stopped in his tracks. His eyeballs darted back and forth. The recollection got stronger. *I remember - Mom stood there with dad's rifle. She arrived in time to witness the flash. I got there right after her.* "I missed it all. Whoa."

Russ plopped down again and straightened up. He stared at Scorpion number two. *Dad and Beth told me the man said his name was Russ.*

"It was me. I have a new memory." But yet, it's like I always had it, ever since I was thirteen.

"My God, I think I just changed history!"

Chapter 23

*M*y body's aching. I can't sleep. *Sixteen days have gone by since I've been here. The two-week allotment is almost up. Daniel informed me the corn harvest is next week and four of the neighboring families will be assisting. He wants me gone by then.*

Sara explained how the machine they use for cutting the stalks operates. The contraption resembles a big sled with sharp blades on each side. The oversized tool gets pulled by oxen and cuts the crops on each side of the path.

Sara brought me to the smokehouse. She explained how the small hut preserves hogs, deer, and fish. We laughed because I thought it was another outhouse.

Another small building, used for storing dried meat and fruit, stood next door. Sara described the process of wrapping the food in cloth. The wrapped items are hung from the rafters to dry.

Every building Sara took me through, she'd ask questions on how we preserve food. I told her about refrigerators, freezers, and microwaves. Later after dinner, I drew pictures of the appliances so she could get an idea in her head of what they look like.

The barn was bigger than I expected. A small part of the building houses the animals during the cold winter. Most of the area is for storing equipment and hay.

The challenge of living on a farm in the 1800s has given me quite a workout. There are muscles in my body now I never knew existed. My body is getting buffed. It's strange, but I've been enjoying the work. I don't miss the hectic work life of the mortgage company at all.

Anna's still not letting me get close to her. In fact, she may be more distant. Because of her fussing, I let her take over with washing my clothes, other than my underwear. Giving in to her is easier. The plus is, every morning I wake to clean clothes.

One of the hardest things for me to get used to - is not having a real bath. Anna offers to fill the tub, but I wash with a pan of heated water. My matted hair I stuff under my cap. No wonder Sara's hair is always in a tangle. So is mine these days. I haven't even put on makeup since I've been here.

Daniel informed me today that tomorrow we will move the outhouse to a different location. We need to dig a new hole. The old one will get covered. Guess who gets to do that job?

Beth put her journal and pen away. While leaning over to blow out the lamp, a strange recollection of her childhood came to her.

She remembered seeing the Scorpion as a kid. *How can that be?* Sitting straight up, she cocked her head recalling the event. *A person was hiding behind the basement door.*

Beth bolted up and put her hand to her mouth *I remember, Bruno was barking. It was my ninth birthday. Dad saw the man too. We ran down to the basement chasing the guy - he got into a machine. He spoke - he told Dad he was Russ. The man was Russ.* "Why am I remembering this now?"

Beth scrunched her brows. *This memory is new. Yet, I've had it since I was nine.*

Her face lit up when a realization hit her. "Russ is looking for me. He has the second Scorpion done. He's looking for me!"

Beth pulled the curtain aside and tiptoed over to Daniel's

bedroom. She knocked on the door - no response. She rapped again a little harder. This time the door swung open.

"What do you want?"

"I need to talk to you outside."

Daniel grumbled something, slipped into his trousers and followed her to the porch. "What's so important that you need to wake me?"

"Russ is looking for me. I've got a brand new memory I never had before. He has the second machine done. He's looking for me." Beth explained the incident she had as a child.

Daniel stood glaring at her. "Sounds like a dream. You woke me up because of a dream?"

Beth could see this was going nowhere. She shook her head, gritted her teeth and waved him off. "Go back to bed."

Daniel returned to his room shaking his head.

Beth sat down and stared at the barn. *Russ will be here soon. At least, now I know for sure he's looking for me.*

Chapter 24

*E*ighteen days since Beth disappeared. I made *a second attempt at finding her. I traveled to the mid-eighteen hundreds - what I witnessed astonished me.*

When I arrived in the past, I landed in a barn being constructed. The building stood framed but there were no walls.

A group of white people stood in the clearing. There were about five men and three women. Two were holding small children.

Indians surrounded them. One savage held a hatchet and had a hold of the hair of a white man down on his knees. The women were sobbing.

All action stopped when they saw me appear in the Scorpion. Every one of them stood motionless with their mouths gaping. They resembled wax figures in a museum.

I realized the savage was about to kill the man, so I grabbed my gun and fired three shots in the air. One of the Indians yelled in their foreign language, and the tribe turned and ran into the woods.

The white people stood in shock watching them disappear. When the Indians were out of sight, they all turned and focused on me.

I hollered, "Have you seen a woman named Beth?"

Well, needless to say, I got no response. I thought it best to leave before I changed history any further.

I returned and checked my vitals. My blood pressure was through the roof. I felt more fatigued than the first time, but no signs of hypothermia.

When Russ finished writing, he sat back and shook his head in disbelieve. *I'm doing it. I'm traveling through time.* He zipped up to the library, got the old encyclopedia, and brought it to the lab. Pulling out a chair, he sat down and thumbed through the worn pages. He hoped to find what tribe and what year it was. After going through the pictures, Russ concluded it to be the Sioux tribe. He set the book aside and kept it close by for references. He had a feeling he would refer to it often.

Chapter 25

It'd been a long day for Daniel and tonight he had a hard time getting to sleep. The moon's rays lit the room enough for him to see his son sleeping next to him. He leaned up on an elbow watching Toby snore. It made him smile, which is something he doesn't do much anymore.

Daniel laid his head on the pillow and observed the moon. The family missed the Full Moon Fun Night this month. He gave the disappointed girls the excuse things had become complicated since Beth came. Daniel shook his head in an attempt to rid the guilt that filled his gut.

His mind wouldn't stop spinning, *what am I going to do with her? I can't send her out on her own with nowhere to go. But she can't stay here. This week the harvest begins. What will I tell everybody?*

Something out of the ordinary suddenly popped into Daniel's head. *Spencer... Spencer Johansson? What? Why did he come to my mind? The Indians killed him - no wait - they didn't kill him. They ran away.*

Daniel bolted upright, his forehead scrunched. *We were building the barn. That thing, it appeared from the middle of nowhere. A bright light came from...*

Daniel jumped out of bed and paced the floor. *What's happening? The apparatus in my memory is the same machine as the one in the barn. It's the Scorpion! It was Russ who scared the Indians away- he fired three shots into the air. He asked about a woman named Beth. Our Beth!*

"Dang, Russ is looking for her."

Daniel slid into his trousers and tiptoed to Beth's curtain whispering her name. There was no answer. Turning, he noticed the open door so he headed outside. Beth was crying with her face buried in the sleeve of his jacket. He turned and quietly closed the door and tiptoed over to her. "Beth..." he called out in a low voice.

Beth shot up out of her chair. "Shit, you scared the hell out of me! What are you doing up?"

"Your brother saved my friend's life."

"What?" Beth stopped crying and wiped her tears on the sleeves.

"Russ, he saved Spencer's life," Daniel observed Beth as she wiped her runny nose on his jacket.

Beth sat on the edge of her chair and sniffled, "What are you talking about?"

He tapped her on the shoulder, "Don't get up." He disappeared into the house.

Beth scrunched her brows - *what was that all about?*

Before there was time to figure it out what he was up to, Daniel came back. He carried a jar of moonshine and two small tin cups. He handed her the cups, grabbed a chair and pulled it over. After plunking himself down, he opened the jar. With a twinkle in his eye, he said, "I've been saving this for the right time and Beth... I think this is it."

Daniel filled the cups, took a gulp and told her his experience. Afterwards, he said, "Now, I have two memories of the same occasion. It wasn't a dream because I was wide awake."

"What happened to Spencer the first time?"

"I'll start at the beginning. I came from Norway when I was a boy. My family settled in the Wisconsin territory. The land was cheap in Minnesota, only one dollar and twenty-five cents an acre. A group of our sect migrated here and bought acreage. We helped each other build our buildings. At the time we were working on my barn."

Beth listened to his story sipping her moonshine. Her puffy eyes were dry now. She wiped her runny nose again on the sleeve of his coat.

Daniel, making a mental note to tell Anna to wash his jacket, took another swig. "Spencer and his wife were there, along with three other couples. Anna was two years old, Kristine was holding her. War parties rarely happened anymore. The Indians signed treaties with the government. Most of them stayed within their boundaries. I guess there were still some disgruntled ones because they surrounded us that day. They were out for blood. We had no means of protecting ourselves. A savage grabbed Spencer by the hair and scalped him right in front of the woman and children. The leader of the tribe spoke little English. It was enough to inform us this is what they'll do to all of us if we stay."

Daniel took another swig and smiled, "But that isn't how it happened anymore. Before the Indian killed Spencer, the Scorpion showed up. Your brother must've seen the trouble because he fired a gun into the air. Well, it sure scared those savages away. They never came around again. That's what happened. Hell... I may be wrong, but I don't think so," he let out a bubbly laugh.

The whiskey was kicking in.

Daniel took another gulp and snatched the jar. He filled his cup and held it out to Beth.

Beth finished hers and raised her cup for him to fill. "You believe me now?"

"I guess I always did, but with the kids, I couldn't let my guard down." A solemn look clouded Daniel's face as he stared at the ground. He stuttered, "I... I... want to say... I'm sorry about how I treated you."

Beth's entire body softened, "Well, it's not every day you

get a time machine in your barn." Beth sat straight up, put a hand on her hip and asked, "By the way, where's the Scorpion? I looked for it the other day. I gotta say you did an excellent job of hiding it."

Daniel grinned and winked, "Some things are best left alone. If anybody should question us, you won't be lying when you say you have no idea where a time machi..."

Daniel stopped in mid-sentence and furrowed his brows. He ran his hand through his ruffled hair and groaned, "We may have a problem. Everyone there the day the machine showed up got this new memory too. Your brother asked if we had seen a woman named Beth. If folks come around and find a Beth living here, it would cause suspicion. We need to change your name so the kids get used to calling you by it."

"Who shall we say I am?" Beth, smiling, crisscrossed her legs and waited for his response.

Daniel leaned over and put his elbows on his knees. "Let's start with your last name.

"Okay, my last name is Nielson. The 'I' comes first. I have to tell that to people. Otherwise, they want to put the 'E' first. Beth relaxed, took a sip of whiskey, and waited.

Daniel said nothing. He gave her a look that said, "Really? Can we please be serious?"

Beth squirmed in her chair. "Did I say too much? I tend to talk too much sometimes..."

Daniel put out his hand, "Seriously now, what's your last name?"

Beth found his sudden somber demeanor funny, and she giggled, "I'm serious." She spelled it, "N I E L SON. The 'I' comes before the 'E.'" She leaned her head toward him, raised her brows, and waited again for his response.

When Daniel realized Beth wasn't kidding, he let out a hearty laugh. "Impossible. Nielson?" He laughed harder as he spurted out, "My last name is Nielson."

The expression on Beth's face was priceless. Her mouth dropped open, and her eyes couldn't have gotten any bigger. "No way." Beth gave him a playful shove and again said, "No way."

Daniel grinned and nodded.

Beth laughed so hard she about peed her pants. "I have my driver's license with my picture and name on it. I can prove it. Can you prove your last name is Nielson?"

Daniel wiped the tears from his eyes and after a few seconds of silence, he asked, "What's a driver's license?"

"That's hard to describe when you don't understand what a car is." She explained to him - in detail - how you need a license to drive a vehicle.

"Well, that's poppycock. That would be like someone telling me I need to pay them so I can drive my cart."

"Why don't we get back on getting me a new name? This explaining of the future could go on all night."

"Oh yeah, you need a name. So, since we have the same last name, why don't we tell people we are cousins? We'll say you live in Minneapolis and ran into some hardships. My uncle, your pa, asked us to take you in for a spell." He paused. "I know... that sounds silly."

"Oh no, it's not silly. It can work. I mean... there won't be that much made up stuff. I'm from Minneapolis, I ran into some hardships. And chances are, we may be related."

"Okay, we need a name." Daniel held up his finger. "Ah... I have one that will fit you. If Toby would've been a girl, Kristine, and I would have named her Emilie." He spelled it, "E M I L I E. Do you like it?"

"Yes, I do. Can we make it with a 'Y' at the end?"

Ignoring her question, he started a new subject. "So Emilie, tell me what's the future's like?"

"I'll tell you what. Tomorrow I'll show you. If you like, I'll give your family a demonstration. I'll bring out the things in my backpack and will explain how everything works. Tonight,

I want to hear more about you. But more important…" Beth lifted her empty cup. "Where can we get more moonshine?"

Daniel sheepishly looked into Beth's cup, and down to the nearly empty jar. He answered in a sluggish voice, "I get it from Mrs. Knutson. We trade for molasses and…" Daniel stopped, he remembered something. He sprang out of his chair.

"The woman was there that day." He leaned close to Beth's face and grinned, "Emilie, tomorrow we'll pay a visit to Mrs. Knutson."

"You mean I get to leave the farm?"

"Yes, Emilie, you get to leave the farm."

As they finished the bottle, Daniel prepped Beth for the upcoming visit - who would be there - what their names were - what to expect.

Beth, about to say something, spotted Anna standing in the doorway looking very confused.

Anna rubbed her eyes and griped, "What's going on? It's almost one in the morning. I thought you two didn't like each other."

Daniel handed his empty cup to Beth and proclaimed, "Anna, get your Sunday clothes out in the morning. We're going to Mrs. Knutson's."

Anna's face lit up, "Really Pa? Beth too?"

He surprised his daughter by picking her up. "Yes Anna, all of us, me, you, Sara, Toby, and Beth. Now, let's get to bed before the sun rises."

He carried her all the way to the loft. All three of them giggling now, bid goodnight and went off to their beds.

Chapter 26

Daniel woke with a slight hangover, but it did not hamper the jubilation of his intriguing expectations for the day. His new memory was stronger, but he still wanted to hear from others it happened how he remembered it now. He was excited to pay a visit to Mrs. Knutson.

Daniel thought Toby, still snoring at his side, must have had quite a day yesterday. The kid was out like a light. *Funny, I don't have a clue about what my own son did yesterday.* These thoughts usually caused additional guilt, but not this time. Instead, Daniel felt elation. Enthusiastic about what the future held for his family, he decided to be done with the self-pity. He made an easy decision. Things were going to change.

Daniel whispered into Toby's ear, "Son, you have a new pa. The pa you should've had since your birth." He rolled out of bed and slipped into his work clothes, eager to get chores done.

Anna seeing her father and Beth having such a good time was confusing, yet exhilarating. First thing upon waking she sat up in bed, put her hands together and prayed it hadn't been a dream. She shook her sister, "Sara, we're all going to Mrs. Knutson's today."

Sara popped up faster than a Jack in a Box. "What? Who?"

"It's true. We're going to Mrs. Knutson's for a visit."

"Really, Anna? Really?"

"Yes, Pa said to get your Sunday clothes ready. I'll tell you more about it later if you're a good girl." Anna giggled and tickled Sara until she laughed so hard she almost cried. Sara broke free and bounced onto the floor. The girl frolicked around the room putting the words to a tune. "We're going to Mrs. Knutson's. We're going to Mrs. Knutson's."

Beth lay on her mattress beaming. She wasn't ready to get up yet. She couldn't stop reflecting on the night before. What seemed like a dream started last evening and ended early this morning. If Anna hadn't come out, no doubt she and Daniel would have stayed up until the rooster crowed.

Beth pulled aside the curtain and saw no one. She tiptoed out the door and sprinted to the outhouse. Once she got back to the house, both girls met her at the door with open arms.

"We're going to Mrs. Knutson's today. We get to wear our Sunday clothes." Sara jumped up and down. "Would you like to see the dresses we picked out? Taking Beth's hand, Sara led her into the bedroom and pointed to the laid-out clothes.

Beth inspected the outfits, "I think you girls did an exceptional job."

"Thank you," said the girls at the same time.

"I'll be right back," said Anna, skipping out the room.

"What are you going to wear Beth?" asked Sara.

Beth was at a loss for words. She couldn't wear her jeans or Daniel's clothes, and she sure didn't want him looking at her in Kristine's clothes. "I don't know ye…"

Anna came back into the room and held up a dress. "How about this dress, Beth? I made it for you. I used different clothes that Ma didn't like much. You'll be the first one ever wearing it."

Beth took the dress and held it up. Tears filled her eyes. She pulled Anna to her and gave the girl a big hug and cried, "You are my Fairy Godmother."

Now that the outfits were ready to go, Anna took charge of the morning. "Beth, Pa says no chores for you today. You get to be the first to bathe."

Anna turned to her sister, "Sara, Pa said to fill up the empty potato sack with vegetables from the garden for Mrs. Knutson and put it in the wagon."

"Can I help with breakfast?" asked Beth.

"Nope, but you can help me heat some water for the tub."

It took lugging fifty pans of heated water to get a bath. It was quite the project. Beth threw her towel over the wooden wall surrounding the tub. Daniel built it a week ago because of her whining of no privacy.

Beth took off the long shirt which served as pajamas and tossed it over the wall. She climbed into the small metal cauldron and sat curled up with her knees just about touching her chin. The scrubbing of her body was quite a challenge. Washing and rinsing her hair was the tough part. That was close to impossible. There was no hair conditioner, but having soft hair wasn't a necessity anymore. As long as she could get a brush through it was all that mattered nowadays.

Back in her private area, Beth dug into her makeup bag for the first time in nineteen days. She balanced herself on the mattress and applied it using her compact mirror. She got the tangles out of her hair, and since there was no curling iron, she let it hang straight.

Beth picked up the dress Anna made and inspected it. It appeared well sewn. The bodice was white with long puffy sleeves and a lace collar. A dark fitted vest, patterned with tiny blue and purple flowers matched the floor-length dark-blue skirt. Beth wondered how Anna dreamed up such an unusual combination. It could be in a fashion show. She slipped into it wishing there was a full-length mirror.

The children were bustling in the kitchen when Beth pulled the curtain aside and stepped out. Anna and Sara stopped in mid-action and gasped.

Anna blew out a sigh of relief, "It fits you perfectly. You can't wear your shoes or Pa's boots with it though. I checked, and your shoes are the same size as Ma's." Anna ran into the bedroom and came out with a pair of fancy black boots which laced up the front.

Beth tried them on and they fit like a glove.

Feeling transformed, Beth stood up and gave Anna another hug, "Anna, how can I ever thank you?"

"You can thank me by watching Toby while Sara and I get ready. And you can set the table for breakfast." Anna grabbed Sara's hand they headed for the tub.

Beth couldn't believe her ears. Anna asked *her* to do something in her kitchen. "Come on Toby, let's put you in your chair while Cousin Emilie makes breakfast."

Toby snuggled into his chair and gave Beth a toothless grin expecting to get another lollipop. His happy expression turned upside down when Beth went into the kitchen instead. Toby cried out and slapped the highchair tray.

Beth realizing what the toddler wanted went to her bag.

Toby's smile came back when she reached in and removed something. She hid it behind her back and Toby's eyes widened as he leaned over trying to see what it was.

Beth gave him a big smile, "I think these will keep you busy for a while." Passing Toby's chair, she dropped onto his tray her clump of keys.

Toby looked down at them and back at Beth for approval.

She nodded, "Yes, Toby, you can play with them, I won't be using them anytime soon."

Toby's smile couldn't have gotten any bigger. He wasted no time inspecting his new toy.

Now that she had Toby entertained, Beth took a stroll around the nook area. A small pantry took up the far corner of the stone wall. The tiny closet was covered with a curtain made of potato sack material. She pulled it aside and found the dishes and the pots, the little bit they had.

Beth grabbed a pan and decided she'd cook the apples but

noticed the fire had gone out in the pot belly. She opened the stove door and loaded it with kindling from the woodpile that she, herself, had put there. Keeping the woodpile filled inside and out somehow had become another one of her chores. Beth didn't mind it anymore. She has a toned up body now because of it. Beth smiled thinking about it while stuffing hay between the kindling. Grabbing a long wick, she proceeded to the fireplace to light it. An idea came to her. It was time to use her birthday gifts. She went to her bag, got the butane lighter and returned to the stove. She lit the wick with her lighter and stuck it in the oven *now that's much easier.*

The house suddenly filled with squealing girls tearing into the house. Wrapped in towels, they raced to the bedroom. Anna stopped long enough to say, "It's freezing when you get out of the tub. We'll be right out, Miss Beth."

Beth watched as they disappeared into the bedroom, *Wow, what a big difference in Anna's behavior. Daniel seemed different last night too. He must be like the old Daniel before Kristine died. Anna must sense that. She knows they have their pa back.*

Beth hummed to the tune of *You are My Sunshine* while preparing sugared apples. Tiny wormholes were in many of them. If the Internet had been available, she could have found a natural remedy that would fix the problem. She chuckled at the thought.

She continuing to hum while stirring the oatmeal and setting the table with mismatched bowls and spoons. As she finished, Anna and Sara came bursting out of the bedroom and halted in front of Beth for approval. "Why, look at you two gorgeous ladies. Good job."

"Thank you." Anna did a curtsey.

Sara did a curtsey as well and turned back to her sister," Anna, will you brush my hair?"

"You want me to brush your hair? You hate to have your hair brushed. I'm not ready yet. Maybe Beth will do it for you?"

Beth put out her hand, "I would love to brush your hair, Sara. Bring me your brush."

Sara handed her the brush and set the ribbons on the table.

Beth examined the brush and remarked, "No wonder you hate having your hair brushed. It looks like this couldn't get through horse hair. Beth went behind the curtain and grabbed her brush and sat Sara on her lap. Beth had never seen hair with so many snarls. The brush wasn't working. Beth went back to her room, and this time she brought out a pink, plastic long-tooth comb.

Sara winced when she saw it and asked in a meek voice, "Is that for a horse's tails?"

Beth giggled, "No, but I suppose it would work." She sat Sara back on her lap and began the endless task of combing out the tangles. Afterward, Beth took the blue ribbons and tied them in bows in her hair. She picked up the mirror and put it in front of the girls face.

Sara's mouth dropped open. She stared at her reflection and ran her fingers down her hair. Turning to her sister, she beamed, "Anna, I can get my fingers through my hair."

"Sara's let nobody comb her hair since Ma passed. Can you fix mine too, Beth?"

Anna's hair had a whole different texture than her sisters. Her blonde strands were long, straight and silky. The way Beth wished hers was. "Anna, I think you should wear it straight like mine. We look like cousins."

Anna turned and smiled, "I think we are."

Sara, noting Toby, asked, "What's Toby playing with?"

Beth glanced at Toby, "Oh, those are my keys, um… by the way, who's supposed to get Toby dressed?"

Sara and Anna looked at Toby still wearing his nightclothes, and they all laughed. Toby didn't care. He was enthralled with his new toy.

"Why don't you girls get Toby dressed while I put all this hair stuff away."

The girls snatched Toby up out of his chair and whisked him off to the bedroom. Beth cleared the table and disappeared behind the curtain taking extra time to clean up her area. She heard Daniel come in from outside and the girls ran out of the bedroom to greet him.

"Pa, look at Toby. We got him all dressed up." Sara was about as wound up as an energizer bunny. She sat Toby in his chair and smiled up at her father waiting for approval.

Daniel put up his hand, "Whoa. Hold on a minute. I don't know about Toby, but dang, what about you two beauties? And what's this Sara?" Daniel ran his fingers through Sara's hair. "How did you get a brush through your hair?"

Turning, he focused on Anna, "And you look as beautiful as your mother. You are a spitting image of her. Did you know that?" Daniel put his hand on her chin giving her a kiss on the forehead.

Beth finished her tasks and came out from behind the curtain. "Good morning, Daniel."

Daniel turned around and his mouth dropped open. His eyes went to the dress wondering where she got it. All he knew for sure was it looked darn good on her. When realizing he was gaping, he forced himself to speak. But he didn't say what he wanted, which was, *Wow, you're gorgeous.* What did come out of his mouth was, "You, you, look… clean, I mean, your hair is brushed… nice." Daniel knew he should stop talking. He was acting like a blubbering idiot.

Beth laughed, "I'm not sure if I should take that as a compliment or not."

"Don't you think Beth looks beautiful too? Anna asked, putting the last bowl of oatmeal on the table.

Daniel, still admiring Beth and with his mouth closed now, pulled out her chair and gestured for her to sit. He answered his daughter never taking his eyes off Beth. "Yes Anna, I think Beth is beautiful too."

During breakfast, they went over the day's plans. More important, the name change for Beth. They would all have to call her Emilie from now on. The name, Beth, must never be spoken again.

Sara waved her hands in the air, "I know what we can do." Let's play a game. Every time we talk to Beth, I mean Emilie..." she giggled. "We have to say Emilie first before we can say anything to her. If somebody doesn't do that, or if they call her Beth, they have to do one of our chores."

Daniel pointed at Sara, "Better watch what you say. You might be the one doing everyone's chores."

"Can't we just call her cousin?" Anna giggled.

Beth took a bite of her sugared apples and spoke while chewing, "So, you all seem super excited to go to Mrs. Knutson's? What do you do there?"

Sara spoke up first, "I'll tell you... Bet... I mean Emilie. Everybody goes to Pastor Bakker's house for worship, and afterward, they all go to Mrs. Knutson's. She lives on a creek, and there are picnic tables everywhere. The kids play games, and we have potato sack races."

Anna raised her hand like it was her turn to talk, "Everybody brings something to share for lunch, and we all eat together."

"Mrs. Knutson and my mother were best friends," Daniel interjected. "She and her husband came from Norway on the same boat as my family. She took over the job of mothering me since Ma passed away. When the group migrated to this area, we built the Knutson's house first. Even before we finished the construction the farmers in our community met there to plan our trade deals. We've been doing it ever since. We make barter arrangements, and we put together our strategy for harvesting. The kid's play and the women gossip, that's it in a nutshell."

Nutshell... the word brought Tony to Beth's mind when he

had said, "That's you, in a nutshell, Beth." Beth hadn't gone three weeks yet, but it seemed like months. She missed her friends, but she didn't miss much else, the traffic, the job, the club, the fast lane of life period. However, she did miss a bathtub and hot running water.

"Beth... I mean Emilie," Daniel stopped in mid-sentence and looked at Sara.

Sara giggled and pointed to her father, "You have to do one of my chores."

Daniel laughed, "Please don't make me clean the pig pen." He looked at Beth, who also was laughing now and started over, "Emilie weren't you going to show us some stuff in your bag?"

He didn't have to ask her twice. Beth got up and went behind the curtain and came out with the small handheld camcorder. All eyes were on the new contraption. They didn't recall seeing this gadget yet.

Daniel pulled the girls over to him, and they all smiled like they were going to have a picture taken.

Beth chuckled. "You don't have to be still for this one. Keep doing what you're doing." Beth turned the camera on and looked through the lens. She had to laugh because they still sat there staring not sure what to do next. So Beth instructed, "Anna and Sara, why don't you stand up and show me your dresses."

The girls looked at their father - he nodded. They stood up looking at each other still confused about what they should do.

"Okay, the camera's running. Do a curtsy for me and let me see the back of your dresses."

Anna curtseyed and turned around and Sara followed suit.

"Now get Toby and show me how cute you have him dressed."

Sara looked at Anna and shrugged her shoulders. Unsure of what to do, she picked up Toby and faced Beth.

Beth giggled. "You can talk if you want to. This isn't a silent movie." Beth shut the recorder off and rewound the film and returned to the table. Pointing to the viewing window, she instructed them, "Everybody look into this window."

They all huddled around her, and she hit the play button. Daniel and the kids couldn't believe their eyes when they watched a repeat of themselves.

Sara's eyes got huge, "Wow, look at me. Toby, look at you. Aren't you so cute?"

Anna watched the recording, "Can we do it again? I'll talk this time."

Daniel, shaking his head in wonderment, stood to his feet, "How about we continue this later? We'd better get on the road before the gang gets to Mrs. Knutson's."

Daniel and Sara laid out blankets in the cart. Anna handed her father the picnic basket, and both girls climbed into the wagon wrapping themselves in the quilt. Daniel tucked Toby and the basket between the two of them.

All eyes were on Beth now. She was having trouble getting on the bench. She wasn't used to wearing long skirts. On one attempt, she got the heel of the boot stuck in the hem of her dress.

Daniel got there in time to keep her from falling backward. "Let me help you."

"No thank you. I need to do this." She made another failed attempt and giggled.

"Are you sure you don't want me to help?" he asked, chuckling.

"No, it can't be that difficult." She took a firm hold of her skirt, pulled it up, and finally yanked herself up onto the chair.

After getting comfortable and smoothing the wrinkles of her dress, she folded her hands in her lap. With raised brows, she gave Daniel a look that said, "Well… what are you waiting for?"

Her chuckle that followed made them all laugh.

And so was the beginning of their first trip together off the farm.

Chapter 27

Once on the dirt road, Beth kept turning around. Her gaze rested on the house as it got smaller and farther away. It was surreal being off the farm but yet scary.

She squirmed and shifted her position. Beth swore there were splinter's in her behind. Sitting on the wooden bench was like sitting on a porcupine. After getting comfortable, she relaxed and let the warm breeze caress her face. She gathered a deep breath and exhaled like she does when doing yoga. Turning to Daniel, she said, "I can't believe I'm actually breathing oxygen with no harsh chemical pollutants."

Sara, listening to every word, asked "What is chemi... chemic... what you said, Emilie. What is that?"

Daniel's attention perked up. He turned to Beth, waiting for an answer as well.

"What are chemical pollutants? Well, without going into too much detail, we call our carts automobiles. Some are cars and the bigger ones are called trucks. They don't need horses or oxen to pull them. The engines run them. Kind of what's in the Scorpion. The vehicles use a chemical called gas to power the motor. The gas makes the car run and it comes out the back of the vehicles as exhaust. That's what pollutes the fresh air."

"What do they look like... these automobiles?" Daniel's forehead wrinkled, he couldn't get his mind past the Scorpion.

"Okay, imagine the front part of the scorpion, that's the

cab, the place you sit and drive. Imagine the interior twice the size. So now the cab fits five people. Instead of a hard bench, imagine sitting in comfortable leather cushioned seats. Reins aren't needed to steer the vehicle. A steering wheel does that. Beth raised her brows, "Are you with me so far?"

Daniel gave Beth a blank stare. "A wheel?"

"Yes, a small wheel. Like the ones on your push cart. Here's the part you'll like Daniel. The back of the vehicle is about the size of your wagon. That's called the bed. *This* vehicle is a truck. Men love them. They can carry lumber, move furniture, and get all kinds of work done." Beth paused for a moment and chuckled *he must imagine something good. He's grinning from ear to ear.* "Daniel, you would no doubt own a truck."

"Will they get invented in my time? Will I get one?"

The question caught her off guard. Beth contemplated the answer. She figured it to be in the early nineteen-hundreds when cars became popular. "If you're still around when you're eighty, you may ride in one. Sorry, I know that's not what you wanted to hear, but..." Beth turned and faced the children, "You kids will more than likely, all own one."

The girls' looked at each other beaming. Toby continued sitting trance-like licking his lollipop.

Beth's gaze went to the outfit Daniel wore. The black slacks had suspenders and went well with his gray pullover top. *The man cleans up well.* She wondered how he got such a clean shave without a mirror. She noted the nape of his neck needed trimming. She reached over and ran her fingers along the scruff. "I can trim this for you. I used to cut Russ' hair."

Daniel didn't respond. He just looked at her and smiled.

"Tell me about yourself, Daniel. How'd you end up in America?"

Daniel looked at her to gauge the depth of interest.

She shifted in her seat - careful not to get a splint - and faced him.

"My parents had a farm in Norway when the economy couldn't be worse. We were told to go to America where land was being given away. When I was nine, Ma and Pa sold everything they had, and we left Norway and came on the boat to America. The journey took forty-five days. Many people got sick and died. About the time I thought the worst was over, we had to travel the rough terrain by wagon train to the Wisconsin Territory. My parents built and ran a good size farm. They died thirteen years ago from an illness that spread through the area."

"Both died from the same disease?"

"Ya, it was a rough year. But Kristine and I got married the same year so I guess it wasn't all bad." Daniel paused and gave himself a few moments to reflect and continued, "Ten years ago, Kristine and I, along with a host of people moved here to Minnesota. We understood after ten years of maintaining the land we might get our acreage for free. Daniel glanced at Beth and grinned, "Maybe you can tell me? Will that happen, Miss Soothsayer?"

"Slow down tiger. I can't tell you all the future in one day." Beth could find the answer - within one minute - if she had the Internet.

Daniel shifted his weight and glanced at Beth, "We're almost to our destination. I'm hoping we'll have plenty of time to speak with Mrs. Knutson before the others arrive." Daniel steered the oxen off the beaten path onto a narrow trail.

Anna and Sara knelt with their arms folded on the bench. Grins lit up their faces as they watched for the house to come into view.

Toby pointed and shouted, "Menuteson."

All heads shot Toby's direction.

"Did he say, Mrs. Knutson?" Sara reached for her brother and hugged him. "Yes, Toby, we're going to Mrs. Knutson's."

When the hitching post came into view, Daniel's jaw

dropped. The lot wasn't empty. In fact, he never saw it so full. Men and women huddled together in groups. Upon seeing a wagon coming down the drive, their conversations halted. All eyes fixated on the wagon. Even the kids in the field stopped kicking the ball to watch.

Anna brows furrowed and her lips puckered, "What's going on Pa? Why are they here so early?"

"I'm not sure, but there's Bradley Borthem and his wife, Inger. Next to them are Ollie and his wife, Eva. Dang, they're all here. Everyone that was there that day the Scorpion showed up is here now. They're all here!"

Chapter 28

"Daniel Nielson." Arne Egner, a lanky man well over six foot, two, waved to Daniel. He left his group and with long strides, headed toward him. His wife Nina trotted behind him along with his friends Bradly and Ollie.

Daniel leaned over and whispered in Beth's ear, "That's Arne and his wife. The other two are Bradly and Ollie. I wonder if they're here because of the new memory. Oh boy... this days going to be interesting."

Anna climbed out of the wagon. Sara leaned over and handed Toby to her and jumped out herself. She was about to run toward the children when Daniel stopped her in her tracks.

"Remember, Sara. No talk of the machine, and no talk of the gadgets. More important, don't say Beth. Got it?"

"Yes Pa, can we go play now?"

Daniel frowned as he watched the girl squirm like a worm. Her hands shook so fast they looked like hummingbird wings. *This wild stallion of a girl needs taming, but I'm not sure that's possible.*

Anna, holding Toby's hand, stood fixated on her father waiting for the go-ahead.

He was nervous about letting them out of his sight. Afraid they might slip up and reveal their family secret. If anybody gets a whiff Beth's the woman the man was looking for, it could start a riot. Daniel remembered stories as a young boy in

Norway of women found guilty of being witches. Dozens of them were burned at stakes. He didn't want the girls to witness the pandemonium he had a feeling was coming.

"Anna, take your sister and make sure nothing's said. Leave Toby with us."

"Okay, Pa." Anna took Sara's hand, but Sara shook if free and raced toward the kid's. Anna ran behind trying to keep up.

Arne, dressed in gray slacks and suspenders, trotted to Daniel and shook his hand. Arne towered over him giving Daniel the biggest grin revealing two missing teeth. "We haven't seen you in ages." Arne put his attention on Beth, now. His eyes widened as he raised his brows. He turned back to Daniel waiting for an introduction.

Daniel took Beth's elbow and drew her close. "Hello Arne, this is my cousin, Emilie Nielson. My uncle, Emilie's father, is going through a rough spell. She'll be staying on with us for a time and will be teaching the girl's schooling."

Teach his girls schooling? Beth almost giggled.

Daniel looked down at Beth and gave her a nudge which Beth took as "Play along with me." She had a hard time not laughing. *Only two days ago he didn't want me near his girls, and now he is telling people I'm their teacher.*

Nina stood beside her husband, Arne. Beth thought they made a comical couple and didn't look well suited. The thin, wiry man was two feet taller than his short, plump wife. Beth could tell this woman was a nosey one. The woman stood all tight-lipped with her hands folded. She twiddled her thumbs while eyeing Beth up and down.

Inger Borthem, the first to greet her, was a stout woman. She wore a black, full dress with puffy long sleeves. With her matching black bonnet, Beth thought the woman looked as if she were going to a funeral. Inger led Beth a few feet from the group and stirred up a conversation, "It's so nice to meet you.

Will you be here long? Where are you from and how on God's green earth did you get here?"

Before Beth had a chance to answer Inger's many questions, Eva, a tall, thin woman with a pointy nose asked, "Are you a teacher?"

Beth gave a nervous chuckle, "I… I'm not sure which question you all want me to answer first. But no, I'm not an official teacher. I mean I haven't been to college for it…" *is there such a thing as an official teacher or a college in 1860? Stop talking.*

Daniel, seeing her dilemma, reached out and took Beth's elbow. He brought her back to his side and introduced her to the rest of the crowd.

Beth felt Inger eyeing her up and down and Eva stood with a blank look with her head cocked to the side. Beth guessed the woman was still trying to figure out what a college was.

Daniel trying to sound naïve, asked, "What brings you here so early Arne? I thought you'd all be at the Bakker's."

"Well Daniel, we were at Pastor Bakker's place earlier, but the strangest thing happened. Do you remember Spencer Johansson?"

"Yes, of course."

"Well… you remember the day the Indians came?" Arne wanted to hear the facts from Daniel before he continued.

"Yes, I remember it. A savage was about to scalp Spencer. Then, out of nowhere, a man showed up in that apparatus. He scared the Indians away."

Arne, Bradley, and Ollie looked at one another, and their eyes settled back on Daniel.

Arne spoke, "Why is it none of us remembered it like that before? I remember the Indians killing Spencer. Now, it's like… like… it didn't happen that way."

Ollie, the pillar of the community, always wore coveralls. The man had a wide brim hat pulled down over his forehead. He tilted his head back when he spoke, "Ya, we have two memories of the incident now. What do you think is going on Daniel?"

"I remember the machine showed up saving Spencer's life. Call it an act of God."

Daniel turned to Bradly, a big, stocky man with a mustache and a full beard, and shifted back to Ollie. "What do you two think? You were both there that day."

Ollie expounded, "I remember it like you Daniel, but I also remember Spencer got scalped that day. It's not just me. Tell him, Bradly."

Ollie passed the buck to Bradly, "Ya, we are here to straighten this out. We all went to pastor Bakker's place today, but we had no worship, no we didn't. Everybody's talking about that gizmo thing. Where'd it come from? Where's…"

Daniel interrupted, "Do you know how ridiculous you all sound? You've seen and talked with Spencer since then. He went out East after it happened and is alive and well. Am I not correct?"

The groups surrounded Daniel and Beth. Trouble was coming. If this didn't stop, it could end up with a witch burning. Daniel wished he'd left Beth home and prayed the girls wouldn't say anything.

"But, Daniel." It was Ollie again. "What about that thing? Why haven't we discussed this all these years? We all heard him ask if we've seen a woman named Beth. We need to find this person."

Bradley started in again, "Ya, we figure if we can find this Beth, we can get answers."

"Bradley, are you listening to yourself? It was nine years ago. It has nothing to do with today. So why don't we forget about it and have some fellowship while we're together? Now, if you excuse us, we got some shopping to do." Daniel picked up Toby, took Beth by her elbow, and pushed their way through the crowd.

Chapter 29

Mrs. Knutson's large, two-bedroom home was the comfiest one around with its multiple fireplaces. The place also served as the much-needed community store. The big enclosed porch had shelves equipped with miscellaneous products such as molasses, flour, oatmeal, tobacco, and such. Cash or bartering covered her compensation. Mrs. Knutson did not have a farm or a garden, so she received plenty of vegetables and meat in exchange.

The woman did well for herself considering she survived being a widower for twelve years. She was in great shape for being forty-nine with forty-three being the average life expectancy in 1860.

Mrs. Knutson stood behind the sales counter when Beth and Daniel entered the store.

It surprised Beth to see the woman was so tall and big-boned and thought maybe the forest green dress she wore made her appear larger than she was. The long sleeves were big and puffy. A large oval hoop underneath made the skirt full and ample. Beth almost giggled thinking the dress material looked like the drapes that hung in Russ' formal dining room.

The color of the dress complimented her dark green eyes. Her dark, almost black hair parted straight down the middle.

Beth guessed it must be thick because a big, black crochet hair net was needed to hold up the mammoth bun.

"Daniel." Mrs. Knutson brushed some long strays of hair away from her face as she scurried around the counter to greet him. After giving him a hug, the pleasant woman turned to Beth, "My, who is this lovely lady?"

Beth put out her hand to shake.

The woman stared down at it. Her lips tighten and her brows furrowed.

Beth quickly put her hand down. *Women don't shake hands in this era, dummy.* "I'm Emilie Nielson, Daniel's cousin."

To Beth's surprise, Mrs. Knutson held out her hand and said, "I admire a woman who shakes. I'm pleased to meet you. Where are you from?"

"I'm from Minneapolis. My father's going through some rough times. He sent me to help Daniel with the children. I won't be here long."

"I didn't realize you had any family left, Daniel." She walked back the other side of the counter and folded her hands on the platform.

Daniel sat Toby on the counter next to the woman. "Hell, I probably have more family than I know what to do with." Eager to change the subject, he pulled out a paper from his pocket. "Here's a list of what Anna and I need."

Mrs. Knutson glanced at Beth, meandering around the store. "So Anna's still head of the kitchen?"

"That girl will let nobody take over her kitchen, except you Mrs. Knutson." Daniel gave the woman a warm smile and continued, "Beth helps with the outside chores and schools the girls.

Beth chuckled *there's that school thing again.* The subject got funnier every time he mentioned it.

"Daniel, I don't mean to pry..." Mrs. Knutson had been

waiting for the right moment. "Is it true you don't have two memories of what happened to Spencer?"

"You're not going to start up too, are you? That incident was nine years ago." After what happened at the hitching post, Daniel thought it best to not speak of the subject with her at this time.

"But this is so strange. Why are you the only one who doesn't have two memories? Aren't you curious about that machine? Don't you wonder who Beth is?"

When Mrs. Knutson said Beth's name, Toby squirmed in his father's grip. The toddler outstretched his arms toward Beth and cried out her name. He talked in his baby babble, but the word was clear.

Daniel, thinking fast, asked his son, "What Toby? Did you say book? Is that what you said?"

Toby cocked his head sideways at Daniel and wrinkled his face.

"Do you have any books, Mrs. Knutson?"

The woman noticed Toby's confused face and thought *I swear the boy said, Beth.* "Why yes, I do." Mrs. Knutson pointed and said, "Do you see the books, Emilie?" They're on the lower shelf on the right."

Beth played along. "Yes, I see them. Toby must've seen them too. He loves us to read to him."

Daniel set Toby down, and the toddler ran to Beth. She sat on the floor with him in her lap, and they rummage through the books.

Mrs. Knutson wasn't convinced the boy didn't say Beth. She ignored the subject for now and started collecting items on the list.

Beth and Daniel gave each other a look that said, "Whew, that was close."

Toby squirmed free from Beth's arms and attempted to pick up a big book.

"Oh, that might be too cumbersome for you, Toby. Let me help you." Beth turning it right side up gasped when she read the title.

Daniel hearing her knelt by her side. "What is it?"

"Oh my God," she whispered so Mrs. Knutson wouldn't hear. "This is the book, the encyclopedia at Russ' house. Only it's brand new. We never understood how it got in our home. I must be the one who brought it in. Do you remember me telling you about it?"

"Ya, I do."

"We have to buy this. I can write a note to Russ on the inside cover. Eventually, he'll see it."

Mrs. Knutson strained to listen to their discussion. She couldn't hear much but discerned it had something to do with the book.

Beth took a deep breath and turned around to Mrs. Knutson. Inside she burst with excitement, but on the outside, she appeared calm. "How much is this book?"

"That encyclopedia, I'm sure is expensive. I can check the price if you like."

Daniel, understanding the urgency, walked back to the counter and asked, "Would the vegetables I brought be enough to pay it?"

"Daniel, you would trade your food for a book?"

Beth set the encyclopedia on the counter. She took off her earrings and showed them to Mrs. Knutson, "My mother gave me these for my 17th birthday. They're silver, diamond, and Sapphire. I'm sure you could get a good price. Would you be willing to trade for them?"

Beth put the jewels in Mrs. Knutson's hand. The woman took out a magnifying glass from underneath the counter and inspected them. "All right, if the cost is more than the book, I'll get the difference to you."

Nobody ever accused Mrs. Knutson of cheating, but she

was sneaky. After writing the receipt, she handed the slip to Beth and said, "Thank you. It's been nice doing business with you... *Beth*."

The woman acknowledged her as Beth, not Emilie.

Beth didn't catch it. "I should be the one thanking you, Mrs. Knutson." Then it hit her. She realized she answered too quickly. *Did she call me Beth by accident? Or did she try to trick me?* Busted, Beth glanced over at Daniel.

They weren't fooling this woman one bit and Daniel knew it. When Beth looked at him, he kept his head down and pretended to be fiddling with Toby's shoelace. Daniel so regretted doing this today. They should've waited until Monday. The place would've been empty. He wanted to skip the picnic but didn't want to cause suspicion.

Saved by the bell, the door flew open. Anna came tearing in yelling, "Emilie, Sara threw up."

Sara trudged in next and whimpered, "Emilie, I'm sick. Can we go home?"

"Of Course we can, Sweetie." Beth put her hand on Sara's forehead to gauge her temperature. It wasn't warm. Beth was about to speak when Sara nudged her in the side. When Beth looked down at her, the girl winked.

A whole lot of play-acting was going on with the Nielson family and the time for the curtain call had come.

Beth gave instructions, "Daniel, why don't you finish up your order. I'll take Sara and Toby to the cart. Anna Honey, you stay here and help your Pa, okay?"

Beth turned to Mrs. Knutson and apologized, "I'm so sorry to have to end our visit but..."

Mrs. Knutson interrupted and assured her, "I understand. Poor Sara, she enjoys these gatherings so much."

"Please give everyone our regrets."

"Of course. Now go bundle that girl in a blanket."

Beth grabbed her book and wasted no time getting to the wagon.

Ten minutes later, Daniel and Anna came out carrying armloads of groceries.

Mrs. Knutson leaned on the door frame observing them as they got situated. They didn't fool her for one minute - no one could convince the woman Emilie wasn't Beth.

Back on the trail, Daniel turned to Sara and asked, "What's going on?"

Both girls turned and knelt, leaning against the bench. Anna spoke up first, "Those kids wouldn't stop talking about the Scorpion. They've heard their ma and pa's. They think we're being invaded."

Sara's lips puckered. Close to tears, she spurted out, "Pa, some of them said maybe Emilie was Beth. I did feel sick. I got scared. I just want to go home." She turned around and plopped down crossing her arms over her chest.

Daniel halted the oxen and turned facing them. "It's okay girls. We talked with the adults. It'll be old news by the harvest. When we get home, Emilie can read to us out of her book while we make ginger snaps. How's that sound?"

Anna and Sara felt better and turned back around chattering like two hens.

Daniel didn't feel better. He prayed to God this new memory episode would pass over soon. His crops were the first to be harvested, and he didn't want a repeat of today.

The minute they arrived home, Beth, clutching her book, jumped out of the wagon and disappeared into her private area. Taking the gel pen out of her purse, she opened the book and brushed the inside of the cover as if it were dusty. With legs crisscrossed on the mattress, she prepared to compose a note - which hopefully - one day Russ will find. Beth thought of what to write and began.

Russ, I'm in the year 1860. I found our book at a store. Can you believe it? When you come to get me, you'll land in a barn. Look for yellow ribbons hanging from the rafters. When you see them you'll know you are in the right month and year. Patiently waiting, your favorite sister, Beth (also known as Emilie.) J

Beth ended it with a smiley face to let Russ know she was in good hands. It'd be a matter of time before he picks up the book and finds the note that was never there before. She found the girl's hair box and grabbed eight yellow ribbons and sprinted to the barn and tied them from the rafters.

Later that evening, the three children sat at the table in their bedclothes. Beth read them facts about their history. Who their presidents had been and how Minnesota just became a state. She also read them stories about the wars between the white man and Indians. These incidents brought the Civil War to her mind. Minnesota was the first state to offer troops. She thumbed through the pages for information but couldn't find anything. She remembered reading it in this book.

Okay, I can't find that. How about something on the US-Dakota War? That coincided the same time as the Civil War. I know it took the lives of eight-hundred innocent people. Indians on the warpath came close to Forest Lake and they massacred everyone in their way.

Beth thumbed through the pages but couldn't find anything on either incident. A light bulb came on in her head and she realized that information was from her school years, not from this book. Beth sat back. She tried hard to remember - it came to her. *It hasn't happened yet. The war started in 1861. It's only months away.* Beth's heart pounded *what if Russ doesn't find me?*

Chapter 30

*I*t's been Twenty-two days since Beth's disappearance. *The experimenting with traveling in the Scorpion is paying off. I'm getting familiar with the speed control by observing the sun and moon's rotation through the west-side window. Soon, I'll have the ability to travel to precise dates and times.*

Russ paused and his eye caught the encyclopedia. He pulled the book over and thumbed through the pages. Needing to pick the next year for traveling, he hoped something of interest would pop up. The note Beth wrote stood out like a sore thumb, but before noticing it the doorbell rang. Russ glanced at the clock, 9:30 a.m. Who *would be here this early?* Closing the book, he made his way to the front door surprised to find Silvia standing there.

"Hey, what a surprise. What brings you here?"

Silvia's eyes were puffy and red from crying. Setting her purse on the entryway table she whimpered, "I'm here with bad news, Russ." She walked past him and moved into the living room and sat down on the couch.

Russ followed her and settled in the recliner next to her, "What is it, Silvia?"

She tried to spit out words but could only cry.

Russ snatched the tissue off the end table and gave it to her.

Silvia pulled out a tissue, wiped away the tears and spurted out, "Tony's dead."

"What? What happened?"

"Tony, Lori, and I were having lunch across the street from the mortgage company. Tony said he saw Beth and the next thing we knew, he was running and tried to cross in the middle..."

Silvia paused, blew her nose and whimpered, "Tony got hit by a bus. I didn't want you to hear it on the news. God, I'm such a mess. First Beth disappears and now Tony. I can't handle this. I'm about to have a breakdown. That bitch Steinhart won't give me any time off. I'm thinking about quitting my job. Heck, I may move away, but my therapist says not to make any major decisions right now."

Silvia paused, wiped her nose and cried, "I'm sorry to put all this on you, Russ."

Russ should've been torn up with the news, but he wasn't. He was actually planning his next time travel trip. He saved a man from getting scalped. So, why not travel to the past and save Tony?

"It's all right, Silvia." He got up and sat next to her on the couch and took her hand. "I agree with your therapist. Don't make any big decisions yet. What time did it happen yesterday?"

Silvia looked at Russ. She realized she hadn't looked at him since getting to his house. It shocked her to see how old he looked. "Russ, are you eating? You seem like you've lost weight or something." She stared at him trying to pinpoint what made him look so different.

"I'm okay, just a little tired. So what time did it happen?"

"Oh... it was noon."

Russ took a mental note and offered her a cup of coffee.

"No thanks. My friend lives in Forest Lake. I'm spending the night there."

After Silvia left, Russ jaunted down to the lab and wrote in his journal.

Saturday, October 15, 2016
Travel time: 10:00 a.m.

Today, I'm attempting to travel to yesterday. The challenge is not running into my double which shouldn't be a problem. Yesterday I left at 9:00 a.m. and returned at 3:30 p.m. So I have six hours to accomplish my trip.

I'll leave in plenty of time to drive Beth's car to Minneapolis well before lunch. I'll tell Tony I'm bringing pizza for everybody.

After writing his notes, Russ slid into the Scorpion and gripped the lever. He placed his finger on the starter switch and paused, his hand shook. He was about to change history - on purpose this time.

"Five, four, three, two..." Russ flipped the switch before saying one. The blinding flash emanated from the tip of the tail and rippled through the room. Gripping the lever, he shifted into slow speed. He kept his eyes on the window which would tell him the time of day.

Streaks of different shades of blue swirled around him. They faded to yellow and orange as the sun set. It all happened in a matter of seconds. The darkness set in and a mixture of gray and black stripes took over. When the yellow steaks revealed the light of the sun again, Russ slowed down the Scorpion. When the room came into complete focus, he shut it down. After climbing out he checked the date. October 14, 9:38 a.m. *I did it with time to spare.*

His first mission so far couldn't have gone better, although, he got lightheaded and needed to sit. Russ held up his hands. They looked old - at least older than they should. However, this concern was for another time.

Russ called Tony to let him know he was bringing pizza for the office. Tony said it sounded great and told him lunch was at noon. *Everything is going great. Now, I just need to get to Minneapolis in time.*

Russ arrived in plenty of time to pick up the pizzas and get to the mortgage company. He stayed while they ate making sure Tony didn't leave the building. At 1:00 p.m. Tony still walked among the living.

The drive home had no traffic hang-ups. He pulled into the driveway at 1:45 p.m. He scampered to the lab, slid into the Scorpion and hit the *return* button. When getting back to the correct time, he dragged himself to the chair, plopped down and reclined, *why am I so zapped?*

Two hours later a ringing woke him from what was supposed to be a few minutes of rest. He jumped up and answered, "He... he... Hello?"

"Hey Russ, it's Tony. I wanted to thank you again for the lunch yesterday. You saved me from having to cross the street to that horrid restaurant. The only reason I go there..."

Tony would've gone on and on, but Russ cut him off, "I had a good time too. Let's do it again soon, all right?"

"By the way Russ, are you all right? Are you sleeping okay?"

"Yeah, why do you ask?"

Tony didn't want to say it, but Russ looked quite a bit older to him than a few weeks ago. "No reason. You must be going through a hard time with what happened to Beth. Just know we're all thinking of you."

"Thanks, I appreciate you calling." Russ hung up, grinned and threw the cap he wore into the air. He saved a life - so much for not changing history though.

Russ stared at his shaking hands. The trembling didn't concern him as much as the aging acceleration. He went to the mirror and for the first time in two weeks, he paid attention to his reflection. He had wrinkles where he never did before. *Something's not right. Now I understand why Tony and Silvia were concerned about me. I'm aging every time I travel. My body can't continue to deteriorate like this.*

Now, he had a new glitch to work out.

Chapter 31

*C*hallenges make you stronger. Isn't that what *they say? This issue of rapid aging is more a threat to my life than a challenge. My body is declining at an accelerated rate.*

I've had many sleepless nights because of the ceaseless time travel experimenting. I can now calculate the time it takes to go weeks, months, and years. The machine travels one year in five seconds at full throttle.

I stocked the trunk with extra weapons and the usual necessities. On my trip to Minneapolis, I purchased two grenades, a switchblade, and a can of pepper spray. It all fit in the pouches of my bulletproof vest.

Next travel time is today at 1:00 p.m. My goal is to search for Beth in the year 2116. After doing the math I figured if I count to 500, the Scorpion should materialize in that year.

Russ zipped up the vest and stuck his pistol in his waist wrapped holster. He slid into the Scorpion and leaned back. Gathering a deep breath he reminded himself, *I must remain unseen. I can't change history. I've done enough of that already.*

Flipping the starter switch the brilliant light lit up the room. When the glow disappeared, the gray and black streaks of the darkness emerged.

"One, two, three..." He shifted the lever to the maximum. The streaks twisted into a tornado. "235, 236, 237..." The waves of color blended into a dark grey, reminding Russ of melting steel. "492, 493, 494…" Bands of colored lights reappeared as he slowed. They became a soft yellow, then blue. The slower he moved the more they took shapes. A room appeared. When it became focused, he shut down the machine. He leaned in close peering through the windshield.

The structure of the basement hadn't changed much. The sun shining through the mud-smeared window made Russ guess it to be about noon. Opening the door, he leaned over and glanced down. The Scorpion hovered above a pile of rubbish. Russ breathed a sigh of relief *so far the hovercraft is working*. Russ slid onto the heap of rubble and scanned the area. His lips grimaced, the room looked like a bomb had hit.

There were no signs the first Scorpion had been there so he doubted Beth was here, but his curiosity got the best of him. He climbed down the debris and headed out to the hallway. Russ kicked trash out of his way as he crept toward the stairs. He pulled out his pistol and proceeded up. Standing on the last step, he peered down the corridor to the living room. From what he could tell, the layout of the house had changed little too.

Turning his gaze to the opposite side of the house, he surveyed the kitchen. It was nothing like the room in his time. His much-loved bright corner nook - where he ate many meals - was no more. The entire walls and ceiling were made of stainless steel. There was no conventional stove or refrigerator. Lined up on the inside interior were - what looked to be - empty vending machines. A built-in round steel table took up the center. Shredded black leather cushions covered the attached booth.

Russ jumped when a loud pop came from the front yard. His grip on the gun tightened. Getting down low, he advanced toward the living room. He peeked around the corner and wasn't surprised when the room was in shambles. Stones from the fireplace crumpled in piles. Much of the large picture window lay in shards.

Another loud pop shot through the air.

Russ crawled through glass fragments to the window and peered out. Forty feet away from the deserted porch, three men and three women stood with hands tied behind their back.

A giant of a man, hair styled in a Mohawk with a long thick braid falling to the side, taunted the petrified victims. He aimed something resembled a metal pipe at them.

Russ figured the big dude was the one in charge. Eight guys, huge as well, held the same vessel-like gadget and were huddled around their leader.

Another popping ripped, then two more.

Russ watched as a forceful stream of liquid blasted from the weapon. The victims screamed in agony watching their limbs melt into nothing.

Witnessing the terror of the bodies disintegrating, Russ's plan now was to get the *hell* back to the Scorpion as quickly as possible. Standing, something to his left caught his attention. He cocked his head, and not even five feet away hid a young woman - scared to death - crouched behind a decrepit chair. They spotted each other at the same time.

Through the window, he said in a low voice, "Can you hear me?"

She nodded.

"Can you make your way to the back door?"

She nodded and scurried out of sight.

He turned to head for the kitchen but halted in mid-action. Another humongous gang member stood only fifteen feet away aiming a pipe-weapon at him.

The man bellowed, "Who in the *hell* are you? Whatever's in your hand slide it over to me. Don't try anything asshole because I will liquefy you before you can say fucker."

Russ slid the gun.

The guy picked the pistol up, examined it and glared at him. He focused on Russ attire from the baseball cap to the sneakers. The big guy's brows scrunched, and his face grimaced. "What the *hell* are you wearing?"

The same question could've been asked by Russ. This futuristic person wore a body suit that appeared to be spandex. A wild pattern of black and gray odd shapes covered the outfit.

The guy kept his eyes on Russ as he took two steps closer to the window. "HEY, ZANE, GET IN HERE, THERE'S ANOTHER ONE."

Russ looked outside, his suspicion of the Mohawk man being Zane proved to be correct. The leader, along with the others headed for the porch. If Russ moved his hand - even an inch - toward his vest, the big guy would zap him in a flash. But he needed to defend himself *now*. If he waited until the rest came inside, he wouldn't stand a chance.

CLUNK!

The horrifying noise made Russ' head spin around just in time to see his attacker fall hard to the floor. He glanced up, the woman towered over the giant holding a bloody bat.

"We'd better get out of here." She said, throwing the bat aside.

Russ rushed over and picked up his pistol along with the man's weapon. He stuffed the gun into his holster, grabbed the female's hand and headed for the basement.

The murdering mob came rushing through the front door and stopped in their tracks when they saw their buddy's body sprawled out.

Russ stopped long enough to pull the pin out of a grenade and toss it.

The surprised gang glanced down at the object rolling towards them.

That precise moment proved to be all Russ and the lady needed. They sprinted down the stairs. The explosion showered ceiling particles on them as they flew to the time machine.

Screams came from the mutilated men. The unscathed ones shouted curses as they trampled down the basement steps two at a time.

Russ assisted the woman to the rear seat of the Scorpion. He slid into the front and slammed the door shut. Without waiting another second, he smacked the *return* button.

Irate gang members skid into the room spotting the machine. Light exploded throughout the room blinding them. They shielded their eyes and when they put their arms down, the apparatus was gone.

Chapter 32

The Scorpion reappeared in 2016. Russ turned and asked the woman if she was all right.

She squeaked in a barely audible voice, "Wh - wh - what happened?" She leaned forward and peered through the windshield. It stunned her when the room was undamaged and organized. "Where are we?"

Russ climbed out and assisted her. "You are in the same place you came from, only a different year, 2016. By the way, my name's Russ."

He helped her stand to her feet and held onto her while she steadied herself. Standing aside, he gave her a moment before saying anything else. He considered it best to let her get over the initial shock first.

"We traveled almost a hundred years into the past?" She asked casually.

By her tone, he thought traveling through time didn't come as a big surprise to her. "Well, that was my goal. What year did I bring you from?"

"2115."

He grinned, "Damn, I'm good."

Zena's brows crunched, "What do you mean?"

"I meant to go to the year 2116, and I came darn close, just one year off." Something dawned on him and his grin disappeared, "If I'd arrived a year later - as I planned - I don't think you would be alive. What's your name?"

"I'm called Zena from the twenty-sixth section of tube boomers."

"Tube boomers?"

"It's a long story for a different time. Are you sure we're safe here?" Zena's voice trailed off as her eyes scoured the entire room.

"Yes, you're okay, this is my home." Russ remembered the futuristic weapon and reached into the Scorpion. He pulled out the unique device and examined it. The thing resembled a metal pipe which measured about two inches in diameter and twenty-four in length. There was a pull lever, an extended scope, and a place for bullets. The gadget reminded Russ of a water gun only much more sophisticated.

"It's called a disrupter."

Russ' eyes shot to the woman. "A what?"

"It's a disrupter. The compartment fits six capsules filled with carborane acid along with three other deadly acids. When you pump the tension lever, it builds up enough pressure to pulverize the cartridges. It shoots up to twenty-five feet. If a person gets hit, even by a drop of the fatal mixture, their body cells disintegrate within seconds. And Russ, I'm sorry you had to witness those murders."

The horrific memory had never left his mind. "Yeah, me too. Who were those guys?"

Zena didn't answer. She already probed the entire room and was now fixated on the Scorpion. Her eyes moved up the slope of the five hulls and paused at the tip. She stared up at it for a few moments and working her way back down, she stopped mid-section and pointed to it saying. "Electromagnetic propulsion - fascinating. Are you using mercury superfluid or helium?"

Russ' brows pulled up and his mouth dropped open, *this lady's getting more interesting by the minute.* For once in his life he was tongue-tied. Nobody but his parents and Beth have ever stepped foot in his lab. Now, here in the forbidden area was this mystifying female. Not only did the woman have an incredible knowledge, she was beautiful besides. He liked her short haircut which was styled in a pixie. Long pointed bangs fell in angles to the right accommodating her well-shaped face. The auburn color made her dark-brown eyes appear intense and focused.

He glanced down at what she wore and noted *it's the same strange spandex suit the others had on.*

Zena sensed him eying her, but it didn't make her uncomfortable. She turned and faced him. Raising her brows, she waited for an answer, "Mercury or Helium?"

"Um, oh, I use Helium."

"Good choice. So what do we do now, Russ?"

"Huh?... um..." He hadn't figured out what to do with her since rescuing her. He put up his hand and said, "Slow down there girl... give me a minute." Russ reflected for a moment and gave her an option. "I can take you to any year you want to go. Maybe when it's safe?"

Zena stared at the floor and brushed the long bangs from her eyes. The corners of her mouth drooped. "I don't recall there ever being a time of peace. Would it be okay if I stay here until I figure things out?"

Russ ran his fingers through his hair biting his bottom lip, *now what? I can't keep her here.* Not sure how to answer, he redirected the subject, "Let's go to the kitchen. I'll get you some water. You may experience some fatigued for awhile so it's imperative you rehydrate."

Zena sensed bad vibes, "Look, I understand you didn't plan to bring back someone with you while doing your time-travel today, but you did. Please, you can trust me. We'll figure out what to do after we get some rest."

Russ knew she was right. They were too exhausted for any more commotion. He stepped aside and gestured with his hand, "Let me show you to your room."

Chapter 33

Theodore had been out and about and now returned to his apartment building. He trudged down the mold filled hallway shaking his head in disgust. The stalker unlocked the door to his studio and flipped on the light. A cockroach scurried by as Theodore plopped down on the only chair at the small kitchen table. He pushed aside the stinking ashtrays and rotten food and put his elbows on the surface and rubbed his temples.

Since Russ built the new Scorpion, Theodore was getting more impatient with every passing day. Russ, with all his time travel experimenting, was no closer to finding Beth. It made him so mad he could spit. Now on top of that, while spying through the lab window, he saw the time traveler brought home a total stranger in the Scorpion. Some sexy broad. Probably from the future, he guessed.

Theodore kept up with everything Russ did. He read every entry noted in his journal up to two days ago. Russ made a trip to Minneapolis, and unbeknown to him, Theodore made himself at home for hours. He predicted from Russ' calendar - and the fact he's habitual - Russ would be in Minneapolis for most of the day. So he took full advantage of the empty house. He even allowed himself to leave the confines of the laboratory for the first time. The man hobbled up to the second floor finding Beth's bedroom. Just as he imagined it looked like the room of a princess. Theodore was in heaven while going through her drawers and closet. He picked through her dresses and found the perfect one for the day he kills her.

After smelling her perfumes, the crazed man returned to the lab and slid into the Scorpion. He sits in it every time he's there. He memorized the control panel and knew he could operate it if need be. If Theodore knew where Beth was, he wouldn't waste any time going to her to finish the job.

He must kill this new woman even though she doesn't fit the profile. This female had brown short hair, but she would be in the way. There was no other option but to get rid of her too.

Chapter 34

How can ten days make such a difference in our lives? Only ten days. It did in Beth's. Her life switched from bad to wonderful overnight, ever since Daniel got his second memory.

Last night, Beth, Daniel, and the kids had a party. They took turns using the video camera while licking on lollipops and taking lots of goofy pictures using the Polaroid. The camera and photos still lay on the table.

Lunchtime was over. Daniel busied himself in the barn preparing for the harvest. The girls assisted him while Toby napped.

Beth, doing chores inside the house, was in her own happy world. She wore her blue mohair sweater, jeans, and sneakers. With the music player attached to her belt and earphones snuggled in her ears, she sang to Adele. The lunch mess got cleaned up while dancing to the music. The extra work of fetching water wasn't a big deal anymore. Nor did it bother her having to heat it on the pot-belly stove. The stove Beth now adored. In fact, every time it got used, Daniel's deceased wife came to her mind. *God bless Kristine for bringing it.*

Beth was in a great mood. She loved her life. It wasn't a simpler life, by far, but it was more satisfying than in 2016.

As she twirled around the room, something caught her eye. She froze coming to an abrupt halt.

Mrs. Knutson was standing in the doorway with her head

cocked. Staring at Beth's clothing, her head leaned further as she noticed the music player.

The music was loud. No doubt Mrs. Knutson heard it. Beth shut the player off and pulled out the earphones.

"You are Beth, aren't you⸮" the woman asked in a non-threatening tone.

Beth's mouth dropped open. Feeling like a deer caught in headlights, she thought *busted again by this lady.*

The matronly woman, nonchalantly, walked past Beth to the table. She pulled out a chair and motioned, "Have a seat, Beth."

Rubbing her hands together, Beth leaned over to get a view out the window. Mrs. Knutson's buggy sat there. She peered past the cart towards the barn, *is anybody aware this woman is here⸮ Where's everybody⸮* Her heart pounded. *How will I explain the headset, along with the watch⸮ And the pictures are still on the table from last night.*

After giving up on getting any help from the rest of the clan, Beth saunter to the table. She surrendered in the chair, folded her hands in her lap and waited.

Mrs. Knutson set her purse on the table next to the photographs. Her head shifted sideways glancing at them. "Uh, huh..." she muttered. Turning, she made her way to the kitchen and took two cups from the shelf filling them with coffee. She set one in front of Beth and settled down in a chair. "Beth, take some deep breaths. Your hands are shaking like a leaf on a tree."

The woman reached into her handbag and pulled out a balled up roll of dollar bills and placed it in front of Beth. "I made a run to Minneapolis to speak with a jeweler about your earrings. It turns out they were worth twenty-six dollars. The book cost five, so twenty-one dollars is your change. The jeweler is interested if you have any other jewelry to sell. He claims he's never seen diamonds and gems with such clarity.

Beth looked at the money and then back at the woman, and muttered, "Thank you. You didn't have to come all the way out here Mrs. Knutson." *Why is this lady holding back? Why doesn't she come out and say what's on her mind?*

Beth decided since the lady wasn't beginning the subject, she would. So Beth slid the disk player off her belt and set it, along with the headphones, on the table. "I suppose you would like an explanation?"

"That's unnecessary. But I'm curious who the young man was in the machine? The thing the Indians called the Scorpion? He asked about you."

Perplexed with Mrs. Knutson's matter-of-fact attitude, Beth guessed lying to her wouldn't help. "He's my brother."

"Did he find you?"

Beth scrunched her brows.

"Your brother was looking for you. Did he find you?"

Beth didn't answer. She just stared at the door and thought *where is everybody?*

"There's no reason to be nervous, Beth. Let me tell you something. My late husband, Henry, believed in traveling through time. He claimed he had an experience with helping a time traveler. The story right now isn't important, but he stood by it until the day he passed." She stopped long enough to sip her coffee and continued. "The contraption we saw your brother in, I figure was a time machine. Apparently, that's where your object that makes music came from and these images on the table. From the future, am I correct?"

Since the woman wasn't expecting an answer, she kept talking, "Somehow your brother lost you and that part I haven't figured out yet. Someday when you and Daniel are confident you can trust me, you can tell me all about it."

"Wow..." Beth rubbed the nape of her neck. *This is too bizarre. Where's Daniel?*

"Not to worry. I will go about my business now and leave your business to you two. Mrs. Knutson stood up, paused for a moment and asked, "You do understand I love Daniel as a son, don't you?"

Beth was unclear where this lady was going with the conversation. It sounded like she wouldn't tell anybody and at the same time, was giving a warning.

At that moment, Daniel rushed in and skidded to a stop. He shot Beth a "What's happening?" look. He knew it wasn't good when noticing the music player and earphones sitting on the table.

"Hello, Daniel." Mrs. Knutson picked up her purse and walked towards him. "I'm sorry we didn't get time to visit. I came to give Beth her change. You must be busy with everybody coming tomorrow so I won't keep you."

"We always have time for you, Mrs. Knutson. We'll come by real soon."

The lady patted Daniel on the shoulder as she walked past him. "You can trust me." She looked at Beth and smiled saying, "If either of you would like to talk, you know where I live."

Daniel and Beth walked her out to her buggy and saw her on her way. Daniel turned to Beth and asked, "What the heck was that all about?"

Beth returned to the porch and plunked down on a chair. She leaned over, put her head in her hands and rubbed her temples. Looking up at Daniel, she mumbled, "She knows." Glancing down at the bills in her hand, she added, "And we have twenty-one-dollars, which I think… is about six-hundred in 2016."

"That's great. Let's take you shopping for some clothes."

"Oh no, Daniel, I can't spend this on myself."

"Now Emilie, is there anything we lack? And you need

some clothes of your own until Russ finds you." Beth leaving was something he didn't want to think about anymore.

Beth pondered Daniel's question. He was a good provider. So she compromised, "As long as the children get new outfits too."

"Okay, it's settled then."

"Can I get split skirt pants?"

Chapter 35

Zena followed Russ out of the lab. Her eyes didn't miss a thing as she scoped the workshop and the laundry room. Once upstairs in the kitchen, Zena scanned the room from one end to the other. Spotting the stove, she grabbed Russ' sleeve and pulled him to it. "I've seen pictures of these." Zena raised her brows and asked, "Do you actually use this?"

"I try not to," Russ answered, nonchalantly.

Zena looked at him confused. That is until Russ chuckled. "Oh, you are a jokester." She chuckled too and took off again.

Russ couldn't help but smile watching the woman skip from one appliance to another inspecting each one. She got more intriguing with every passing minute. She reminded Russ of him - a female Russ. "What did you do for work?"

"I'm a quantum physics professor."

"Whoa, are you serious? Did I just die and go to heaven? You are a Quantum Physics Professor from the future?" He about went down on his knees pleading with her, "Can we please retire to the library? We can have a glass of wine. I'll make a nice fire, and you can relax... while I pick your brain."

"Pick my brain?" Zena scrunched her brows.

"Okay... I guess that phrase isn't used in the future. Anyway, I'd like to hear what happened to the world. From what I saw in 2115 it hasn't been good."

Zena scooted to the large kitchen window and peered out.

The backyard, surrounded by oak trees and tall pines, appeared quiet. "You're sure it's safe out there?"

"Yes, it's safe." Russ hoped for a response to his request for retiring to the library, but Zena kept moving. So, he followed her through the living room and up the stairs to the second floor as she inspected each room. When they came to Beth's bedroom, Russ took her inside and opened the closet door. "You seem to be the same size as my sister. While you're here, I'm sure Beth wouldn't mind if you wear her things."

Zena entered the walk-in closet and rummaged through the clothes. She turned to Russ and asked, "Where's your sister?"

"That's a long story. She may have got lost in time," Russ' smile turned to a frown.

Zena, noticing his concern, figured he could use some venting. "What's a library? And where's it at? I could use a glass of wine."

Russ' face lit up, and he gestured with his hand, "Right this way my dear." As Russ led the way downstairs, he asked, "Don't you have libraries?"

Zena peered into the room and gasped when she saw shelves and shelves lined with books. She hurried to a shelf, shifted her head sideways and began to read titles. She spoke while still reading, "No, we don't have libraries. I've seen pictures of them but I can count on two hands the books I've seen in my lifetime."

Russ couldn't believe his ears. "There're no books in the future?"

"They're scarce."

Zena strolled from shelf to shelf while Russ got a cozy fire going. After setting the poker aside, he rushed to the wine rack and picked out a bottle of Merlot. He motioned for Zena to have a seat on the sofa and set the bottle on the coffee table. Russ was so excited at what Zena had to say that he practically ran to the shelf to fetch the wine glasses. At last, he sat down next to her, poured the wine, and handed her a glass. Russ raised his and toasted, "To new friendships from different centuries."

Zena smiled, clanked her glass and took a sip, saying, "Your sister, you were going to tell me about her." She crossed one leg over the other and got comfortable.

Russ didn't want to be the one talking. However, he spewed out words for a half hour. He explained how the assumed serial killer stalked Beth and may have chased her into the machine. He told her about the madman committing suicide and how everyone assumes Beth is dead too. Russ picked up a picture of him and Beth and showed it to her. "I took this picture a few weeks before she disappeared."

"Where did she get the blonde hair?"

"Beth got my mom's hair. I got my dad's dark hair. So tell me. What happened to the world?

"So much has happened in the last hundred years. There were many wars. They began with Russia bombing America." Zena paused, unsure how much she should share about the horrific events. She felt it might be too heartbreaking for him.

"Are you all right, Zena?"

"Yes, but I'm concerned about you."

"Why?"

"These events I'm about to tell you begin in your lifetime. If you have family and friends living in these years, you'll worry. It may give you additional stress."

"Don't worry about me. Please, keep talking."

"All right. The destruction began in 2050. Russia bombed Yellowstone and the San Andreas Fault that ran through the country, the California Republic."

"What's the California Republic?"

"California's a separate country. So are the east coast states. The East being wealthy didn't want to fund the rest of the country. But that's history that'll have to wait for another time." Zena chuckled and kidded, "I can't tell you the whole future in one night."

"You're right. I'm sorry, keep talking. I won't interrupt you anymore."

"It's okay if you do. I'm sure you'll have lots of questions. But for now, I'll give it to you like a short story. Okay?"

"Yup, let's do it. But before you skip ahead too far, what happened to Russia? Did we get them back?"

Zena raised her brows at Russ giving him a "Really?" look.

Russ, getting the hint, zipped his lips and picked up his wine. He reclined, got comfy and gave her his attention, once again.

"So... because of the bombing, America became a third-world country. The volcano explosion - along with the eight-point zero earthquake - killed sixty-five percent of the United States population the first day. Within twelve hours, every continent in the world had after-effects. There were more earthquakes, tsunamis, and multiple volcano eruptions. One after another the calamities destroyed cities, farmland, and towns.

"Within one month, the death toll zoomed to seventy-five percent. That's not to mention the lives it took in other countries. It brought global cooling by twenty degrees to the entire earth that lasted decades. It destroyed farms for thousands of miles. The ashes clogged roadways and blocked sewer lines. The eruptions spewed out sulfur dioxide, and that caused respiratory problems and a high percentage of the elderly died. It changed rainfall patterns and caused severe frosts and mass starvation."

Zena looked down and paused like she was praying, "You asked about Russia. The United States struck back, and it was enough to wound them. Russia became a third-world country also.

Russ got up, took the globe of the world off a small round

table and set it in front of her. "What else is different compared to this?"

Zena ran her hand over the ball turning it with the other. She stopped it and pointed to New Orleans. "New Orleans is gone. It's underwater along with Miami Beach and the southern tip of Florida."

Zena paused. Russ looked like he was going to cry. "How about we change the subject?" She picked up the picture Russ had shown her earlier. "This was taken only three weeks ago? Are you okay, Russ?"

"No, I'm not. The Scorpion has a glitch I can't fix."

"What is it? Maybe I can help."

"How old do I look?"

"I don't like those questions. I'm not good at guessing peoples age. Got anything else for me?"

"Seriously, I need your opinion."

Zena cocked her head and looked him over. "I guess, I would say you're about forty-six."

"I'm thirty-one. I've time traveled about fifteen times. That means I must age close to a year every time."

"The time travel is aging you?"

"Yes, and I don't know how to fix it, or if it's fixable. I suspect the body cells get teleported through time-space, and they're trying to adjust to the change."

"You're right. Every time a body travels through space, the body cells get scrambled. In order to recreate themselves, they make copies."

"Exactly. The thing is, the replicas of the cells are making weaker copies and those models make more fragile duplicates. All this is causing my body to age out of control."

"Your body's recreating atomic matter. I hate to tell you this, but that was the major glitch in my time. It's the reason the government stopped machine time travel. I'm sure there are some crazy people out there still doing it, but it isn't safe."

"Well... I don't have a choice. Beth's lost somewhere in time, and I have to find her. I'm starving. Let's go to the kitchen. I'll fix us some lunch."

"Okay, but I'm taking this bottle of wine with us."

Once they got back to the kitchen, Russ reached into the refrigerator and took out the cheese. "How about grilled cheese sandwiches and tomato soup?"

"It's been a long time since I've eaten real food." Zena peered into the refrigerator over Russ' shoulders.

Russ grabbed the bread and moved to the counter.

Zena stayed at the refrigerator and examined the condiments.

Russ buttered the bread. "What were those things that looked like vending machines in the kitchen?"

"More or less, that's what they were." Zena continued to go through the refrigerator. "We buy our pre-made food in huge warehouses. Everything comes in single serving packages for filling the containers. There're dispensers for everything. The cold items are in refrigerated machines, and the hot items are in heated ones. We don't need conventional stoves and refrigerators."

"Did you live in that house?" Russ asked, getting a can of soup from the pantry.

Zena shut the refrigerator door and started going through the pantry while she talked. "No, my friends and I found it empty. It became our temporary shelter. As usual, the gangs come from every direction and bombard their way through peaceful places and leave them in complete destruction."

"What gangs?" Russ had the soup heating and the sandwiches frying.

"To list a few, there're the *Fire Dragons*, the ones trying to bring communism back into the country. That gang is more of a nuisance, but dangerous just the same. Many smaller ignorant groups, like the one you saw, are everywhere. The worst of them is the *United Blood*. We see little of them, but the destruction is massive. This movement is the main reason we stay out of the inner cities."

Zena paused, the memories were painful. The tears she had been fighting back now slipped down her cheek.

Russ picked up a napkin and handed it to her.

Zena wiped away the tears and moved next to Russ watching him stir the soup. "No where's safe. Even the underground homes get discovered by the scum. They move in and kill everybody in their way. They pillage and move on."

After stirring the soup Russ walked to a cabinet and pulled out two plates and bowls. Handing them to Zena, he reassured her, "You're safe here."

Zena took the dishes and set them on the table and excused herself to use the bathroom. When she returned, lunch was ready.

Russ looked at her outfit as she slid into the booth, "So what's up with your clothing? I have seen nothing quite like it," he chuckled.

Zena chuckled too, "Oh, you think my suit's funny? Well, listen up big-shot. This suit is body armor."

Russ, still smiling, raised his brows, "Body armor, really?"

"Yes, the outfit's a computer. The material protects our body from the weather. It cools down when we overheat and heats up when our body temperature falls. Electromagnetic waves circulate the blood and clean the pores."

Russ realized his mouth hung open again and quickly closed it. He picked up his sandwich and took a bite. Still chewing, he said, "That outfit's awesome. If my life hadn't been so focused on building the Scorpion, I would have invented it. I hate doing laundry. How long can you wear it?"

"Only a week and this suit got used up two days ago. Since

I have nothing to plug into, I may need to go through Beth's closet."

"You charge it up?" Russ asked, taking another bite.

Zena didn't respond. She watched Russ eating his grilled cheese. It made her mouth fill with saliva. She grinned and told him, "I can't talk right now." She picked up her sandwich and took a huge bite.

Russ watched Zena tear into her lunch. She ate like she hadn't eaten in days. Chuckling, he said, "Take your time girl, there's plenty more where that came from."

Zena, with a mouthful and about to take another bite before swallowing, eyed Russ over her sandwich and muffling she said, "I know, I'm rude, right?

"No, you're just hungry, apparently."

After finishing their meal and cleaning up the kitchen, they went up to Beth's closet. Russ, wanting to give her some space, offered to go downstairs while she tried on clothes.

"No, Russ, I have no idea of what outfit to pick. These are 100-years-old. You sit on the bed. I will try them on and will come out and model them. You say yes or no."

"Okay, let's do it."

While Zena searched through Beth's closet, Russ twiddled his thumbs and waited. He shouted, "Find anything yet?"

"Yes, I'm putting it on." Zena smoothed out the wrinkles as she observed her outfit in the full-length mirror. She hadn't expected to find something that wasn't frumpy, but she did. Feeling quite satisfied with her choice, she yelled through the door. "Okay, I'm coming out."

Russ' first glimpse of what she wore made him grin, he almost laughed.

Zena, thinking he was making fun of her, turned to go back into the closet.

"No... hold on." Russ jumped up grabbing her hand. "Listen to me. This outfit looks awesome on you." He sat down on the edge of the bed and explained, "What you're wearing is for exercising. You like it because it's spandex. It looks like your body armor."

"So it's something I can wear all the time?"

"As long as you wash it every day. You look fantastic in it."

Zena found a pair of sneakers that completed her outfit. "Do you mind if I clean up?"

"I thought you'd never ask." Russ chuckled, "I mean you've been wearing the same clothes for over a week." With a more serious tone, he crinkled his nose, "I would think you'd smell, but you don't." Russ stopped talking before he embarrassed himself any further. "I'll be in the lab when you're done. Yell if you need anything."

An hour later, Zena came through the door wearing a different spandex than the one she had modeled. She noted Russ' confusion and said, "Yeah, Beth must have exercised a lot because she has several of these outfits."

"I don't know what Beth has up there, but it works well for you."

"Good, I have to admit, I was worried about what I would wear. Russ, I have an idea."

"What is it?"

"Can we go out for a while? You can show me the town. I'm dying to see what it looks like now."

Russ stood up and walked towards the door, "Hell yeah, let's grab a jacket."

Chapter 36

Zena made her way down the porch steps while Russ secured the front door which was a breeze using the new lock. She scampered to the two cars parked in the driveway and tried to decide which one was Russ'. Out of the two, she picked the Silver 2012 Sebring convertible. Being sure of her decision, she walked to the passenger door and waited.

"Where are you going?"

Zena turned and saw Russ was unlocking the passenger door of the other one. "That ancient car is yours?"

Russ stood beside a red 1994 Subaru station wagon. It made him laugh seeing the look on her face. "This was my dad's car, so it has sentimental value. Besides, I can haul a lot of stuff in it. It's better than having a truck."

"Wow, that's like a hundred-and-twenty-year-old car." Zena strolled around the car inspecting it.

Russ put his hands in his pockets and meandered behind her, "Well, in my time its twenty-two years. Nevertheless, I take care of it. It's good on gas and gets me where I need to go. But if you like we can go in the convertible. It's a warm, sunny afternoon. We can put the top down."

"NO!" I mean... I don't want to be in the open. Did you bring the disrupter?"

"We don't need it here. Zena, nobody's going to jump out of the woods or anywhere else for that matter. I have a carrying license, and there's a gun in the glove compartment. So we're cool."

They were back at the passenger door now and Zena made one more swipe at the surrounding woods before sliding onto the seat.

Before closing her door, Russ bent over and asked, "Are you sure you want to do this?"

"Oh yes."

"Would you like to go to Forest Lake which is about eight minutes away or Minneapolis which is an hour drive?"

She shook her head. "No big cities."

Russ took a right and headed toward town. "So, you told me you were a tube babe, what's that about?"

Zena shifted and faced him, "Thirty-three years ago, the socialist government banned natural childbirth. At birth, all females got fixed. If a couple gets approved to have a baby, they would be allowed one, but only one. Eggs from the woman's ovaries, along with her partner's semen were extracted and transferred to a birth tube at one of the Population Growth Facilities. The fetus develops in a cylinder while the parents monitor the growth of their baby on a computer. It was imperative there be bonding. Children came into the world this way for twenty-six years, for every letter of the alphabet."

Zena paused and spied out the window. There wasn't much to see, only woods, so she turned back to Russ. "I was born the last year of the tube babies, which is why my name begins with Z. After the country became the United Union, communism ended and so did the tube babies. Now, females born the last seven years will have a natural childbirth. Every infant still gets a chip implant in their heel though. That replaces the social security number system.

Again, it took Russ a minute to realize his mouth was wide open. Sitting up straight, he regained his composure. "Wow, do you still have the implant?"

"Yes, but it won't do my government any good. They've no control over me anymore." A puff of laughter escaped her mouth.

"No, I guess they don't. Has anybody tried to remove the chip?"

"Nobody I know. You'd have to remove part of the Achilles tendon. That would impact your ability to run. We couldn't risk that."

"So... you mentioned the parents monitored the baby through their computers? How have computers evolved?"

"There are many types, but the popular one is the eye contact. They're our connection to the world. All of our devices are controlled by them. The eye computer works through a *wet connection*. Engineered nerves linked organic material to computer material and..."

Russ interrupted, "What do you use for a keyboard?"

"The eye computers come with a virtual keyboard. It's all new. Technology didn't skyrocket until the world had time to recuperate."

"Are they in your eyes now?"

"Yes, and I can read your mind with them. So be careful what you think."

Russ' head shot in her direction.

Zena giggled, "I'm kidding. I don't have them in my eyes. They wouldn't do me any good in this year anyway.

Zena sat at the edge of her seat and peered out the window. They passed the sign announcing, "You are Entering Forest Lake, Population, 18,375." A handful of Mama and Papa restaurants along with a few small businesses seemed almost empty. Zena thought the sidewalks were quiet too. It made her uneasy. *Something's going down. Maybe, it's an attack from the Baldies.* Feeling foolish, she remembered, the gang didn't exist yet. She took in a deep breath and blew it out slowly.

Russ, picking up on her anxiety pointed, "Zena, watch, straight ahead."

Zena squinted through the windshield and caught the view of the lake as they arrive downtown. Quaint outside sitting areas were everywhere now. People strolling, jogging and bicycling filled the sidewalks and streets. Zena found it peaceful and non-threatening. So at last, she let her guard down and relaxed - somewhat.

After driving through the round-about on Lake Street, Russ took the first available parking spot. "Would you like to walk a while?"

"Oh yes."

Russ and Zena sauntered, mesmerized with the stimulating activity within the park. They strolled down the busy boardwalk and stopped to lounge on a bench to enjoy the view of the tranquil lake. Shades of violet and blue streaked across the sky casting its reflection on the water making it appear as a polished mirror.

Zena couldn't remember ever feeling such peace, although she still caught herself looking behind her. Her eyes darted staying focused on every motion. She watched a man and a boy acting strangely. The man held a phone out in front of himself. He and the boy followed something using the cell. She turned to Russ, pointed to them and asked, "What do you suppose those two are doing?"

After observing them Russ presumed they were father and son. They would aim the phone at nothing and would laugh. "They're playing 'Pokémon Go.'

Zena crinkled her nose and asked, "Pokey what?"

"It's a game that's played on your phone. They're fictional characters that capture other beings, and you try to catch as many as you can. The makers of Nintendo put them in tourist traps like here."

"But it looks like they see something."

Russ shrugged his shoulders, "I guess it's like your eye computers, there's nothing there. It's virtual. I know little about it and have no time for it."

Zena breathed a sigh of relief, "For a minute, I thought they had a virtual keyboard."

"That's all we need," Russ chuckled, shaking his head.

A warm gust of wind brought with it the mixed aromas of cooked beef and seafood. Zena sat straight up and sniffed. Her mouth watered and her stomach growled."

Russ turned and looked at her belly and laughed, "Was that your stomach talking? I think we better find a restaurant to feed it. That sounded scary."

Zena elbowed him in the ribs and laughed as well. She hopped to her feet and asked, "Which way?"

They walked until they came to a restaurant that appealed to her. "I like this one, but I don't know if I'm dressed up enough for it." Zena stared at the rear end of a woman standing in front of her while waiting for a table. The shapely lady wore a tiny black dress that showed her every curve. Her heels were so high Zena wondered she walked in them.

Russ, noting her concern whispered in her ear, "You could wear rags and still look fantastic." Taking hold of her elbow, he led her inside following the hostess. She led them to a window booth with a magnificent view of the lake.

After a few moments passed the waitress came with menus. Russ ordered a carafe of Merlot and handed Zena a menu. "Get whatever fancies you, my dear."

"Are you sure? Because I'm so hungry, I could eat a horse."

Russ acting like he was ignoring her, read the menu, and without looking up, he said, "Mm... nope... no horse on the menu."

Zena giggled, "Smart ass."

"Let's see, that would be donkey... hm, nope, no donkey on the menu either." Russ looked up, and they both laughed.

They decided on *All you can eat Crab*, and Russ taught Zena the painstaking art of getting the meat out. They laughed repeatedly as they squirted each other while snapping the claws. Russ loved watching Zena eat. She couldn't get enough.

Zena sighed and pushed her plate away and moaned, "If I eat anymore, I'll explode."

Russ agreed and filled their glasses with the last of the wine. They leaned back and enjoyed the dazzling sunset. The multiple shades of amber had taken over the sky. The sun resembled a big yellow lollipop. And somewhere, in the mirrored image of the orange horizon, was the sleeping lake.

"Breathtaking isn't it?" Zena asked, just a little louder than a whisper.

Russ watched her. He marveled how beautiful she was. Without taking his eyes off of her, he answered, "Yes, breathtaking."

They returned home exhausted and called it a night. Russ walked Zena to the guest room and made his way to his room. He changed into his tee shirt and boxers and crawled under the covers of the king-size bed. Folding his arms behind his head, he laid grinning. He couldn't stop thinking about this extraordinary day even though he broke all his rules. Although the rule on not mingling with the inhabitants left him with no guilt, he felt Zena came into his life for a reason. His thoughts got interrupted by a knock.

"Russ?"

Russ jumped out of bed and opened the door, "What is it, are you okay?"

"Yes, can I please sleep in here?" Zena asked with pouty lips.

Russ opened the door and glanced down at what she wore. It was another one of Beth's spandex exercise outfits, just a different color this time. "Yeah sure, I'll sleep in the other room."

"No, I mean, can I sleep in here with you? I don't want to be alone."

"Oh, right, yeah sure, I can sleep in the chair. You take the bed." Russ headed to the closet for a blanket.

"You have a huge bed. I think we can both fit on it. I just don't want to be alone."

Russ watched Zena as she skipped to the bed and pulled the blankets aside and crawled in. "Okay... no problem." Russ went back to his side, crawled under the blankets and said, "You know Beth has pajamas right?"

"Yes, I know. Oh, by the way, thank you for the great evening."

"No, thank you."

"No, thank you." Zena giggled.

"Oh, I see how you are." Russ kidded, "Always got to get the last word. Good night."

"Good night, Russ."

Chapter 37

Daniel was right when he said it would take three days to complete the harvest. With his oxen pulled sled cutter, he and Arne, cut down the corn stalks. Bradley and Ollie bound the stocks into shocks for drying. Pastor Bakker and two other farmers came to relieve the men halfway through the day. There're still plenty of chores on their own farms with the upcoming wheat harvest.

While the men worked, the women husked, shelled and ground much of the corn into animal feed.

The older children watched over the young ones and kept them busy with games.

The families worked as one large household and harvested three and a half acres of corn. One hundred and fifty bushels, it was enough to provide each family for the long winter months.

Right from the start, Daniel announced there'd be no talk of the new memory. He made it clear they're here for the harvest, not for storytelling.

Daniel instructed Anna that none of the children were to go near the barn. The Scorpion was well hidden, but he wasn't taking any chances. They already had to deal with Mrs. Knutson, who Daniel invited for dinner. They planned on telling her everything.

Beth was writing in her journal when Sara came tearing into the house.

"Emilie, she's here. Mrs. Knutson's here."

"Go get your pa." Beth stood and tossed the car keys onto Toby's tray. "Okay kiddo, keep yourself occupied." Beth put her pen and tablet in her room and smoothed the wrinkles on her dress. She took a deep breath, scooped up Toby and proceeded to greet their company.

Daniel assisted the woman off her buggy while the girls cooed and petted her magnificent Shetland pony.

When Beth came out and spotted the Shetland, her face lit up. She rushed down the steps and handed Toby to Daniel. She headed for the pony and slid her hand down the long smooth mane. "My goodness, she's a beautiful animal."

"Thank you. Her name's Elsa. I rescued her from pulling carts through the coal mines."

Beth's forehead crinkled. "Coal mines?"

"Yes, Shetland ponies get imported to America for that purpose. I traded my husband for her."

Beth, Sara, and Anna's heads all shot toward Mrs. Knutson.

The woman chuckled, "I'm kidding."

Daniel shook his head and smiled. He was familiar with the woman's humor.

Anna ran her fingers through Elsa's blonde bangs. She turned to her father and begged, "Pa, can we get a pony? Please?"

Sara jumped up and down so hard two rocks flew out of her pocket. "Ya, Pa, can we?"

"When we get a horse, it'll be a big one. A horse that's strong enough to pull our cart." Daniel turned to Mrs. Knutson, "I don't think a pony can handle that, right?"

"No, I don't," she chuckled. But if you consider getting a workhorse, I can get you a fine one for ten dollars. I'm sure my friend won't have the mare for long, so you'll need to let me know soon."

"Ten-dollars? That sounds cheap enough."

Now both girls jumped up and down begging, "Can we get it? Please, Pa."

Daniel glanced at Mrs. Knutson and gave her a "Thanks a lot" look. He turned to Beth, who was trying to stay out of the discussion. "So Emilie, how about it, should we buy a horse?"

Is he asking me to take part in making such an important family decision? "Huh, well… we have twenty-six dollars."

"That's your money," Daniel said, giving her a warm smile. "Mrs. Knutson, when can we see the animal?"

"I can set it up for next Sunday. If you like, I'll bring the owner and horse to you."

"Sounds like a plan." Daniel put his arm around her shoulder. "Mrs. Knutson, would you like to take a stroll to the barn?"

The magnificent Scorpion towered above the woman. She strained her neck upward to the top and back down to the cab. "Yep, that's what we saw that day. But wait… how can it be here? Where's your brother, Beth?"

"First thing to remember Mrs. Knutson, Beth goes by Emilie now. We'll tell you about it at dinner. Shall we retreat to the parlor?"

During dinner, Beth told of her ordeal. She also brought out the encyclopedia, explained its history and read her written note. "Mrs. Knutson, you said your husband encountered a person who time traveled. Can you tell us about it?"

"Well… I wasn't one hundred percent truthful about that." She paused for a moment as she recollected and continued, "My husband Henry was the time traveler, himself. But he didn't have a machine. It happened when they were experimenting with wormholes. The scientists had no problem sending Henry to the past, but retrieving him was impossible. The hole he traveled through closed up and he got stuck in the past. I guess like you did Emilie."

Beth's eyes were as big as silver dollars. "Oh, good Lord, what happened after that?"

"When I met Henry, I was seventeen, he was twenty-four. I lived at home with my parents. I found Henry hiding in our barn. He had pictures and gadgets from the future, kind of like your things, Emilie. I had no reason for doubt when he told me he was from 2111. I brought him food and water every day for over a month. We fell head over heels in love. One day my dad caught him and ordered him to leave. Henry begged me to go with him. He had a pouch of high-quality diamonds for the worst case scenario. He promised we'd never lack for anything. So I left with him and we had a wonderful life together."

Daniel put his hand up, "Whoa... you have me dumbfounded. Did my parents know about Henry being a time traveler?"

"Oh no, we never told a single soul. I'll tell you more about it one day." Mrs. Knutson turned to Beth and said, "I don't mean to change the subject, but I'm dying to see your gadgets. Maybe after dinner, you can take some out?"

As soon as the kitchen got cleaned, Anna and Sara put on a show. They assigned acting parts for everyone, and the play turned out to be hilarious. Beth recorded them and Daniel took pictures - now that he could operate the Polaroid. Afterward, they settled at the table and enjoyed apple dumplings while viewing recordings and passing around pictures.

Mrs. Knutson sipped the last of her coffee and turned to Beth, "I've been admiring your dress. I know it wasn't one of Kristine's. I would've recognized it."

Beth explained how Anna designed and sewed it.

Mrs. Knutson turned to Anna, "My, my, Anna, you have quite a skill. I can send more work your way if you like. It wouldn't take long for you to have a successful business as a seamstress."

Anna beamed, "I'd love that. I have another dress started for Emilie."

Beth wondered *when does this girl sew?*

Mrs. Knutson stood, "This has been a fascinating day. But I don't want to wear out my welcome, and I want to get home before dark." She hugged the children and bid goodbye to Daniel. Turning to Beth, she shocked her by asking, "Emilie, would you consider staying here in our time? For good?"

"Um... I... I don't know..." Beth looked at Daniel.

He smiled and raised his brows.

The woman hugged Beth and said, "You don't have to decide now, but please consider it. You have a family who loves you very much right here."

Beth's mouth hung open, but no words would come out. She'd be okay if Russ never found her. But if he comes, *would I stay? Could I stay? Is that what Daniel wants?*

"Oh, by the way," Mrs. Knutson whispered in Daniel's ear, "There's a bottle of moonshine in my buggy."

Daniel grinned and thanked her as the group walked her to the cart.

Later that evening, after the children got tucked away in bed, Daniel and Beth retired to the porch. Daniel brought two cups and the jar of moonshine. After pouring the whiskey, he handed one to Beth. He let out a big sigh and said, "Looks like we got the corn harvest done just in time, any day now there'll be a freeze. I got to say, you did an excellent job with the women and children. You fit right in."

"It sure was better than the other day at the store. Thank God."

Daniel cleared his throat, "Emilie, what Mrs. Knutson had to say about you staying on... the children would love it if you made this your home."

When Beth and Daniel's eyes caught she quickly turned away. She wasn't ready for this conversation.

Daniel, nervous she would say no, assured her, "I wouldn't mind it either."

A nervous laugh came out of Beth, "Russ may never find me. So you all may get stuck with me anyway."

Daniel chuckled, "We would love it if you got stuck with us. Besides you fill that empty spot in our home."

Beth stared at the ground and without looking up she said, "Let's deal with it if and when Russ comes."

"I guess that sounds sensible." Daniel's half smile turned upside down. He stood to his feet, stretched his body and said, "Well... I'm beat, I'm heading to bed. Tomorrow we need to cover the Scorpion. We're low on pork so I'll need to butcher a hog too."

Beth looked in Daniel's cup. It was still half full. She wished she could say yes to staying, but making that kind of a decision wasn't that easy.

"Good night, I'll see you in the morning." Daniel turned and disappeared into the house.

Alone on the porch with almost a full jar of moonshine, Beth took a swig and fixated on the barn. She worried about Russ, Silvia, and Tony, but living a life without Daniel and the kids sounded horrible. Her motto had always been, 'When in Doubt, Do Nothing'. For now, it was an easy rule to follow. She didn't need to decide yet. However, when Russ comes for her, she would. The longer she stayed in 1860, the more attached she would get.

Beth sighed and swallowed the rest of her moonshine. Picking up Daniel's cup, she finished that too and tiptoed off to bed.

She lay there for a half hour, arms folded behind her head, pondering the question *they all want me to stay? Stay to be a friend to Mrs. Knutson, a mother to the children and a wife to...* Beth shook her head, *Okay, that's crazy thinking. Stop it right now.* Turning onto her side, it wasn't long before the whiskey kicked in putting her out like a light.

Chapter 38

The morning sun shining through the window woke Zena. She reached for Russ, but he wasn't there.

The aroma of fresh coffee wafted under the door. Eager to see what was cooking, she sprung up and slipped her feet over the edge. Before reaching the floor, the door opened.

In came Russ carrying a breakfast tray of pancakes with all the trimmings, complimented with a yellow rose. "Back into bed," he demanded.

"Breakfast in bed?" Zena swung her legs around faster than one can count to three.

"You've never had a meal served to you in bed?"

"I consider myself lucky to get breakfast period," Zena said, with her wide eyes gazing at the full tray. "Russ, you don't have to make me breakfast every day."

"Are you kidding? I've never seen anybody who can eat as much as you first thing in the morning. Besides, this is only your fifth day. I won't be spoiling you forever."

"Keep spoiling me, please." She picked up her fork and dug into the scrambled eggs and bit off a piece of bacon at the same time. Talking with a mouthful of food, she mumbled, "What's on the agenda today, boss?"

"We need to get groceries. You're eating me out of house and home. Would you like to go to the grocery store with me?"

"Oh yes. I love real food. Is the supermarket filled with real food?" Zena asked stuffing her mouth with more eggs.

"Not really, only the outer edges. That's where you find the dairy, meat and produce. Everything in the middle is processed."

Russ watched as Zena stuffed a big bite of waffle and took another before swallowing the first. "You understand that food isn't going anywhere. You don't need to rush every time you eat."

Zena stopped mid-motion with the fork at her mouth. She set it down and giggled, "Am I rude?"

Russ laughed, "No, you're never rude. You eat as fast as you want. I'm joking with you."

Russ plopped down, slouched over and became serious. "What if I never find Beth? If I keep traveling my body will be ninety years old in no time. I have no idea of what year to go to next. I think I need to put a graph of some sort together."

"That's a good idea. I can help you with that. I can share in some runs too."

"You mean you go in the time machine? No, it's too dangerous. Promise me you'll never go into the Scorpion without me."

"Okay Russ, calm down. Let's go to the lab. I'm going to get dressed." Zena gulped her coffee and jumped out of bed.

Russ watched as she ran out wearing the blue spandex, *what's she going to do? Change from the blue into the red?*

Russ was sitting at his desk when Zena came into the lab. This time, she wore spandex with a wild pattern. He chuckled, "That outfit almost looks like the one you wore here."

"Yes, doesn't it? Beth has great clothes." Zena strolled to the table and plunked down. She pulled over the encyclopedia and rested her elbow on it. "Russ, maybe we should take a trip to 2110."

Russ looked up, raised his brows and waited for her to continue.

"Have you heard of nanorobots?"

"Yes, they're molecular components that kill cancer cells. It's in the experimental stage. I doubt they'll be in use anytime soon."

"Well, they are in the future. Cancer is unheard of in my day. A swarm of nanorobots gets injected into the bloodstream. They kill injurious cells, which include the ones causing you to age. Every newborn gets a shot and a booster every five years. My friend works in a health facility and will get as many dispensers as we need."

"I need to find Beth first. Then we'll talk about it, all right?"

"Okay, but if we got you better first you could travel more to search for her."

Zena opened the book and suggested, "Let's see what time you should go to next. I'll randomly pick a page, and that'll be the year we'll start the graph." Zena opened the book in the middle and put her finger on a page.

"That encyclopedia will do no good, Zena. I already traveled to the mid-eighteen-hundreds. There wasn't anything but wilderness. The book goes up to 1850. Next time I'll try after the turn of the century, around 1905."

"When did this book get published?" Zena flipped to the front when something written on the inside cover caught her eye. At first, she didn't comprehend what she read. She re-read it and realized it was a note from Beth! "Uh... Russ... you need to see this."

"I told you already, that book won't do me any good."

"Russ, it's a note from Beth."

Russ' head shot up, "What?"

Zena grinned and nodded her head saying, "I think we found her."

Russ flew to the table and stared at the writing. "That's never been there." He sat down, pulled the book closer and read it again.

Russ, I'm in the year 1860. I found our book at a store. Can you believe it? When you come to get me, you'll land in a barn. Look for yellow ribbons hanging from the rafters. When you see them you'll know you are in the right month and year. Patiently waiting. Your favorite sister, Beth (also known as Emilie.) J
P.S. every month I'll change the color of the ribbons. They're orange now for October.

"It doesn't appear she's in much distress. She drew a smiley face," Zena commented.

"Damn, Beth found this book, and she wrote in it. What are the chances of that? She's okay!" Russ paused for a moment and looked up scrunching his brows, "I must have been within ten years of her when I traveled to the wilderness."

Russ jumped up and dashed to the Scorpion. He opened the front hood and checked the trunk for supplies. "If the other machine isn't working, I'll need extra parts." Russ went to the closet and grabbed a handful of wires and connectors and threw them in. "Let's go."

"Russ, the Scorpion only fits two. If the first machine is broken she'll need to come back with you. I'll wait here for you."

Russ didn't want to leave her. What if she wasn't here when he returned? He wanted to kiss her, but instead, he slid into the Scorpion. "I need to travel back 156 years. That means I count to 750 and watch for ribbons. Is that correct?"

"Yes, it sounds right. Good luck and please return to me."

"I'll be back before you know it."

"In case you don't..." Zena bent over, took his face in her hands and kissed him.

He gave her the biggest grin and drooled, "Wild Indians won't keep me from coming back to you."

"I hope you're bringing the disrupter."

Russ already thought of that. The weapon was at his side. He winked at her through the window and gave her a thumbs up. He flipped the switch and when the bright light subsided, he counted.

Chapter 39

Sara was collecting eggs when the barn lit up, She let out a loud scream, "PA, THE BARN IS ON FIRE."

Daniel tore out the door. He would've ordered Sara to go into the house, but he was sure the little stinker would run after him. So he said nothing. He raced to the barn and pushed open the door. There was no smell of smoke and no sign of fire. It occurred to him, he had been through this before. He trudged to the far corner, and sure enough, there sat the second Scorpion. Daniel's heart sank.

Russ climbed out and stood next to the time machine and yelled, "Hello my name is..."

Daniel cut him off, "Ya, ya, I know who you are."

At that moment, Beth came tearing through the barn and halted when she spotted her brother.

"Russ, oh my God, you're here."

They ran to each other, and Russ lifted Beth off her feet and twirled her around. They laughed and cried at the same time.

Beth took her brother's hand, led him over to the family and introduced him. "Russ, this is Daniel, and these are his children, Sara, Anna, and Toby. They were kind enough to let me stay here."

Russ shook Daniel's hand, "Hey man, I can't thank you enough for taking care of my sister."

He looked Beth over and chuckled, "At least it appears

like you've been taking care of her, she doesn't appear to be starving."

"They've taken excellent care of me."

Anna took a step forward and being the little hostess whom she is, all grown-up like, said, "I can make coffee if you like."

Russ gave her a big smile and said, "A cup of coffee sounds good about now. Thank you, Anna. You're a great hostess."

When coming out of the barn, Russ surveyed the grounds. He couldn't imagine how Beth made it as long as she did. "Wow, this place is so out of your realm, Beth. Have they made a farmer out of you yet?"

Beth flexed her biceps. "Hey, I have muscles now. You don't want to mess with me." She laughed and wrapped her arm around Russ' as they walked to the house.

Once inside, Daniel pulled out a chair at the table for Russ while Beth and Anna got the coffee and cups.

Sara perched across from Russ and stared at him. She put an elbow on the table and rested her chin in her palm and mumbled, "I've seen your picture."

Russ furrowed his brows wondering how that could be. He was a little uncomfortable with the way the whole family seemed to be staring at him. No... it was more like they were glaring at him.

Beth, sensing his dilemma, put a cup of coffee in front of him and sat next to Sara. "Russ, remember my birthday party the night I disappeared? Well, my co-workers gave me white elephant gifts. I had them in my backpack when I got chased. Plus, I had my phone in my purse, and your picture's in it."

Russ not hearing much of what Beth said put his forearms on the table and leaned closer. "Beth, what happened? Why did you take the Scorpion?"

He listened to her story and it happened like he figured. His eyes scrunched wondering how the killer got out of his house. It looked like nobody had been in it. Snapping out of his thoughts, he told her, "The serial killer's dead. You don't have to worry about that bastard anymore. Silvia, Tony, and all your friends assume you are dead too. Silvia slipped into a deep depression and hasn't come out of it. She took a little time off of work but she only got worse. Tony worries about her. He's afraid she may try to commit suicide."

Beth's hand flew to her mouth. She had thought little about the pain they suffered.

Russ held the cup in his hands like he was trying to warm them. He blew lightly on the coffee and continued, "But one good thing has happened. The Company fired Steinhart and brought in somebody else. I guess after you disappeared, your co-workers became distraught. They ganged up and wouldn't take her crap anymore. Tony says it's a great place to work for again. But there's a big hole missing, and that's you. I guess they have a temp working your job, so it'll be open for you to pick up where you left off."

Beth didn't reply. She wasn't sure what to say.

The room got silent as everyone waited. Toby even stopped playing with his gadgets and looked up to see why nobody was talking.

Beth broke the silence saying, "I don't care about the job anymore. But I care about Silvia. She needs to see me, to know I'm al…"

Her sentence was cut short when Sara got up from the table and ran into the bedroom slamming the door behind her. Beth stood up to go after her, but Daniel stopped her.

"I'll take care of this." He grabbed Toby and took him into the room.

Anna stood up and followed her father.

So now Russ and Beth sat alone at the table and stared at the closed door. She heard the girls crying, and it was breaking her heart. Turning back to her brother, she tried to pinpoint what was different about him. "Russ, are you okay? You look terrible."

"No, I'm not. But that's a long story. I have so much to tell you, but let's wait until we get home. By the way, where's the first Scorpion?"

"It's in the barn," Beth glanced at the closed door. Once again she felt like an outsider, separated from the ones she had come to love. "Come on, I'll show you." She yelled through the door, "Daniel, Russ and I are going to the barn. He's going to take a look at the other machine. Would you like to come along?"

Daniel shouted back, "No, you two go ahead. I'll stay here with the kids."

Russ observed Beth's expression. Her lips quivered and he was sure she was about to cry. "Maybe you should get your stuff together Beth. It won't do anybody any good to delay the inevitable."

Beth didn't want to leave Daniel and the kids, but Russ was right. Silvia needed her, and so did Russ. He was sick, and she knew it was because of the time traveling. He couldn't continue doing it. Staying here was no longer an option. She reluctantly threw her stuff into the Rhinestone bag. Beth talked through the closed door again, "Will you please come with us, Daniel?"

She got no response. So she ventured to the barn once again, fearing this may be the last.

Beth slumped on a hay bushel staring into space while Russ inspected the broken machine.

"I found the problem." Russ motioned for her to come over.

Beth stood and sighed. She trudged to the Scorpion and looked over his shoulder.

"See this wire? Somehow it got disconnected." Russ proceeded to re-connect it when Daniel and the children came into the barn.

"Were you going to leave without saying goodbye?" Daniel refused to let his eyes fill with tears.

Anna and Sara stood with bloodshot eyes. Toby, next to them looked perplexed.

"No, of course not," Beth outstretched her arms to Sara and Anna, and both ran to her. Beth fought hard to hold back the tears but lost the battle. Now all three females were bawling.

After Russ repaired the Scorpion, he stood and waited until the girls stopped crying. When the sobs diminished, he took a step forward and announced, "All right, we have working lights and fans. The Scorpion can travel once again."

Daniel walked over to Russ, "How'd you fix it?"

"It was a loose wire." Russ saw by Daniel's confused face that he didn't understand, so he showed him where he reconnected it.

"That little thing caused all the trouble?"

Beth turned to the machine and mumbled, "I guess if I had paid attention, I would've figured it out."

Turning to Daniel, she wiped away the tears and cried, "I don't..."

Daniel put his finger gently to her lips, "Don't worry, the girls and I understand you have a whole other life and you have obligations there. We'll be all right. It was a pleasure we got you as long as we did."

Daniel reached out and pulled Beth close to him, embracing her. He held her close for several moments not wanting to let go. Noticing Russ waiting, he pulled away and whispered, "You should go now."

Beth took a step back, wiped tears from her eyes and reached into her backpack. She pulled out the bag of lollipops and knelt down to Toby's level. She locked eyes with him and said, "Now don't you eat these all at once, okay little man?" Beth beamed when Toby gave her a big toothless smile. Something caught her eye. She looked closer and noticed Toby wasn't toothless anymore. "Oh, lookie here, Toby's finally getting a tooth."

Both girls came right away and examined their brother's tooth.

Tears came again to the corner of Beth's eyes, *I won't be here when Toby gets the rest of his teeth, or when Sara gets her two bottom teeth...*

Her thoughts were interrupted by Russ, "Beth, are you comfortable taking a machine back? It's ready to go. All you have to do is push the *return* button."

Beth's shoulders sagged as she spoke, "No problem."

Russ put up his hand, "Okay, but wait a few minutes after I leave. I'll need to move my Scorpion to make room for yours."

Shaking Daniel's hand once more, Russ said, "Thank you, for taking such good care of my sister."

He turned to the girls and patted the top of their heads like they were puppies. "It certainly was a pleasure meeting you."

They didn't respond. They stared at Russ with scorn.

Russ wanted to tell them Beth could come back for visits, but he knew it wasn't a good idea. Both families needed to move on in their own centuries. Russ left it alone and told them, "Cover your eyes, the flash will be blinding."

Both girls covered their eyes and Daniel put his hands over Toby's.

Russ got into the machine and flipped the switch. The flash filled the barn, and Russ, along with Scorpion number two, disappeared.

When they all uncovered their eyes, Anna stared at Beth with pleading eyes and tears spilled out.

Beth reached into her bag once again and took out a picture Mrs. Knutson had taken of Beth, Daniel, and the kids. She studied the photo one last time. They looked like the perfect family. Beth held the picture out for Anna and told her, "I'll never forget you. You'll be in my heart forever."

Anna stepped back. She wouldn't take the picture.

Even though Beth understood, her heart felt like it was being ripped from her chest.

Turning to Sara, she put her hands on her tiny shoulders. She bent over and locked eyes with her little guardian angel and told her, "Sara, now make sure you brush your hair every day. Then it won't get so matted. Okay?"

Sara stared at the ground and nodded without saying a word. Her shoulders slumped, and her little arms hung at her sides like a Raggedy Ann doll. Then, barely moving one arm, she snatched the picture from Beth's hand continuing to stare at the ground.

Beth's heart was about to burst and if she didn't leave that second she knew she would change her mind. But for Silvia and Russ' sake, she had to go. She gathered a deep breath, made her way to the scorpion and slid in. Before pushing the button, she paused to take one last look at the family she'd come to love.

Daniel wore the most dismal look. Toby wrapped his little arms around his Pa's neck and both girls' stood with their arms wrapped around his waist. Each had the same sad face. *I can't leave. I love this family. Take your eyes off of them and think of Silvia, think of Russ.* Beth shut her eyes and hit the return button.

Chapter 40

Zena was still standing right where Russ left her when the Scorpion showed up.

He hopped out, "Quick, help me move this machine."

"Did you find her?"

"Yes, she's coming right behind me."

After moving the Scorpion, Zena grabbed Russ and hugged him. "Oh, thank God, you returned."

"I was only gone a minute."

"Thirty seconds to be exact and it was the longest thirty seconds of my life."

The lab filled up with the blinding light once again, and the next Scorpion appeared. Russ ran and opened the door.

Beth slid out clutching her backpack. It stunned her when she saw Zena standing there. Beth's eyes shot at Russ and then did a double take at what Zena was wearing *is that my spandex?* Her eyes shot back at Russ with her brows raised high.

Russ moved next to Zena, "Beth, this is Zena."

"Zena?"

"Yes, and if you're wondering if the outfit's yours, well it is. Zena's from the year 2115. It's a long story, would you like to hear it here, or in the kitchen where we can have a cup of coffee?"

"I've had enough coffee for one day. Let's sit here on the

couch. Beth never took her eyes off Zena while walking to the sitting area.

Russ sat next to Beth on the couch, and Zena settled on the chair. The two told Beth of Zena's rescue. Beth watched as they took turns talking and wondered if something romantic was going on. It was something about the way they looked at each other. *Daniel used to look at me like that.*

"Zena's a Quantum Physics Professor," Russ said, giving Zena a look of admiration.

"Really? Well, you must be in heaven, Russ."

"That's funny, that's what Russ said when I told him," Zena said, giving Russ the same look he gave her.

Russ snapped his fingers, "Listen to this Beth, I went to the past and saw you as a little girl…"

Beth rolled her eyes. "Yes, I know, Russ. I got a new memory that day. You also went to 1851 and saved a man named Spencer. You saved him from getting scalped."

"What? How'd you know that?"

"The day you saw me on my ninth birthday, I got a new memory. And when you traveled to 1851, one of the men you saw was Daniel. He got one too. In fact, everyone there that day got the second memory. It caused quite a stir."

"I knew I got a different memory, but I didn't realize it would happen to everyone involved. Well, I bet you don't know I saved Tony."

"Tony?"

"Yes, I saved him from getting hit by a bus," Russ explained the rest of the story.

"Wow, I guess Tony should be thankful he's got you as a friend. But… your goal was not to change history and not to mingle with the inhabitants. So, how's that working out for you, Russ?" Beth raised her brows and gave him a sly smile.

"I call it *fate*. I had to find you and while searching for you a few other things happened." Russ didn't want the subject on him anymore so he passed the buck, "Zena, tell Beth about your body armor."

Zena spoke and Beth half listened. Her mind wasn't in the future. It was about what would not happen, and that was a life with Daniel and the kids.

Zena, seeing she didn't have Beth's full attention, asked Beth about her experience of living in the past. So Beth shared the life of living on a farm in 1860. She told them about her friend, Mrs. Knutson and how Beth came upon the book at her store. When the subject of Daniel and the kids came up she had to stop. It was too painful. "I need to lie down a while, that bit of time travel wore me out." She turned to Russ, "Did I just age a year?"

"Maybe ten months. I'm just going by how I look every time I travel."

They walked Beth to her room and while going up the stairs, Beth asked, "I still have a room here, right?"

Zena told her, "Oh yes, I sleep in Russ' room."

Russ noted Beth's brows rise, and quickly said, "Her room's the guest room. She sleeps with me because she doesn't want to be alone. That's it though, we sleep."

As they walked down the hallway, they passed the guest room, and Beth got a glance at Zena's body armor hanging up. Beth stopped and stared at it for a moment, "Is that the outfit you wore here?"

"Yes, it is."

"Well, I guess I can see why you like my spandex."

"Yup, it's all she wears," Russ chuckled.

Beth went into her bedroom and found her bed scattered with every spandex outfit she owned.

Zena scooted ahead of her and gathered them up. "I'm sorry about this mess. I can put them in your closet if you like."

"No, it's ok. Take them to your room? I won't be jogging anytime soon. In fact, take whatever you want from my closet."

A dark heavy cloud loomed over Beth. *What have I done? Nothing here matters anymore.* She tossed her bag onto the bed and plopping down she planted her head on the pillow covering her eyes with her arm.

Russ patted Beth's foot and said, "Zena and I are going to the grocery store. Would you like to go with us?"

Beth, not moving a muscle, mumbled, "No, you two go."

After hearing the front door shut, Beth sat up in the middle of her bed. She reached for the bag and dumped out the contents. She picked up two loose pictures, and for the longest time, she stared at them. The left was a photo of Daniel and the girls when she first got there. They all had confused looks on their faces.

Beth then studied the right picture. This one was Daniel and the kids also, although, this time they were making goofy faces. Beth giggled as she recollected how funny they were once they got the gist of it.

Beth dropped her hands and pictures to her lap. She slumped over and didn't have the energy to straighten up. It made her think of her mother. She would always scold, "Sit up straight, dear." She knew her mom was the reason she has good posture to this day. *Who will teach the Anna and Sara such things?*

Beth sighed and gazed out her bedroom window, but she more or less stared into space. She visualized Anna and Sara's faces. Beth didn't like the fact they may have to grow up without a mother.

She snapped herself out of her thoughts, and the backyard came into focus. It was a large area surrounded by tall Pines. She helped her father plant them when she was young. She had a good upbringing. Beth wondered how the girls' upbringing would be. Would every day be spent sad and separated from their pa again? It seemed every remembrance Beth had as a child brought her back to Daniel's children.

Tears seeped from the corners of her eyes. She wiped them

away and put the pictures aside. Now she reached for the video camera and turned it on. Watching the last video taken by Daniel's family, she couldn't help but laugh. Mrs. Knutson was the main star and her humorous side came out like never before. They had laughed until their stomachs hurt. *What a fun night that was. I miss her too.*

Beth rewound to another recording. Daniel had Sara, with her mussed-up hair, sitting on his shoulders while little Toby clung to his dad's legs. He was yelling, "My turn, my turn."

In the video, Anna came to Beth and said, "You go over there with them. I'll record."

So now, Beth watched herself in the video. She was wearing the dress Anna made. Beth pushed the pause button and studied the uniqueness of the outfit. With a little direction, Beth felt positive Anna would make a fine seamstress and could bring in a little cash. Mrs. Knutson would help her get clients. Beth wished she could be there to help her get started on her new adventure.

Beth resumed the video and watched herself pick up Toby. She raised him high in the air and set him on her shoulders. Sara played tug-a-war with Toby and the room was full of laughter.

Beth stopped the recorder and peered out the window, staring into space once again. She recollected Toby on her shoulders and remembered how sore her body was the next day. Daniel gave her such a good message. She remembered it well. Daniel's strong fingers rubbing her shoulders, *it was heavenly. Stop it. I have to get them out of my mind.*

Beth's focus returned to the room. She couldn't watch anymore, it was breaking her heart. Throwing the camcorder on the bed, she leaned over, put her head in her hands and sobbed.

After five minutes of indulging herself with self-pity, she sat up. She wiped the tears away with the sleeve of her blue mohair sweater. The one she'd been wearing and washing for thirty-some days. It could come off now. She could put on a clean, fresh one. But there's no way anybody would get it off of her now. It still smelled like Daniel's house and the scent was all she had left. Beth took another whiff of her sleeve and sniveled, *yup, this sweater won't get washed ever.*

She spotted one stray lollipop. Picking it up, she stared at it and twirled it. It made her think of Toby. More tears, she didn't bother to brush them away anymore.

Beth scanned her entire bedroom. The room she grew up in. She didn't see one thing she cared about anymore. Taking a deep breath, she sat up straight. *Why did I return? Everything I want now is in 1860. I came back for Russ, Silvia, and Tony. Russ doesn't need me anymore. Zena's filling that empty spot in him nobody else could do. I don't want that job back, and I hate the horrific traffic. I no longer want to live alone and living at Russ' is out of the question.*

Now that Beth knew Russ would be fine, her mind went to Silvia and Tony. It bothered Beth to think of her best friend so awfully depressed. Once again, she stared into space. After a few trancelike moments, an idea came to her.

Beth threw all her stuff, except the phone, back into the backpack and bounced off the bed. At the dresser, she found the charger and plugged in her phone. After it had a charge, she made a call to Russ and put her plan into action.

Two hours later, Russ and Zena arrived home. Russ called out to Beth but got no answer. They went into the kitchen and set the groceries on the counter and Russ set out to find her. The first thing he did was to look down the basement stairs. A light glowed from the lab, so he made his way down and found Beth in front of the Scorpion.

"Beth, what are you doing?"

"Oh, you startled me. Did you do what I asked?"

"Yes, but I'm not sure it's a good idea though."

"It'll be okay."

They stopped talking when the doorbell rang. Russ and Beth shot each other a look before Beth went flying down the hallway.

Russ, right behind her, grabbed her arm and said, "Let me go first. I can prepare them."

Zena answered the door and let the guests in just as Russ got there.

"Hey Russ, what's up?" Tony stood there checking out Zena.

Silvia came in after Tony, and she also eyed the woman up and down.

Russ briefly introduced her. "Hey guys, this is my friend Zena.

Tony and Silvia, hoping to get a little more info on her, stood waiting.

Zena made their introduction quick, "It's splendid to meet you. Now if you'll excuse me, I'll give you some privacy." Turning, she disappeared down the hallway.

Silvia put her purse on the entry table and took off her jacket. "We got out of work but we have to go back. The new boss gave us three hours. It wasn't easy, but you told us to come no matter what. Have you heard something? About Beth, I mean."

Russ thought Silvia looked fragile. She had lost weight and looked like she hadn't slept in weeks.

"Um, yeah, about that... why don't you come into the living room and sit down." Russ turned to lead them, but they didn't follow.

"No, you can tell us here." Silvia wouldn't budge. "I don't have to be sitting when you tell me they found Beth. That's what you're going to say, right?"

Beth couldn't stand waiting in the kitchen any longer. She couldn't bear to hear Silvia sound so hopeless. She stepped out into the hallway. "Silvia."

Silvia dropped her jacket and cried, "Oh my God!" She ran to Beth and hugged her so tight it almost took Beth's breath away.

Tony gave Silvia a little time, but now he wanted in too. He put his long arms around them, saying, "Group hug."

After a few minutes of laughing and crying, Russ brought them a box of tissue. All three reached in, grabbed one and blew their noses as Russ led them into the living room. Silvia and Tony sat on the couch, and Beth picked the chair next to the sofa, turning it to face them.

Beth wiped the last of her tears away and spoke, "What Russ and I are about to tell you must stay here. We're going to confide in you because we trust you not to tell anybody."

"What is it, Beth?" Tony asked.

"First swear. Swear you won't tell a single soul."

Tony put up his hand, "Give us a Bible, and we'll swear."

Silvia pushed Tony's hand down, "You can depend on us. Tony and I swear Bible or no Bible."

Silvia and Tony listened as Beth and Russ revealed everything. They heard about the serial killer and how Beth got chased into the time machine. Russ explained in detail how he searched for his sister and about his endless time travel experimenting. He told them about going to the future and saving Zena. He thought it best to leave out the part of saving Tony's life.

After Russ and Beth agreed they'd heard enough, Russ brought them down to the lab where Zena waited.

Tony, seeing Zena, put his index finger on his bottom lip. He was sure he and Silvia were the objects of a hoax. He strutted to her waving his finger and drooled, "So, you're the woman whom Russ saved in the future?" He waited for Beth to fess up and turned to say something when big as all outdoors, the two Scorpions stood on the platform right in front of him. His jaw dropped, "No way! I thought you were going to tell us it's all a joke."

Silvia saw the Scorpions too. Her mouth dropped open as well. "Beth, this whole time I thought that monster buried you somewhere." She was still emotional. She couldn't stop the tears no matter what, good or bad.

Beth gave her friend a long hug and turned to the group. "Now that you all realize I'm alive and well... I'm returning to where I belong, with Daniel and his children. I have no doubt I love that man. And I love his kids like they're my own and they need me. I already have the Scorpion filled with what I'm taking and I'm leaving today."

"You're leaving us again?" Silvia's brows raised high and her lips pouted.

Tony put his arm around Silvia's waist, "Beth, you gotta do what makes you happy. Silvia and I will miss you, but it'll also make us smile every time we think of you cleaning a pigpen."

That remark made everybody laugh.

It didn't take Russ by surprise Beth chose to go back. He couldn't remember seeing her so excited about anything in her entire life. "Okay, so what kind of stuff are you bringing?"

"Well, for sure batteries. You picked up some more for me, right Russ?"

"I got everything on the list you gave me over the phone."

"Good, I took all the flashlights I could find in your house. I hope you don't mind. You may have to buy some more for yourself. I packed some more clothes, two long skirts, some jeans, and oh, my dolls for Sara. Hm, let me think, oh yes. I'm bringing my battery alarm clock and some utensils from your kitchen. And I took the wine from the rack. I left one for you guys. Oh, I almost forgot... you may find some of your curtains gone." Beth chuckled.

Russ chuckled as well, "Are you sure you don't want to take the kitchen sink too?"

Giggling, Beth answered, "No, I don't need that. I tried taking the bathtub, but it wouldn't fit in the Scorpion."

Beth turned to Silvia and Tony, "Now, let's go upstairs. I believe Russ and Zena brought home pizza. Let's have one more party for the road."

For an hour and a half, they either laughed or cried, or they did both. The visit was dying down. Silvia and Tony sat in a private discussion about work. Russ and Zena, deep in conversation, sat on the other side of the table. Beth watched as Russ leaned in and listened to Zena's every word. She could tell her brother adored the woman. *Where there's love...*

Silvia looked at her watch and jumped up. "We need to go, Tony."

Beth stood up, and they all followed suit. They headed back to the lab. Tony and Silvia insisted on seeing Beth off. They refused to believe the story until Beth and the Scorpion disappeared.

Silvia gave Beth one more long hug. "I can't believe my best friend is leaving me to go live in 1860. It's so bizarre." Silvia reached behind her neck unfastening the clasp of her dainty diamond teardrop necklace. She put it on Beth saying, "I want you to have this. Think of me when you touch the teardrop."

Beth clasped the teardrop and said, "Don't cry any more tears for me, okay?"

"All right, but I will miss you so much."

"What do I have to give Beth to remember me by?" whined Tony.

Beth hugged Tony and chuckled, "You're already unforgettable."

She turned to Russ, "Promise me you won't do any more time travel until you fix the aging issue."

"I can't guarantee anything. We still need to visit you."

"I will miss you. But if you age almost a year every time, I don't want you doing it. How about you come once a year?"

"I'm not sure I can wait that long. How about every six months? Maybe we'll have the problem solved by then."

"Okay, that'll be April." Beth walked to the Scorpion and threw her Rhinestone bag into the rear seat.

Russ reminded her, "Don't put too much stuff in there. Don't forget you have to sit there."

"You don't have to go with me."

"Yeah, I think I do. It took practice to travel to a precise time. If you do it, you may wind up a year too early or a year too late."

"Don't I just look for the orange ribbons?"

"What if Daniel took them down? Besides, I don't think Daniel would feel comfortable knowing he has a machine hiding in his barn forever."

Beth hadn't thought about that. "All right, I guess I'll have to hold all the stuff on my lap."

"Don't forget the Scorpion has a trunk."

"I know. It's full too."

Beth faced Zena and hugged her. "Take whatever you want in my bedroom. I won't need any of it." Then she whispered into her ear, "I left something special for you on the bed."

The time had come. Beth climbed into the rear seat and maneuvered all her goodies around so she could fit herself. Once situated, she worried *what if Daniel took the ribbons down? How will we return to the correct day? To the moment I left?*

Russ slipped into the front seat, flipped the switch and began his count to 756. When getting to 750, he slowed the machine to a crawl.

Beth searched for the ribbons, praying to God they were still there.

"753..."

Beth noticed something hanging from the rafters. "I think I saw one."

Russ saw it too. When the streamers came into focus, he turned it off. Russ slipped out and assisted Beth.

Beth stood in awe as she looked up. At least fifty ribbons were hanging from the rafters. They were everywhere, red ones - yellow ones - blue ones - all kinds of colors. Beth grinned from ear to ear *where in the world did they get them all?* It took all she could muster up not to race to the house and throw her arms around him that second.

Russ gazed up at the ribbons too. He stood grinning with approval, *way to go, Daniel.* Turning to Beth he said, "Let me help you get this stuff to the house."

Beth, still staring at the ribbons, said, "No, its okay. Just set it on the ground, Daniel will help me."

After the two emptied the machine, Beth gave her brother a long hug, "I love you so much. I know you and Zena will be triumphal together."

"Are you sure you don't want me to walk you to the house? To make sure we're at the right time?"

Beth looked up at the ribbons as she brought her hand up to her newfound necklace. She clutched the teardrop and replied, "No, that won't be necessary. I'm at the right time."

After saying goodbye, Beth made her way to the house. She crept up the steps to the closed door, knocked and waited.

The door swung open. Daniel stood there. His mouth dropped as he ran his hand through his mussed-up hair.

Beth smiled and in a nonchalant way, asked, "Can you give me a hand? I have a bunch of stuff to carry in from the barn."

Daniel stepped outside closing the door behind him. Grinning, he picked her up and twirled her around. He set her down and pulled her close, wrapping his arms around her tight.

Beth could feel her whole-body go soft as she molded right into his frame.

After a few moments, Daniel took her chin with his fingers,

tilted her face up and gazing deep into her eyes he purred, "You know this means we must get married?"

"Is that a proposal?"

"Yes, it is, Beth."

"Does that mean I will have your last name?" Beth giggled.

Daniel smiled and whispered, "Shut up and kiss me."

When he kissed her and her knees almost gave way. She wrapped her arms around his firm shoulders and snuggled right in. She couldn't get close enough.

Before things got passionate, the door opened, and Sara let out a howl, "Beth, Pa told us you'd be back."

Daniel released his hold and Beth bent over with outstretched arms. Sara ran into them and wrapped her little arms around Beth's waist squeezing her with all her might.

"Beth, we knew you would be back." Anna also flung herself into Beth's arms.

Toby came toddling behind, yelling, "Emawee."

Beth looked at Anna, "Did Toby say, Emilie?" Beth picked him up and lifted him up in the air, "Toby, you're the only one who called me by my correct name."

They all laughed and pointed at each other saying, "You have to do one of my chores."

Beth cupped Sara's chin, "I need some help. I have something for everybody, but it's all in the barn."

"Really, Emilie? What did you bring me?" Sara jumped up and down like a jumping bean and it reminded Beth of one of the many reasons why she returned. So, together as a family, they ventured out to the barn once again.

Chapter 41

Russ returned to the lab with-in thirty seconds of leaving, causing Tony and Silvia to become believers. Zena and Russ walked the two to the door, promising to keep in close contact.

Zena, eager to find what Beth left on the bed for her, headed straight to Beth's room. Standing at the foot of the bed she viewed the contents lying on it. Her whole face lit up. Wearing a huge smile, she shook her head at Beth's incredible insight.

At the top of the stairs, Zena yelled down, "Russ, the evening's early. What'd you say we get more of those crab legs?"

Russ walked to the bottom of the stairs and yelled up, "Sounds good to me."

"I'm going to take a shower, give me thirty minutes," Zena said, skipping off to the bathroom.

Russ looked down at the jeans and tee shirt he wore. He figured his outfit would suffice since it's a restaurant you can dress up or go casual. So having a little time to spare, he headed for the lab. It was imperative to get the notes of today's activities into his journal while they were fresh in his mind.

Thirty minutes later Russ looked at his watch. He stood up and turned off all the lights except the one above the Scorpions. He locked the door and jaunted up to the living room. Seeing no sign of Zena, he headed for the stairs. Looking up at to the second floor, he saw her standing there. Stopped in mid-motion, his mouth dropped.

Zena stood with a hand on her hip looking and feeling sexy as hell. She wore a seductive, tiny, black dress revealing her every curve. She had to laugh at Russ' expression because it looked like his eyes were popping right out of his head.

Russ' bulging eyeballs aimed in on her sexy black high-heeled shoes, then to her delicate ankle bracelet, and upwards to her well-shaped legs. "Wow," was all he could muster up to say. Taking a step back and with fingers locked behind his head, he stared upwards at her. "Whoa, you're gorgeous." He put his hands back to his side and looked down at what he wore. It would no longer do. Russ looked at her frowning.

Zena, noting his dilemma, said, "Come on up. We'll find something for you to wear."

Upon entering Russ' room, they spotted on top of the bed a laid-out outfit, right down to the shoes and socks.

Zena laughed, again impressed with Beth's intuition.

"I guess I'll need about fifteen minutes."

"I'll pour us a glass of wine." Zena left the room and descended the stairs. Before making it to the kitchen, she heard Russ yelling from the top of the stairs.

"Hey Zena, have you seen my razor?"

At the bottom step, Zena hollered up, "No, Beth's are gone too, and the blades. She left us a cheap one though. Zena chuckled at the thought of Daniel shaving with Russ' shaver.

Zena carried the wine-filled glasses up to the room.

Russ, all dressed, sat on the edge of the bed slipping into his black shiny dress shoes. After tying the laces, he stood, smoothed out the wrinkles from his trousers and straightened up for Zena's viewing. "I'm not sure about the pants. I haven't worn these for years."

Zena looked down at the tight fitted black dress slacks. They made his butt look cute, but she kept that to herself. She observed his maroon button-down shirt. Russ had the sleeves rolled up to his elbows. Zena deciding he cleaned up well, remarked, "You look sizzling hot."

Russ gave her a sexy smile and sauntered over to her and purred, "Well, there you go, one hot dude and one hot chick, out for a night on the town."

Zena ran her fingers over Russ' chin, "And your five o'clock shadow's sexy too."

"How do you think I got ready so fast? I didn't have to shave." Grumbling, his voice trailed off as they left the room. "I don't have a shaver to shave with. Some other guy's using it."

After leaving the house, Russ informed Zena they needed to make a pit-stop at the corner store for gas. When arriving, Zena decided to buy a bottle of water while Russ gassed up.

As Russ pumped the fuel, he watched Zena walking to the door of the convenient store. The door opened, and a hunched over man rushed out bumping into her knocking the black clutch out of her hand.

Russ continued watching and was prepared to intercept if necessary.

Zena glared at the man and glanced down at her purse. He didn't make any attempt to pick it up. So Zena bent down, grabbed it and disappeared into the store.

Russ was taken aback when the man peered through the window and followed Zena with his eyes. It startled Russ even more when the guy spun his entire body around frantically searching the parking lot. At first, Russ assumed the man forgot where he parked his car. The guy scanned the lot from one end to the other until his beady eyes settled directly on Russ. Their eyes locked giving Russ a creepy feeling. The man turned away, lurched to his car, and drove off. Russ noted the vehicle was a white Ford Focus.

Russ sat in the car waiting when Zena came out of the

store. She slid in and grumbled, "Did you see that jerk? Some guy almost knocked me down."

"Yeah, I saw him. What an asshole. I didn't like the way he looked at you. It made my flesh creep." Russ glanced at Zena. He would do whatever it took to protect her. Marveling at her beauty, he took a moment to check her out. "Are you sure you want to go out tonight? I mean, we can always go home and watch your little black dress hit the floor."

Zena grinned and put her hand on his shoulder and said, "Down boy, down."

Chapter 42

Theodore couldn't believe his luck. He hadn't been able to get into Russ' lab for days. Ever since that bitch came, Russ wasn't making trips to the big city anymore.

However, Theodore just saw them all dressed up. He figured they must be out on a date. This was his chance. He needed to get to the lab and read Russ' most-recent notes.

Theodore hid the car in his usual spot. He trudged the rest of the way to the basement window. Once inside, he pulled out a small flashlight out of his pocket. He found his way to Russ' journal and sat down. Today's entrée sat open. Theodore read it, and re-read it. Thinking his eyes deceived him, he read it one more time. It was true, Beth had come and gone.

"WHAT THE FUCK! Theodore sprung from the chair and whipped the journal across the room. Now, he was irate because he broke his number-one rule. Never move anything. Theodore hobbled over, picked the book up and returned it to its place.

Not knowing what to do next, he stood there all hunched over with his shoulder's sagging. Putting his hands on his hips he hung his head. The madman breathed heavily and hollered out curses. As quickly as he'd started, he stopped and glared at the Scorpions. His mind spun in circles *how did Russ find her? How did I miss it?* Theodore smacked himself on the forehead *you weren't paying attention, idiot!*

Theodore sat down, bent over his already arched torso, and rested his head in his hands. After a few moments, he straightened up and stared at the two machines again. *Think, think.* He stood and scowled, "Fuck Russ, I'll get the bitch myself." He chose the closest Scorpion *I know I can do this. I can work this piece of shit. I need to count and look for the ribbons like Russ instructed in his fucking book.*

Theodore reached down into his pocket and pulled out his switchblade, making sure it was ready for use. Next, he pulled out a syringe filled with synthetic opioid etorphine and inspected it.

Theodore's new plan would be to find Beth, shoot her in the neck with the catatonia drug - which will induce unconsciousness. He'll bring her back to the future and carry her to the bedroom. The dress he picked out will be displayed on her. He'll prop her up on the bed - *maybe like she's reading a book, or smoking a cigarette. I haven't decided yet. There are so many options.*

Next, he'll take pictures before he slices her face and will finish her with three-deep stabs to the chest. That'll have to wait until she wakes. Watching them squirm and wither in their blood is his favorite part. When she's dead, he'll set her in a new pose and will take after pictures.

When he finishes with her, Theodore plans to hide around the living room corner; right off the front entryway. Equipped with Russ' baseball bat, he'll wait for the lovebirds to come home. After clubbing Russ in the head, he'll slice Zena's throat.

Theodore thoughts wandered, *the best pose for them might be in the living room on the couch. Perhaps with Russ' hand up the whore's little black dress.* He wasn't sure how yet. It'd come to him.

Satisfied with his plan, Theodore slid into the machine and peered at the dashboard. After studying it for several seconds, he put his stumpy finger on the switch and sat back. He took a deep breath and flipped it up. The room filled with the flash and Theodore began his count.

Chapter 43

Beth and the girls spread a large quilt in front of the stone hearth. They wanted room to sprawl out while they burrowed their way through the goodies Beth brought from the future.

Blazing orange and red flames crackled and popped in the fireplace setting the mood for the event. The warmth radiating from the glowing embers took the chill out of the air.

Anna and Sara sipped on mugs of warmed apple cider, and Beth treated her and Daniel to hot toddies. Toby couldn't be bothered with anything to drink. He pre-occupied himself with snooping into the boxes and bags.

The time came for the revealing of the mystery contents. Beth kept the family in anticipation long enough. Daniel got comfortable in a rocking chair, and the children sat cross-legged on the blanket. They waited patiently acting all giddy.

Beth began the unmasking with a small bag. She peeked inside and closed the sack again watching the children. She purposely kept them in suspense. Beth smiled at Toby, who watched her every move. "We'll give Toby his first. That way he won't want everybody else's stuff."

Toby, hearing his name mentioned, sprung to his feet. Standing tiptoed, he placed his tiny hand on Beth's shoulder peering into the bag.

"Hold on, little man." When Beth dumped the contents onto the blanket, Toby's eyes got as big. In fact, so did everybody else's. In a heap on the floor were outdated cell phones, calculators, remote controllers, and two handheld video games.

Toby let out a holler, plopped himself down and grabbed for them.

"Toby may be a little young for these, but I figured since he loved my car keys, these gizmos might keep him busy. There are songs on the old phones, and the games still work. At least until the batteries wear out. We'll put them in this bag when he's not playing with them and hide them under your dad's bed, okay?"

Beth wasn't sure anybody was listening. They had all grabbed a gadget and were examining them. So, she continued, "All right, moving right along… I have one more thing for Toby."

Now all eyes were back on Beth as she reached into a bigger sack and pulled out a stuffed panda bear. A squeal came out of Toby. He leaped to his feet with outstretched hands, grabbed the bear and plunked himself down squeezing it to his face.

Beth paused to observed Daniel and the kids as they watched Toby. They all had such big smiles on their faces. Beth beamed *this is my new, wonderful family*. Bringing her thoughts back to the unraveling she said, "Okay, Sara, this one's for you." Beth pulled over a sack and handed the bag to her.

Sara seized it and wasted no time digging in. The girl gasped pulling out a Raggedy Ann doll. Sara reached into the bag again and lifted out a baby doll that looked like a real infant. "Ooh, I love them." Sara hopped up and flung her arms around Beth. "Thank you, Emilie, thank you, thank you, thank you. I'll take good care of them."

"Today feels like Christmas," said Anna, waiting for her gift.

Beth told Anna, "I'm going to give your father's stuff next. I'm saving yours for last." Beth reached behind her, grabbed a package and handed it to Daniel.

Daniel squeezed the sack and teased the girls making them wait, "Well, well, well… what could this be?"

The girls chanted, "Open it, open it, open it."

Daniel peered into the bag and scrunched his brows. He dumped the contents out. Russ' expensive shaver along with two packages of new blades along with an almost full can of shaving lotion sat on his lap.

"That's a shaver, and if you like, Russ will bring more next time he comes. I took mine too because I got scared using your razor every time I shaved my legs."

"Well I got to say, this shaver looks somewhat safer. You'll have to show me how to use the thing."

"No problem. Okay, Anna's turn." Beth pointed and said to Anna, "The large bag next to you is yours, but first I want to give you this." Beth reached behind her and pulled a gadget out of her Rhinestone bag. "This is a battery handheld sewing machine. I used it for mending, but you can use it for whatever you sew."

Anna took the machine and turned it every which way trying to figure out how the gadget could make stitches.

Beth pointed, "Now look in that bag."

Anna dug in and pulled out two sizeable pieces of material. Standing up, she unfolded one and held the cloth in front of her.

"Those are curtains. If you like, you can cut them up and make a new covering for the pantry. And maybe some valances for the windows."

Daniel, Anna, and Sara all glanced from the material over to the window above the counter. Visualizing the forest green color panels as window coverings, they all concluded they liked the idea.

Beth motioned to Anna, "Something else is in the bag."

Anna reached in and removed a sewing kit about the size of a laptop computer case. The kit supplied Anna with multiple color threads, all sizes of needles, sewing pins and a sharp pair of scissors.

"Oh Beth, I mean Emilie…" Anna giggled. "Can you show me how to use the sewing machine now?"

"Not yet." Sara yelled, "We haven't seen what's in the rest of the bags yet."

"When we finish going through everything, I'll show you. Now Sara, will you push that box over to me?"

Sara thought the box would be heavy, but it wasn't.

Beth said to the girls, "You two are going to love what's in here." Beth opened the lid, and both girls peered into the container. They stared blankly and looked at Beth crinkling their noses.

The box was stuffed full of toilet paper. She held a roll up and stated, "This will replace the corn husks in the outhouse. You will thank me later. But, a word of advice, use it sparingly."

Next Beth reached for her Rhinestone bag and pulled out a six by eight-inch hand mirror, and both girls cheered.

Daniel liked the mirror too and said, "Don't you women go hiding that with all your girly stuff, I can use that when I shave." Daniel put a hand on his face and felt his chin, "Yup, I need a shave. Give me the mirror," he teased.

Sara knelt up and pointed to her pa and shouted, "No Emilie, don't give that to him. He'll hide it with his shaving stuff."

Giggling, Beth turned to Daniel, "Looks like you're outnumbered. The mirror stays with the ladies."

Sara, still kneeling with a doll in both arms, asked, "What else did you bring?"

Beth dumped most of the remaining things from the bag and one by one she picked them up and explained what they were.

"This little thing that looks like a black box is called a portable speaker. It amplifies the sound so everybody will hear the music." Beth set the speaker aside and picked the next item. "This is a battery alarm clock, so we'll always know what time it is. I took a load of batteries, which are also on the list of things Russ will bring. I brought more lighters. These are not butane like the other lighter. Once these are empty, we throw them out."

Dread enveloped Beth. Was she beginning the pollution of the generations? Use the item up, throw it out, and let the dumps pile up with stuff that never breaks down. Beth decided to stick with the butane.

She removed a manicure set, "This will help keep our fingernails clean." When she removed a handful of new toothbrushes and three tubes of toothpaste she stressed, "We want to keep our teeth as clean as we can."

Next, Beth dumped out a variety of music disks. She didn't need to explain those. The family already knew what they were.

Beth looked around, "We're just about done. We have two boxes left." Out of the closest box, Beth pulled out two large, thick books. A history book titled, 'Discovering Minnesota,' and one on organic gardening. Beth looked at Daniel, "I noticed the apple trees have worms, so this book will instruct us on how to get rid of them. The rest of the stuff in this box is personal hygiene products, clothes, and my parka."

Sara pointed, "We have one more box."

"That one is for me and your pa."

Daniel got up, peeked into the box and saw eight bottles, "Is that moonshine?"

"Seven of them are wine, and the other one is champagne for our honeymoon," Beth gave Daniel a sexy smile. She took one last glance around the area and stated, "Looks like we're done."

No sooner did Beth say that when Anna pleaded for her to show her how the sewing machine worked. Sara at the same time begged Beth to play house.

Toby put up a fuss, so Daniel bent over, picked the little guy up, and sat him on his lap. Daniel put his hand out for Beth to take, and while holding it, he announced, "I need everybody's attention."

The room became quiet.

He kept his eyes on Beth and announced, "Emilie and I, as

you girls know, are getting married. So as a family, we need to pick a date for our wedding. The sooner we do it, the better."

Anna stood up, "Pa, I bet Mrs. Knutson can marry you cause last year she married a couple, remember?"

It amazed Daniel how his eldest daughter was about attentive as a grown woman. However, now he wanted her to be his little girl again. He let go of Beth's hand, set Toby down on the floor and motioned for Anna to come to him. When she did, he sat her on his lap, "Anna, when did you get so smart and grown up?" He leaned over and gave her a peck on the cheek.

"Tomorrow we're all going to Mrs. Knutson's. We'll talk things over with her. Since she's planning on coming Sunday, we should get married then. That would be October 14th. What do you think?"

Anna put her arms around her father's neck and said, "If it's warm you could get married out in the yard. We can decorate it with pumpkins and fall colors, and the wildflowers are in bloom now."

Sara asked, "Can I be the flower girl?"

Beth cupped Sara's chin and said, "You being our flower girl would be awesome."

"What about me?" Anna asked, with lips pouting.

Beth turned to her with a warm smile, "Anna, will you be my Maid of Honor?"

Anna's eyes got big and round, "You want me to be your Maid of Honor?"

Daniel bent over and looked Anna in the face, "Do you know what the Maid of Honor does?"

"Yes Pa, she cares for the bride throughout the wedding process."

"What?" Daniel wasn't expecting an answer quite like that. He raised his brows and turned to Sara, "Where does she learn this stuff?"

Sara raised her shoulders, and with a goofy smile, she shrugged.

"It's settled then. Tomorrow we'll make the final arrangements."

"Can we go play now?" Sara asked, wiggling like a fish out of water.

"Yes, go play."

Sara ran off to the loft's ladder hollering, "I'm putting my babies down for a nap."

Beth and Anna moved to the table, and Beth instructed her how to operate the sewing machine. Anna picked right up on the skill, and in no time at all she was sewing.

With both girls busy doing their own thing, Beth walked over to the box of wine and took out a small, black pouch. She sat down on the chair next to Daniel, who was busy inspecting Toby's electronics. "Daniel, these are for emergencies." She emptied several pieces of valuable jewelry into his hand. My mother left these for me. I think Mrs. Knutson can get us a good price for them."

"Are you sure about that?"

"My mother would be happy to know the jewelry will be used for my well-being." Beth reached for the diamond teardrop and said, "All I want is this new necklace Silvia gave…" Beth stopped in mid-sentence. The diamond teardrop was not there. "My necklace is gone."

Beth sprung to her feet and desperately tossed boxes and bags around. She stopped, straightened up and turned toward the window, "It must have come off in the barn."

"Maybe it fell off in the Scorpion."

"No, I remember holding the teardrop after I got out of the machine. I'm going to the barn." Beth picked up a flashlight.

"Why don't you wait and we'll come help you."

"The girls are occupied. I can go. I won't be long."

"Okay, I'll stay here and watch the little man."

"I'll be back in a flash." Beth disappeared out the door for yet another trip to the barn.

Chapter 44

Beth was glad she didn't wait to search for the necklace. The sun was making a rapid descent and the outbuilding would be dark enough as it was. She trotted to the barn, slid the heavy door open, and peered into the musty smelling interior. The last of the sun's rays shimmered through the wooden slats of the roof casting a prison bar shadow on the straw-covered ground.

Aiming the flashlight, she bound for the far corner. Every step caused the crispy straw to snap beneath her feet.

A loud crack came from her left. She halted, turned an ear and flashed the light in the direction. The noise stopped. *Okay, calm down. It's just the chickens.*

Shaken up, she brushed off the weird vibes and resumed her mission. Before taking two more steps, the cracking started again - closer this time. *Something's out there.* Again she swung around and the sound quit. It was like the red light, green light game. Something or someone was playing her. She considered retreating to the house, but she was almost to the ribbons.

Hurry up and just find the necklace. As she picked up her pace, a movement caught the corner of her eye. She twirled around fast hoping to catch it by surprise. That didn't work, she saw nothing. Even though she suspected it to be an animal, her heart pounded so hard she was sure whatever was out there could hear it.

She shined the light and squinted hard. Farm equipment casting their shadows prevented her from seeing who or what it was. She crouched down flashing the beam in-between the machinery aiming at every nook and cranny.

Crunch, crunch, crack!

Beth jumped back and just about peed her pants. Her first impulse was to turn and run. But she didn't. Instead, she turned an ear and her eyes narrowed in on the area of the noise.

Suddenly, a high-pitched squeal filled the air. Out of the shadows bolted a monster of a hog. The pig ran amok, dodging Beth missing her by two feet. She let out a yelp and froze in her tracks. *Shit, how'd that pig get out of the pen?* She bent over putting her hands on her knees and waited until her heartbeat slowed.

Once her composure was back, she took long strides wanting to get the job done. With no warning, a flock of chickens strutted toward her clucking up a storm, thinking they were getting fed. Beth muttered, "These animals are going to be the end of me." She waved her arms and hollered, "Damn chickens, get out of the way!"

Beth made it to the rainbow of ribbons unscathed. She searched the ground where she was standing earlier and found the necklace right away. She examined the hook. It wasn't broken, so she put the chain around her neck and fastened the clasp and turned to head for the door.

Her heart skipped a beat when the barn filled up with the Scorpion's blazing flash. Beth swung around, wondering why Russ returned. She sauntered over to greet him and was several feet away when the door opened. She squinted focusing on the figure, but white spots from the flash hindered her view. *Something's not right.* The person didn't have Russ' frame, and he wasn't saying anything. A lump built up in her throat. When the spots disappeared and her eyes focused, she realized, *that's not Russ.*

The mysterious person turned and came into view. She had seen that face before. That distorted mouth with the narcissistic smirk revealing brown crooked teeth wasn't hard to forget.

Oh my God, it's him. He's not dead! Beth turned to run, but Theodore, in a split second, lurched forward and grabbed a handful of hair. As he yanked her backward, she got a glimpse of the needle in his other hand. She snapped her entire body around, pulling hairs from the roots as she pivoted. Shoots of pain veered to every hair follicle nerve ending causing her to scream out.

Flailing her arms around, she got a good grip on his shirt. With all the strength she could muster, she shoved her knee deep into his crotch.

Both his hands clutched his groin as he wailed out bending over in pain.

The needle dropped to the ground. Beth grabbed it and raced for the barn door. The last light of the sun coming through the door was all she concentrated on as she ran the fastest she'd ever run in her entire life.

A chicken hobbled out of nowhere and ended up beneath her feet causing her to fall face first to the ground. The needle flew up in the air. She lay dazed and stunned. But like a boxer down in a ring, she forced herself to her feet. She dove for the needle but wasn't quick enough. The crazed man grabbed her from behind putting a knife to her throat. He slammed the front of her body up against the wood planked wall and leaned into her putting his contorted mouth on her cheek. With a gravelly voice, he whispered into her ear, "Listen bitch. I can kill you right now and bring you back dead. I assure you, I'll get the rest of your family too. Come with me now and I'll leave them alone."

He leaned in harder on her backside causing her to gasp for air. The offensive odor of his body sweat and the horrific smell of his foul breath caused her to gag.

Theodore growled with his heinous voice, "I can lug your dead body back, or you can walk. Now let's go."

"I wouldn't be seen dead with you, you fucking asshole," Beth turned and spat at him.

"Have it your way, Princess." Theodore raised the knife.

Beth scrunched her eyes shut as her body tensed waiting for the stabbing pain. But it never came.

The weight of his body was no longer there. She turned around in time to witness Daniel heaving the sleazeball to the ground. Daniel jumped on top of him and slugged him repeatedly in the face, his knuckles cracking with each blow.

Using both arms, Theodore protected himself as the jabs kept coming. He turned his head sideways to ward off the punches and spotted a piece of wood. With one arm blocking his face the other reached for the weapon. He could feel it, but before grasping it another blow hit him square in the jaw. Another hit, to the ear this time, filled his head with a shrill ringing. Ignoring the pain, Theodore concentrated on stretching until he got a good grip on the timber. With all his might, he swung it around hitting Daniel on the side of his head, knocking him out. A new surge took over. He shoved Daniel's limp body off and leaped to his feet.

Beth frantically crawled around digging her hands in the hay searching for the syringe.

Theodore spotted her and lunged at her.

She rolled over in time to miss the impact of his body and pushed herself to her feet. Spotting the wood, she dove for it and clutched the weapon so tight her hand turned white. At once, she sprung to her feet and charged at him swinging.

Theodore grabbed her by the wrist and flung her to the ground like a ragdoll.

Beth pushed herself to her knees, but before she could stand, Theodore, pushed her back down and hurled himself on top of her. His knees straddled around her waist pinning her flat on the ground.

Beth squirmed and attempted to scream.

Theodore covered her mouth with his hand, making it impossible for her to breathe. He grabbed a handful of hair and yanked her head back. He hissed in her ear, "The more you fight the worse the outcome will be, bitch."

His putrid breath filled her nostrils. White spots filled her eyes. She was blacking out, and she welcomed it.

Theodore sensing this, removed his hand and growled, "Oh no, you're not going to pass out and miss this, my dear. I have such good plans for you. I've already been through your closet, Beth. Remember your lacy summer dress you love so much? That's for your photo shoot. The white color will complement the dark red from your blood, don't you think, my Princess? I will make you the prettiest of them all." Theodore smashed her face into the ground and knelt up straight. With the knife at her side he ordered, "Now, you're going to stand up and walk in front of me to the Scor…"

Thwack!

The full weight of the attacker fell on top of her and rolled off facing her. Puddles of blood spewed from his mouth.

Theodore never got to finish his sentence.

Beth turned and her eyes darted up.

There stood Daniel holding a pitchfork dripping with blood. He threw the weapon aside and pulled her up.

She collapsed in his arms sobbing.

Daniel led her to a bundle of hay, sat her down and pulled her close to him. He took her hand and held it tight.

Beth, noticing blood on Daniel's hands cried out, "Oh my God, are you hurt?"

Daniel looked at his blood-splattered palm. He leaned back and checked Beth's backside. The dead man's blood saturated her sweater and jeans. He sat forward again and assured her, "We're okay, come here." Daniel pulled her closer and held her tight.

She laid her head on his shoulder wrapping her arms around his waist. Every bone in her body shook. For half a minute they sat there until Beth's sobs subsided. She wiped her nose with her sleeve and whimpered, "That monster must have been stalking Russ' home." Sitting straight up she wiped her face with the back side of her hand and shifted her body to face Daniel. "I need to take the Scorpion back. I have to make sure Russ and Zena are okay."

Daniel's shoulders fell. He nodded, "Of course you do. Just come back all in one piece, okay?"

"I'll return in one piece, but I'll be a year older."

"That's okay baby. You're catching up with me."

Beth wondered how she would return to this precise moment and not a minute earlier. After giving it a thought, she said, "Daniel, stand by the Scorpion and as soon as I leave wave your arms and keep waving them. When Russ brings me back, we'll see you."

Daniel kissed her and said, "Now, skedaddle. We've got a wedding to plan."

So once again, Beth slid into the Scorpion and hit the *return* button.

Chapter 45

The Scorpion reappeared in the lab at 3:45 p.m. Beth rushed up the basement stairs calling Russ and Zena. She went to the living room window and glanced out at the driveway. Her brother's car wasn't there. She skipped up to the second floor to her bedroom and found the black dress gone. She checked Russ' room and wasn't surprised when his bed was void of clothes too.

Guessing they were on their hot date, Beth headed back to the lab. Her eyes scanned the room. *How did that scumbag get in?* She moved from window to window and came to the one above the hope chest. Standing on the bench, she pulled aside the curtain and examined the lock. That's when she found the little tin piece lodged between the latches. "There's the culprit." She secured the window and set the metal on the desk.

Sitting down, Beth skimmed Russ' journal. The thought of that horrid man's torso on this chair sent shivers down her spine. She could still smell his retching odor on her. She shook herself free of the bad images and continued reading the notes. He wrote precise details on everything. *Now I understand how he learned to operate the Scorpion.*

Beth glanced at the clock. 4:00 p.m. She had hours to wait before the two came home. Locking the door to the lab, she headed for her bedroom.

The sweater was the first apparel to come off. After

inspecting the blood-stained top, she decided it wasn't worth saving. It got dumped into the garbage. The recollection of the killer dying on her made her shiver.

A nice hot bath was the next thing on her list. Beth sauntered into the bathroom and ran the water in the tub. She locked the door and jammed a chair against it.

At the mirror, she focused on her reflection. Her face was bruised but what made her eyes widen and her mouth drop was when she saw how much she aged. Her newfound wrinkles added years to her face. Shaking her head in disbelief, she removed the blood-stained jeans and threw them aside. A huge black and blue mark on her hip stood out like a sore thumb. Back at the mirror, she inspected herself - bruises covered her body.

She climbed into the tub and slid into the steaming hot water. *Awe… this is heaven.* Beth laid her head on the headrest and closed her eyes. She couldn't remember a bath ever feeling so good. Every muscle loosened right up. She became so relaxed she ended up falling asleep.

Someone or something was chasing her and the only escape was the elevator in front of her. She hit the button repeatedly. The door opened but the shaft was empty. She leaned over and peered down. It was filling with water. Beth sprinted down a long hallway coming to a dead-end. There was no going back. The water rose and was now flowing out of the elevator towards her. With nowhere to run, she was about to drown.

Beth woke and bolted upright gripping the sides of the tub, her eyes darting around the room. After getting her bearings, she washed and got out. She wrapped a white plush bath towel around her and glanced at the clock. 5:20 p.m. She had a few hours to kill before the lovebirds get home.

She strolled into the walk-in closet to her underwear drawer and picked out her sexiest undergarments. She chose a lace semi-sheer bra and bikini style panties. Those, Beth decided, would be for her wedding night. For today, she picked out her beige cotton stretch bra with matching undies.

While sifting through the clothes on hangers, Beth came upon the sundress Theodore had tucked away. She shuddered at the thought of what would've happened if Daniel had not come to the rescue. She yanked it off the hanger and tossed it into the same garbage as the bloody sweater.

Returning to the closet, Beth picked out her gray jeans and a black pull-over sweater which hung loosely around her hips. In the bathroom, she dried her hair and put on eye makeup.

With her fingertips, Beth picked up the stained jeans and carried them to the bedroom. She grabbed the bag from the garbage containing the sweater and dress and threw the pants into it as well. Afterward, she headed for the kitchen feeling like a new person.

Once downstairs, Beth tossed the bag into the kitchen garbage. She wanted a drink and thought *there's no sense in searching for any wine since I took all of it.* So she made herself a Manhattan along with a lunch meat and cheese sandwich. Beth took her cocktail and dinner to the library and sat on the couch with her laptop. For the next hour, she researched certain past events and printed off information she could bring back for Daniel to read.

When her eyes couldn't take any more strain, Beth turned off the computer. She stood and stretched and decided to bake something. After rummaging through the kitchen cabinets, she found the ingredients for peanut butter cookies. The entire time she took to bake the cookies, her thoughts were on Daniel and the children. Beth could no longer envision her life without them, or them without her. Beth's reverie ceased as she searched for a bag to bring some peanut butter morsels back with her. She set the jar of peanut butter next to them. *This is a good time to introduce the family to nut butter.*

After cleaning her mess, she sauntered into the living room and reclined on the chair. She shut off the lamp which left only the dim-glow of the hallway nightlight. Closing her eyes, she planned her wedding in her head. *It'll be small, just the family and Mrs. Knutson. I like Anna's idea of having it outside. That is if our Indian summer lasts. And I need a wedding dress, what will I wear?* All her thoughts drifted into one as she fell asleep once again.

Zena and Russ' giggles woke her. Groggy and discombobulated, she sat up and listened. Russ said something about it being time for the little black dress to come off. Beth peered into the hallway and saw the two kiss. As Russ began to unzip Zena's dress, Beth turned on the lamp.

Instantly, they stopped what they were doing and glared into the living room. It gave Russ the heebie-jeebies when he saw Beth sitting there.

"Damn, you scared the hell out of us. What are you doing here?"

"The serial killer, he never died."

"What are you talking about?"

"Russ, you have to bring me back and help us clean up the mess. The monster who chased me into the time machine has been stalking you. He's read your notes, and he knew how to operate the Scor..."

"Wait a minute, calm down." Russ took Zena's hand and led her to the couch. "Are you telling me the serial killer's still out there?"

"Not anymore." Beth tried to stay calm as she explained the terrifying incident. Afterwards, she stood and said, "I don't mean to rush you, but can we go right away? I've been here for hours. I need to get back. We have a dead body to deal with."

"Yes, of course," Russ and Zena stood as well.

Beth smiled at them and commented, "I must say, you two clean up well. You make an adorable couple."

Without taking his eyes off of Zena, he replied, "Yes, we do."

Back in the kitchen, Beth grabbed her baked goods, "I left some homemade cookies on the counter. But you'll need more peanut butter." She grabbed a handful of baggies, and they made their way to the time machine.

Beth bid goodbye once again to Zena and slipped into the seat of one of the Scorpions.

Russ gave Zena a kiss and whispered, "You know the drill. I'll be right back."

Beth reminded Russ they must watch for Daniel waving his hands.

More experienced now, Russ flipped the switch and counted. When he got close to 740, he slowed down. Beth watched as the yellow streaks of the sun zoomed by and the dark-gray stripes of the night took over. Her heart skipped a beat when the rainbow of ribbons appeared.

"Another tad further, I'm not sure I can get you to the right..." Russ stopped in mid-sentence. Daniel appeared in a blurry fog. Russ slowed the machine down almost to a halt and when Daniel was in focus, he shut it down.

The flash subsided. Russ opened his door, climbed out and assisted Beth. He walked up to Daniel and shook his hand. "Great idea about the arm waving thing, guys."

"Yeah, I just started when the Scorpion returned. Sorry, you had to travel again so soon. You probably didn't recuperate from the last time."

"Not a problem. I think my body's getting used to it. So where's the body?"

"It's over here." Daniel led Russ to the spot where the nightmare happened. Daniel suggested that Beth go to the house and stay with the kids while he and Russ bury the corpse.

Beth handed Russ the baggies she brought. "You guys put these on your hands when you handle that repulsive body." She gave Russ a peck on the cheek, "Come inside when you finish and spend some time with your future nieces and nephew. I'll make you a hot toddy."

"Sounds fantastic."

Even though Beth was at Russ' for hours, it was not even fifteen minutes for the children. All three were still occupied with what they were doing before Beth left.

Anna, busy sewing, looked up at Beth and did a double take, "When did you change your clothes?"

"We had an emergency, but everything's fine. Your Uncle Russ is here to spend some time with us. Would you like to heat up some water?"

Anna sprang out of her chair, scurried to the stove and lit the wick with the butane lighter. Beth, right behind her, got a plate out of the pantry and dumped the cookies onto it.

Sara came down the ladder, "Do we have company?"

"Yes, my brother's here."

Sara ran to the door, and Beth stopped her, "Sara, can you put plates on the table? I have a surprise for everybody,"

Sara stopped in her tracks and did a complete turnaround and headed for the kitchen. "How many more surprises do you have?" Then she did a double take at Beth - as Anna had - and asked the same question, "When did you change your clothes?"

Meanwhile back in the barn, Daniel threw Russ a shovel. They found a burial spot far enough away from the house. At the edge of the woods, they dug the hole and returned for the cadaver. Daniel turned the body onto its backside.

Russ' face turned ashen white. "I just saw that guy today! He bumped into Zena at the corner store. It makes sense now. Why he gawked at her the way he did. The creep recognized her. And that's why he did a frantic search around the parking lot. He was looking for me. He must have gone straight from the store to my house."

Russ put two baggies over his hands, bent over and reached

into the dead man's pocket. He pulled out his wallet and looked at the driver's license. "Theodore James Collins. He must have framed Jimmy Grey. I'm taking this wallet with me." Russ stuck it into a bag. He yanked a few of the dead man's hairs and added them. He stuffed the contents in his pocket and handed Daniel two baggies. Russ grabbed the legs while Daniel took his arms and they carried Theodore to his grave.

After burying the body, they camouflaged the pile of dirt with tree branches and marched to the well and washed up. Afterwards, they proceeded to the house stopping at the bottom step. Facing each other, they drew in a breath and paraded into the house as if nothing happened.

Russ stayed for an hour while the children showed him their new treasures. Most of what had been his. He didn't care though. The whole scene with a family from the 1800s using his things was surreal. He relaxed at the table with his hot toddy watching the children play. Beth and Daniel informed him of their plans to get married the following Sunday.

Russ tensed up, "There's no way I'm missing my only sibling's wedding."

"You can't be traveling again so soon. You're killing yourself. Please, promise me that you won't do it for a while. We'll take lots of pictures for when you come in April. Okay? Promise me."

Russ made no promises. Standing, he outstretched his arms and said to the girls, "Come and give your uncle a big hug. I don't know when I'll get to see you again."

Daniel and Beth walked Russ to the barn and once again, bid goodbye. When Russ disappeared, Daniel took Beth's hand. As they strolled to the house he said, "We have to do something about your sleeping arrangements. I don't want you sleeping on the floor anymore. Until we get married, you take the bed with Toby, and I'll sleep on the mattress."

"I don't mind Daniel…"

"Nope, I've decided." They got as far as the porch steps when Daniel pulled her aside, "I've been waiting all day to do this." He put his arms around her waist, pulled her close and kissed her. As the kiss became passionate, they heard giggling. They glanced up at the house, and all three children were peering through the window. Daniel laughed, "I think it's time we add-on to this place."

Back in the year 2016, the first thing Russ did upon returning was to write an anonymous letter on the computer. He addressed the note to Detective Tom Watson of the Minneapolis Homicide Dept. He slipped the printed copy into a manila envelope along with Theodore's hair and wallet. The contents of the letter read:

I believe you've deemed the wrong person as the Minneapolis Serial Killer. Enclosed is the wallet and identity of the actual criminal. I'm sure when you find his residence you'll find all the proof you need. The hair also belongs to him. It'll provide you with the DNA necessary to prove this man was in all his victim's homes.

Russ set the package aside. Tomorrow he would somehow get it into the detective's hands. Right now, there were more important things to do. A trail of clothing attire led to the bedroom beginning with the little black dress.

Back in 1860, Beth and Daniel put the kids to bed and retired to the porch. Beth brought out two glasses of wine and handed one to Daniel. "There are challenges coming our way we need to plan for. Next month, Abraham Lincoln will become our president. In April some events are going to happen that will lead this country into a civil war. It'll be between the north and the south and will last four years. I did some research at Russ' and…"

"Whoa. Slow down, Baby." Daniel set his wine on the porch. He reached over, took one of her hands and brought it to his lips and kissed it. "When you tell me things of the future, you need to be gentle with me." Daniel grinned as he took her wine and set it down. Reaching out, he took her other hand and kissed that one just as tender, "You can't just throw this on me all at once." Daniel playfully yanked on Beth's hands trying to pull her over to him.

Not fighting him too much, Beth chuckled, "I'm trying to be serious."

"I understand, but I can't stand it anymore, I've been dying to have you in my arms. You wouldn't deny me, would you?" He resumed in trying to pull her onto his lap.

Beth giggled and then got serious. "Daniel, when we go to Mrs. Knutson's tomorrow, I'd like us to speak with her about a few opportunities she may want to partner with. I don't want to bring it up with her until you and I have discussed it."

"Babe, I have total trust in you. Mrs. Knutson is part of our family, so I trust her too. How about we compromise? Tonight, you sit on my lap and hug and kiss me. Tomorrow you can put forth your plans while we're at Mrs. Knutson's. We can all discuss it together. What'd you say?"

Beth felt herself losing the battle. Daniel with his dreamy eyes and pouty lips made her melt. It took all she could do to not to throw herself on him at that second, and then she realized, *why aren't I?* Before Daniel knew what was happening, Beth was on his lap giving him a passionate, tongue filled kiss.

Chapter 46

Monday, four days later

Russ and Zena woke up naked under the white satin sheets with their legs wrapped around each other. Zena twisted out of Russ' grip, turned onto her side and propped herself up on her elbow, "Hey lover, how about you make me some of your yummy waffles for breakfast?"

Russ turned onto his back, bending one arm behind him to support his head. He gave her a lazy smile, "You sure like to eat, don't you? We still have peanut butter cookie crumbs in our bed from the other night."

Zena lifted up the sheet and looked underneath, "Where are those crumbs? I'm hungry."

Russ flipped around, grabbed Zena by the arms, and pinned her flat on her back and stared into her face. Zena's pearly white teeth glistened as she laughed and Russ thought *everything about this woman is perfect in every way.* "Have I ever told you how beautiful you are first thing in the morning?"

"Well, this is the first time today, what took you so long?"

Russ' eyes went to her mouth, which looked very alluring at the moment, the way her lips parted ever so slightly. He outlined her upper lip with his fingertip drawing an invisible line shaping it like a Cupid's bow. Her full bottom lip gave her a playful pouty look. "I think I like your lips the best."

Zena teased, "The best of what? Your bedroom? The house? My body?" Her grin disappeared as their soulful eyes locked.

Russ bent down and put his mouth over hers. He lightly caressed her soft lips with his, enticing her. It surprised him a little when Zena brazenly parted his lips with her insistent tongue and seductively slipped it in and out, sweeping it over his bottom lip and gently biting on it before moving to the top. The osculation stimulated his mouth and tongue like he never experienced before. It was driving him crazy; he immediately became aroused. Russ kissed her back with a fervent urgency as his tongue got lost in her mouth; her tongue and his, wrapping around one another as if they were making wild love. The foreplay slowed down, and they teased each other with playful moves amorous as an intimate waltz. The graduation of intensity would come again - both breathing heavily - wanting more.

Dizzy from the passionate entanglement of tongues, Russ let out a throaty groan. He moved down to Zena's neck and ran his hot moist tongue along the curves focusing on her sensitive spot causing Zena to writhe with desire. Slipping his hand down, he grabbed her bottom and pulled her closer, pressing her against him.

Russ nibbled on her earlobe; his hot breath on her skin caused her to cry out as she weaved her fingers through his hair. He could feel her body trembling as he moved his thumb lightly down her sternum and toward her breasts, drawing circles. The osculation stimulated them like never before and the intimate lovemaking following left them both breathless and satisfied.

Afterward, Russ turned facing her, "Have I told you lately how much I love you?"

Zena grinned, this was her opportunity. "Show me how much you love me by making me your famous waffles."

"Well, you give me no choice." Russ gave Zena a kiss, rolled over and hopped out of bed.

Zena watched his naked body as he walked away, thinking to herself what a cute butt he had.

Russ grabbed his robe off the door hook and slipped into it and threw the other one over to her. "I'll start the coffee." He blew her a kiss and disappeared out the door.

10Russ faced the stove cracking eggs into a frying pan when Zena came in. She thought his butt looked sexy even in his bathrobe. She sauntered over to him and slipped her arms around his waist. As he leaned his head back toward her, she kissed him on the cheek and whispered in his ear, "So you know... I love you too."

Russ flipped an egg, turned around and put his arms around her waist, "I love you more."

"You love me more? I don't think that's possible."

At that moment, the doorbell rang. Russ glanced up at the clock, "Who would be here this early?"

Zena moved into Russ' spot and flipped the other egg.

Russ trotted to the front door. Upon opening it, Detective Watson stood there along with Officer O'Leary. Russ motioned for them to come in. "We were about to sit down for breakfast. What can I do for you, Detective?"

The detective looked down the hallway towards the kitchen, "We? Do you have company?"

"It's my girlfriend."

"Oh... well, we won't keep you long. If we could sit down I'll explain why we're here."

"Of course, come in." Russ led them into the living room.

"Sure smells good in here." Officer O'Leary said, taking a whiff.

"I would offer you some, but my girlfriend has a huge appetite, and I don't think there will be enough waffles."

Zena hollered from the kitchen, "I heard that."

The detective cleared his throat, "Mr. Nielson, I found a package on my desk. How it got there nobody seems to know. The package revealed something I'd been suspecting all along."

Russ leaned forward in his chair and put his elbows on his knees. Folding his hands, he gave the detective his attention.

"It appears we had the wrong guy pegged as the Minneapolis serial killer." Watson paused trying to read Russ' face.

"What do you mean the wrong guy?" Russ gave the detective a confused look.

"Do you have a printer, Russ?"

"Of course I have a printer? What does that have to do with this?"

"The package contained a note from an unidentified person. We're hoping to find out who wrote it. It was printed from a computer."

"Which is why you're asking me if I have a one? Doesn't everyone these days? Detective, could you please get to the point, if Jimmy Grey wasn't the killer, who is?"

"The man's name is Theodore Collins. The package also contained his wallet which led us to his place of residence. Mr. Nielson, what I'm about to tell you may be unsettling for you and I apologize for any additional pain it may cause you."

Russ didn't say a word, he just nodded.

"Years ago, Collins murdered his mother, father, and sister. He spent twenty years in a mental asylum in Mason City, Iowa. After getting out, he went on a killing spree. Pictures of his victims hung on the walls of his apartment. Most were from Iowa, but some were from Minneapolis. I'm sorry to tell you Beth's pictures were among them. Collins had taken before and after pictures of all of them. It's his trademark. The puzzling thing is there are no after pictures of Beth."

Russ thought about the victims and what they must have gone through. The possibility it almost happened to Beth brought tears to his eyes. He wiped them away, "Where's Theodore now?"

Officer O'Leary leaned over and put his elbows on his knees, "We think whoever delivered the package has that answer."

Watson cleared his throat again, "Well, that's just it, unless we find the person, we won't know. We suspect Collin's is dead. The wallet had his dried blood on it and his landlady hadn't seen him for days now. And the man hasn't shown up to his job in Forest Lake."

Russ, alarmed now, held up his hand, "Wait a minute, did you say he worked in Forest Lake?"

"Yes, he worked a few blocks from his apartment."

"Are you telling me he lives in this area?" Russ couldn't believe what they told him. That scumbag moved to Forest Lake, got a job there, and set out to stalk his home.

"Collins *lived* in Forest Lake, not anymore. As I said, we're quite sure he's dead. Collins fit the profile in every way which Jimmy Grey never did. That's why it made no sense Grey was the killer, but Collins did a good job at framing the poor guy."

Russ clenched his fists and stood up. He was furious the cops had been so ignorant and put Beth in danger because of it. "Before, you told me not to worry because the killer died. Next, you tell me the killer didn't die, but now you say he did? Does anybody know what they're doing down at the homicide dept? And I'm supposed to take your word for it now?"

"Oh, don't get me wrong Mr. Nielson, this investigation isn't over. It won't be until we find your sister and Theodore, dead or alive. We wanted to give you a heads up. It'll be on the news tonight. We wanted you to hear it from us first."

The detective and the officer both stood, and Russ followed them to the front door.

O'Leary turned to Russ, "We'll keep you informed if anything else comes to the surface. You better get back to your girlfriend now before she eats all your breakfast."

"Yeah, have a good day." Russ closed the door behind them and made his way the kitchen.

Zena came out to meet him, "Good job, you even had tears."

"Those were real."

"So, are you ever going to tell me how you got the package onto the Detectives desk¿"

Russ put his arms around her waist and pulled her close and whispered, "I would tell you, but then I would have to kill you."

"Well, I guess you won't be telling me then. Come on. Let's warm up our breakfast."

Later that day, Russ and Zena tuned into channel eleven in time to hear the news. The reporter announced the revised information on the Minneapolis serial killer. Theodore's evil deeds had been exposed, and now his face appeared on all the local channels. When Zena saw it, she flinched, "My God Russ. That's the man who almost knocked me down."

Don't worry. He won't be bothering anybody anymore. That guy's six feet under."

At Forest Lake's Barbeques Joe's Restaurant, the kitchen employees stood around the break room's television in shock. A tall, blonde female former co-worker said, "I can't believe we were working with that repulsive creep." Unbeknown to her, she was to be Theodore's next victim.

Meanwhile, at one of the Minneapolis Downtown Buffet restaurants, Theodore's former co-workers who knew him as George Wilcox stared at the break room television in disbelief. A young male employee said, "That guy was spooky. Poor Jimmy Grey, I knew he wasn't the serial killer. I told that to the detective, but they wouldn't listen. They think they're so smart. At least now Jimmy's name is cleared."

The news also played on the television in the break room of the Willis Mortgage Company. Silvia and Tony stood among several other co-workers as they watched with wide eyes while the identity of the actual killer got broadcasted. The innocence of Jimmy Grey had also come to light, all because of one person who preferred to remain anonymous.

Tony moved in closer to Silvia and whispered, "I wonder if Russ and Beth had anything to do with this?"

Silvia looked up a Tony and muttered, "Keep it to yourself, Tony."

Chapter 47

"The Wedding Dfay"

The fallen orange and red leaves from the surrounding oak trees got raked together to form a twenty-foot wedding aisle runner. It began on the porch and ended in a half circle bordered with arrangements of pumpkins and flowers. At the end of the runner was a white wooden trellis which Daniel built as his contribution. Entwined between the top slots of the arbor were thin oak branches with a conglomerate of amber and crimson leaves. It formed a perfect splashy canopy.

Weaved into the sides of the lattice were multi-colored long stemmed wildflowers. They still attracted butterflies flying from flower to flower gathering the last of the nectar for the year. Their brightly colored wings shimmered in the morning sun. They seemed to change colors right before your eyes. They weren't a part of the planned décor, but their presence was most welcoming.

Daniel was gone quite a bit this week helping with the grain harvest of his fellow farmers, but that did not stop him from doing his part. Besides building the trellis, he repaired the broken railings on the porch and applied a fresh coat of white paint and put a new rung on the ladder to the loft.

For the reception afterward, Beth covered the parlor windows for ambiance. Candles were ready to be lit along with kerosene lamps. The girls decorated the whole room with colorful fall décor.

To prepare a dance hall, the privacy blanket was taken down and the straw mattress got moved to the bedroom floor. Both rocking chairs were put on the porch and the table, which later will be full of goodies, was pushed against the wall.

The ceremony was scheduled for one o'clock. It was only ten in the morning and the day was already warm and sunny. It would be one of the last tepid days of their prolonged Indian summer.

Beth stood on the porch and marveled at the impressive teamwork of her new family. Everything about the wedding so far was perfect except for Russ not being there.

Before she had time to dwell on it, Daniel, Sara, and Anna came out and joined her. Together they stood on the renovated porch admiring their remarkable accomplishment of creating the most beautiful place to say, "I do."

Tonight the moon would be full and after the reception, they would finally have their "Full Moon Fun Night."

While gazing at the marvelous scene, Mrs. Knutson's buggy pulled into Daniel's drive. She was towing a shiny, dark auburn horse with a mane and tail as black as night. Both girls raced straight to the new horse, running right past the Shetland pony and Mrs. Knutson.

"Oh, I guess we're old news now, huh Elsa?" Mrs. Knutson chuckled.

Daniel assisted the woman out of the buggy. "I thought the owner of the horse was coming."

"Daniel and Emilie, I got this excellent horse next to nothing. I know enough about animals to know this one is a jewel. I would like to present this mare as my wedding gift for the bride and groom."

Daniel gave the woman a frustrated look, "Mrs. Knutson, you can't keep buying us stuff."

Beth had the horse chin strap in her hand as she inspected the animal. "My goodness, this mare is a Quarter Horse. She's wonderful."

Daniel looked at Beth scrunching his brows, "A what?"

Mrs. Knutson's brows rose as she answered, "Why, yes it is. Do you know much about horses?"

"I used to ride all the time in my teens. My first job at fourteen, I worked for a local ranch tending the horses. I could ride them as often as I wanted. I practically lived there."

Beth inspected the front hoof of the mare. "This is the type horse they use for horse racing."

"It's funny you should say that. This horse's primary function was for the upcoming pony express which will bring mail throughout the entire country. She hurt her leg while on the boat from Norway. As a result, my friend got an excellent deal for her. She's fine though, just can't run as fast and far as she used to."

Beth ran her fingers through the mare's black bangs and said to Daniel, "This horse will make a decent workhorse, and we can ride her besides."

Both girls, while petting the horse, begged their father into keeping it.

Daniel would not go against four females, so he held up his hand, "Fine, but I'm warning you. I don't know the first thing about horses."

"That's okay Daniel. I'll teach you something for a change." Beth untied the mare and her and the girls walked the animal to the barn.

"What shall we call her?" Sara jumped up and down as if she were on a trampoline.

"Let's wait until tomorrow. We'll come up with a name together, Okay? Your father and I need to finish the discussion we had with Mrs. Knutson. You two keep an eye on Toby. Give us an hour."

When Beth came through the door, Daniel was pouring coffee. Mrs. Knutson sat at the table with the history book Beth had brought from the future. She had it opened to chapter eleven.

"First off, Emilie and Daniel, I'm sorry we got interrupted on Monday and couldn't finish our conversation. I would like to thank you for leaving this book with me. I have read it from beginning to end. You're right. We have preparing to do. Please explain your ideas now that you have my undivided attention."

Daniel sat down and looked at Beth, "You go first."

Beth put her elbows on the table, leaned in and pointed to the title of the chapter. "The civil war starts in April. There's going to be a high demand for wool. Wool blankets, socks, jackets, you name it. Last week at Russ', I did some research on sheep herding. It sounds like something we could do. I printed out information on it to educate ourselves." Beth stopped and looked at Daniel to take over.

"Emilie and I have figured out we can cut the cornfield in half and turn that acreage, along with the connecting five acres of woodland, into a pasture. We can use the wood to add-on to the house or build a new one. Maybe where the barn is now, its higher ground, and we found a natural spring nearby."

Beth leaned back in her chair, "And with the jewelry, we can afford to purchase the sheep and hire some help to clear the land before winter. The price of lamb is the cheapest now. If we buy impregnated females, they'll have their babies by spring. They feed on hay during the winter months and in the spring we'll plant grass seed."

"Mrs. Knutson, Emilie and I need you to find connections for us, someone to buy the jewelry and a place to purchase a herd. We need to find workers who can be trusted and a place to sell our products. If you can do this, we'll be equal partners." Daniel stopped and gave Mrs. Knutson a chance to take it all in.

It didn't take the woman much convincing, "So if you're

saying you want me to be your business manager, you have a deal. I'll get on it first thing Tuesday.

You may have enough wood left over for me to have some cabins built. I've read the next chapter of the history book and it's horrifying. The following year a war with the Dakota Indians will coincide with the civil war. It'll leave an additional eight hundred white people dead. We need to get rifles, and we need to learn how to use them. We're close to the path of the war party. Even if we're lucky enough for it to pass us by, there'll be hundreds of people who'll need shelter and clothing. So we need not waste any time getting started."

Mrs. Knutson pulled her jeweled pocket-watch from her skirt pocket, "Oh, look at the time. You two have to get ready for your wedding.

However, I have two more things to tell you. As we discussed on Monday, I have convinced the community Beth was adopted which means you two are not cousins by blood. So there'll be no problem with marrying.

Second thing, I have one more wedding gift for you, if you like, that is. After the wedding reception, I'd like for you to spend your honeymoon in the quiet confines of my home. I can stay with the children. I've already packed an overnight bag. It'll be your special night, and you should be alone to celebrate the occasion.

Daniel's face lit up with a wide smile, "That works for me, how about you, Emilie?"

"But we have the campfire tonight. We promised the kids."

Mrs. Knutson stood up, "The kids and I can still do that. You two will have many full moons together. You'll only have one honeymoon night. I'll explain it to the girls. They'll be happy for you. Now go and pack."

Beth disappeared into the bedroom, not wasting any time packing a bag.

Chapter 48

"The Wedding"

Toby sat obediently on one of the four bow-decorated chairs placed on each side of the aisle.

Mrs. Knutson stood matronly under the trellis canopy. She wore a royal blue colored dress decorated with a frilly white collar and white lace at the ends of the puffy sleeves.

Daniel stood opposite of Mrs. Knutson. His heart pounded as he waited for the most incredible moment of his life. He didn't feel this way with Kristine. Their marriage had been set up more for convenience. Kristine was shy, quiet and not very imaginative. She was the complete opposite of Beth. Daniel loved his first wife, and she was an excellent mother, but he didn't have the passionate love he has for Beth.

Daniel's thoughts wandered to the kiss Beth gave him the other night. She did this strange thing with putting her tongue in his mouth. He had pulled away at first, but Beth drew him back and did it again. It gave Daniel an instant erection. He had to stop everything for fear of not being the gentleman whom he strived to be.

Daniel forced himself to stop thinking about the kiss because it aroused him again. So he tried to change the subject in his mind and thought of a name for their newly acquired horse. However, it proved to be useless. The only thing on his mind was what Beth had planned for tonight. He couldn't wait for her tongue in his mouth again.

Back in the house, Beth prepared the music for their wedding. She always imagined there would be a beautiful grand piano with an accomplished pianist for this special day. There was neither. Beth only had to line up the preplanned song on her disc player and hit the button. The time had come and Ave Maria played loudly from the door.

Sara, the first to start the wedding procession, walked out the door onto the spruced up porch. The white knee-high dress she wore was a hand-me-down from Anna, but it looked entirely different. Anna had sewn - with her portable sewing machine - yellow bows all around the bottom. She completed the outfit with a wide matching ribbon wrapped around the waist with a huge bow tied in the back. Underneath the dress, she wore matching yellow bloomers.

Her hair wasn't matted as usual. It was free of tangles with a hint of curl. A white beaded headpiece crowned her top making her look like an angel.

Sara turned and looked back into the parlor, and Beth gave her the go ahead. So the little flower girl, carrying her yellow ribbon decorated bucket, stepped in pace with the music and strewed flower petals.

Bursting with pride, Daniel beheld his little girl as she marched to the trellis and stepped off the side next to him.

Daniel's eyes returned to the door as his beautiful Anna appeared on the threshold carrying her wildflower bouquet. She looked so grown up in her floor-length lemon-colored dress. The bodice was decorated with lace and sewn in a fashionable style, designed by Anna, of course.

Tears filled Daniel's eyes.

The traditional Wedding March began. Everyone became quiet as a mouse as they waited in anticipation for the bride to come over the threshold.

What they weren't expecting was the familiar flash of the Scorpion. Before anybody could comprehend what was going on, Russ and Zena came flying out of the barn yelling, "Hold the wedding."

Zena, in a floor-length black gown, sat in the chair next to Toby and said, "Hi everybody, Russ will introduce me when the wedding's over."

Everybody stared at her for a moment and then they shifted and all eyes went to Russ as he disappeared into the house.

The music stopped - everybody froze.

After a minute of silence, the music began again. Beth appeared with her hand slipped through her big brother's arm and a hankie to her tear-filled eyes.

They paused on the porch and Daniel and Beth's eyes caught.

Daniel, positive there wasn't a more beautiful woman in the entire world, wondered where she got the dress. It was a low-cut white chiffon fitted dress that flared out at the bottom. The long lace sleeves sparkled with sequins.

Beth's feet caught Daniel's attention as she lifted her dress to proceed down the steps. Instead of boots or tennis, she wore some odd dainty white shoes. They had high heels, *those are different, and they're sexy*

Never taking her eyes off of Daniel, Beth marveled at his outfit - another one of Mrs. Knutson's contributions to the wedding. The black slacks went well with the light gray silk vest which fit nicely over his long-sleeve white shirt. Beth found him so incredibly handsome.

Russ, dressed in a tuxedo, walked his sister down the autumn leaf path. In a low voice, he asked, "Isn't that Mom's wedding dress?"

"Mom always wanted me to wear it."

"Yes, she did. I'm sure she didn't expect it to be in 1860."

Russ led Beth to the altar, and Mrs. Knutson asked, "Who gives this woman in marriage?"

"I do," Russ answered. He gave Beth a kiss on her cheek and left her at Daniel's side.

Mrs. Knutson versed the simple traditional vows and asked Beth the question of accepting Daniel as her husband.

Beth answered, "I do."

Mrs. Knutson asked the same question to Daniel. After he said "I do," she asked, "Do you have the ring?"

Beth interrupted, "We don't have them yet..."

Daniel put his finger to Beth's lips and turning to Toby, he said, "It's time son."

Toby climbed down from his chair and waddled over to his father. He reached into his pocket and pulled something out, gave it to his pa and returned to his chair.

Beth was baffled. *This isn't part of the practice.* Her brows furrowed as Daniel took hold of her hand and slipped a ring onto her finger. Beth's jaw dropped as she stared at it. She gave Daniel a look that said, "I thought we were going to wait?" Her focus returned to the ring. Examining it she noticed the unique craftsmanship. It was a simple silver band, but there was something about it. Carved onto the ring was a delicate design making it appeared as though it were diamonds.

"I hope it'll do for now. I made it from a nickel." Daniel said, sheepishly.

"You made this from a nickel?" She looked back at her ring, *how many talents does this family have?* Beth threw her arms around him. "Daniel, I adore it."

Mrs. Knutson ended the ceremony with, "I now pronounce you man and wife, you may kiss the bride."

Beth didn't need to wait for Daniel to kiss her. She was already smothering him with kisses.

Mrs. Knutson had the married couple turn to the family and she introduced them as Mr. and Mrs. Nielson."

As instructed, Anna turned up the music player full blast. The traditional recessional wedding march played. The newlyweds made their way to the house for the reception as the family showered them with bird seed.

Chapter 49

"The Reception"

Once everybody congregated into the parlor, Russ introduced Zena. With her impudent personality and whimsical humor, she fit right in. The girls begged them to stay for the Full Moon Fun Night. It took no persuasion. They were in no hurry to leave.

The party began with a smash. Beth inserted her disk and the song *Celebration*, by Kool and the Gang played.

Russ thought it was cute when the girls from the 1800s danced just like the teens in the future. They swung their hips, moved their hands and feet to the beat, and soon they had Mrs. Knutson doing it.

The dance floor was alive. The next tune was *The Twist*, by Chubby Checker. Russ and Beth taught the ones from the past and the one from the future how to do the famous twisting move. The songs *YMCA, Macarena, Chicken Dance,* and the *Cupid Shuffle* were all taught by Beth and Russ. They all laughed, talked, danced, hugged and twisted.

The party continued for two hours. Between dances, they ate. A spread of peanut butter and jelly finger sandwiches, roasted chestnuts, and beautifully done up vegetable and fruit trays graced the decorated table. And of course, the wedding cake which Beth cooked in a pan. She's been practicing with stovetop cooking since there was no oven. The cake turned out better than expected.

When Daniel and Beth cut the cake and fed each other a piece, Sara asked why they did that.

"It symbolizes the first meal for the newlyweds," Mrs. Knutson answered.

"We should feed each other a piece. It will be our first meal together as a family," Sara said, raising her brows high.

"That's a good idea, Sara. We could start our own tradition." So, the two of them handed a piece of cake to everyone and they all fed one another. It turned out messy because now, they were shoving it into each other's faces.

After the party died down, Mrs. Knutson suggested the married couple leave before it gets dark.

Russ took Beth aside, "Before you go, we have something important to talk to you and Daniel about."

Beth instructed Anna to take the kids outside.

The men moved the table and chairs back to the original place, and everybody sat.

After clearing his throat, Russ began, "Zena and I are going to travel to the year 2110. There's an antidote called nanorobots. They're microscopic robots which comprise DNA. When inserted into the bloodstream, they seek and destroy cancer cells while leaving the healthy ones intact. Zena knows somebody in Minneapolis who can help us get some."

"Can't you two just stay put and be happy with coming here twice a year?"

"I saw a doctor. I have cancer, its stage four. He gave me six months. The time travel, I'm sure, caused it. If we don't do this, you are in danger as well since you have traveled several times."

Beth turned to Zena. "Will it be dangerous? Going to 2110? Is the country at war?"

"Yes, I won't lie to you. Peace in my lifetime didn't exist. But in the year 2110, I know somebody who can be trusted.

My friend can get a sufficient supply, enough to heal Russ and to inoculate us."

"We're going to move the Scorpion in a vehicle to an area close to the health facility. The machine will stay in the trailer."

"How in the world will you get that huge thing out of the basement?"

"That isn't for you to worry about. Zena and I have it figured out."

Mrs. Knutson, who'd been quietly listening, surprised the rest by saying, "My husband, Henry, is from Minneapolis. He came to the past from the year 2111. I'll give you his name and address. When you travel to 2110 go to him. He'll help you with the aging problem. He claimed there's a way of warping time back so cells don't scramble. The government wouldn't listen to him. They banned the machine concept and continued with the wormhole theory."

Beth shot up out of her chair. "Really, Mrs. Knutson? You're going to encourage my brother to keep time traveling?" Beth turned to leave the house. She was so mad she could spit fire.

Russ intercepted, "Beth, it's the reason I was born. There's a reason I invented the time machine, there's a reason you traveled to 1860, and there's a reason I found Zena.

Beth's forehead crunched as she grimaced. "Can't the doctors remove the tumor?"

"No, it's spread. We have our minds made up. If we don't succeed, we'll come to see you before anything happens. If we solve the problem, we'll bring the vaccine. So either way, we'll return within a few months."

Mrs. Knutson pulled out her pocket-watch and opened it. Inside was a picture of her and Henry on their wedding day along with an inscription that read, 'To my son, the inventor.' "Henry's father gave him this when he was a teenager. If you take this and give it to him, he'll know you're legitimate. He'll help you."

Daniel shook his head. He agreed with Beth. Now, Mrs. Knutson, whom he had known all his life, was in cahoots with Russ in making time travel plans. *Can this situation get any more ludicrous?*

After saying their goodbyes, Daniel fetched the cart.

Beth walked over and stood by Mrs. Knutson taking her hand in hers. "We appreciate you so much. I don't know where I'd be if it hadn't been for you."

The woman's eyes welled up. She hugged Beth and said, "I cherish your friendship as well. I could never talk to anybody about Henry's time travel. My friendship with you and Daniel is... Oh, pay me no mind. This is your time. Go and have a wonderful honeymoon."

"Oh, we will. I have a special night planned." Beth beamed, with a twinkle in her eye.

Chapter 50

"The Honeymoon"

Alone for the first time in history, the couple traveled the road to Mrs. Knutson's empty and quiet house. The wagon rocked back and forth from the wheels hitting every bump on the rocky path.

Beth and Daniel swayed to the flow with their backside warmed by the setting sun. The lucent rays cast the longest shadows of the year onto the terrain right in front of them. The enslaved dancing shade figures ushered their way down the trail lined with tall ceremonious pines. Their fallen needles blanketed the ground, no longer a dark, lush green. Now the dead refuse was a drab, dull brown.

However, the maple trees in their prime made up for it. With every gust of wind came an abundant color of crimson, yellow, and orange spinning through the air like snowflakes. They settled on top of the pine needles complementing their natural tones.

Beth, so caught up in the beauty of the season, didn't hear Daniel speaking.

"Hello? Are you ignoring me?"

"Oh, I'm sorry, what'd you say?"

"I said, I think you're madly in love with me. Am I right?"

"Yes, I think you're right, and you know what else I think?

These oxen have been to Mrs. Knutson's house uncountable times before. So I say we put them on autopilot, jump into the back and get under the blanket."

Daniel smiled and turned to check if he'd thrown the blanket into the cart. His eyes caught the bag Beth packed. "The overnight bag looks small. What clothes did you pack for us?"

"Not much, clean underwear and clothes for tomorrow. That's about it."

"What bedclothes did you bring?" Daniel sounded panicky.

"Bedclothes? What do we need those for?" Beth laughed, thinking he must be joshing.

"You brought no bedclothes?" Daniel yanked on the reigns, and the oxen halted. Daniel turned to Beth, "What're we going to sleep in?"

"Nothing silly, haven't you slept naked before?"

"No, I haven't."

"Well, what about when you and Kristine slept together?"

"Kristine always slept in her nightgown, and I slept in my bed shirt and long johns."

"Even on your wedding night?"

Daniel flicked the reigns giving the oxen the go-ahead, "Kristine came from a very modest and strict upbringing. I never saw her naked. She didn't deem it proper, so I respected her feelings."

"But what about when you made love?"

"She believed sex was only for conceiving a child and the private areas were for baby rearing, which meant no touchy-touchy." Daniel paused a moment, and with a twinkle in his eye, he muttered, "I was always envious of those babies."

"Are you telling me you two made love only three times?"

"No, of course not, she would indulge me from time to time."

"Indulge you?"

"I don't know how lenient people are in the future, but remember you are in the mid-eighteen-hundreds now."

"I don't think the vast amount of years makes that much difference. All I'm saying is it sounds like neither of us had decent sex lives. So I see this as an awesome opportunity to make our lovemaking whatever we want it to be."

"I guess I'm a little nervous I won't satisfy you."

Beth's mouth dropped open. She could not believe the insecurity of this man. She realized they should have had this conversation ahead of time. Beth put her hand up and shouted, "Stop the oxen."

Daniel halted the animals and turned to her, "What's the matter?"

Beth readjusted her body to face Daniel and cupped his face in her hands, "Let's put away the fear and replace it with desire. Let's do whatever we want. Make our best fantasies come true. I want to feel your naked body against mine. It's a beautiful thing between two people in love. I won't be shy if you're not."

Daniel gave the oxen their go-ahead flick and grinning, he said under his breath, "I wasn't the shy one."

The sun was set by the time they arrived. The oxen knew where to go and when to stop at the hitching post. Daniel jumped off the cart, tossed the rope around a pole and went to his wife's side to assist her. As Beth lifted her dress to step off the cart, Daniel got another look at her sexy high-heels. He didn't know what it was about them. But they put tingles in his stomach and desire in places which he wasn't prepared for yet. *Think of something else. Our horse, it needs a name, maybe Tim, no it's a mare -*

"Are you okay, Daniel?"

Daniel mumbled something under his breath about the damn horse and pulled the bag out of the cart, thankful for the distraction.

They made their way through the path leading to the

humble abode and Daniel set the bag down. He unlocked the door, swung it open and tossed the sack into the room. Daniel turned, scooped up his bride and stepped over the threshold kicking the door shut. Still holding her in his arms, he kissed her. Her lips were soft and warm, and he wanted a lot more of them. But it led to an early arousal again. Daniel set her down and slowed down the swelling desire by starting a conversation. "Do you know why I carried you through the door?"

"All I know is it's a tradition."

Daniel smiled and took hold of her hands, "In this era, a woman deems it improper to have any interest in the wedding night procedure. In fact, she fights upon entering her husband's home. So he picks her up and carries her over the threshold."

Beth opened her mouth to speak, but Daniel started up again. "However, another belief is, if the young woman appears to be too eager to consummate her marriage, it is the husband's job to get her in the house before anybody gets suspicious. So the guy picks her up and carries her through the doorway to save face."

"That would be me. It's taking everything I can muster not to jump your bones."

"Well, don't forget what you said on the way here. We can do whatever we desire. So please…" Daniel held both his arms out, "Don't let me hold you back."

Beth rubbed her body against him and seductively whispered in his ear, "Let's get the lamps lit."

Daniel threw his hands up in the air. "Okay, have it your way, sooner or later though you'll have to jump my bones."

With her butane lighter, Beth lit the kerosene lamps dimming each one. Next, she grabbed the Rhinestone bag and took out everything needed to provide them with music.

In the meantime, Daniel got a red-hot blaze going in the

fireplace and rearranged the furniture. Tomorrow he would return it to its place. For now, they needed a dance floor.

Once the tasks were done, Daniel took Beth's hand. "Come on. Let's go see the guest room." Daniel led the tour through the house, which was three times the size of theirs.

When they came to the open door of their room, Beth peeked inside and her hand flew to her mouth as she gasped. Mrs. Knutson went through a lot of trouble to prepare the room. Daniel, right behind her, saw it too and grinned shaking his head in disbelief.

A beautiful multi-wine colored quilt covered the Victorian mahogany full-size bed. Rose petals covered the top and a path - made up of red scattered pedals - disappeared around an alcove. Daniel and Beth followed the trail like a scavenger hunt. Glimpsing around the corner, their faces lit up.

Two glasses and a bottle of wine sat on a mahogany bistro table. Daniel read the wine's label and raised his brows, "This is expensive stuff." A small box was next to it. After opening it, he held it up, "Chocolate." Next, he picked up a jar, and unsure of what it contained, he held it up to the light and guessed, "I think this may be honey."

Beth picked up a jaw she was sure was oysters. Scrunching her brows she wondered, *why would Mrs. Knutson put out such an odd combination of hors-d'oeuvres?* It didn't take long before she figured it out, "Duh, everything on this table is an aphrodisiac."

"What's an aphrodisiac?"

Beth knew Daniel wouldn't need these. She pushed her body against him and ran her hand over his chest, "It's something that stimulates you sexually. It gives you desire."

Daniel laughed and put his hand up, "Get that stuff away from me. Don't make me have to think of horse's names again."

"What are you talking about?"

"Never mind, let's get back to the fire. I got the wine, you grab the glasses. Oh - and get the chocolate."

Daniel spotted a spare blanket at the end of the bed. He grabbed that too. Once in the sitting room, they laid it out in front of the fireplace and got down on their bellies propping themselves up on their elbows. The warmth coming from the subdued, glowing orange embers felt good on their faces.

They kissed, talked, laughed, ate chocolates and drank wine.

Daniel had to laugh when Beth's words began to slur. "Baby, this wine is stronger than the moonshine Mrs. Knutson makes. Slow down or I'll have my way with you once you're passed out."

Beth laughed and leaned into Daniel, "Oh…is that one of your fantasies? I can pretend to pass out."

"I'll keep that in mind. Right now I feel like dancing. Do you have any waltz music?"

Beth wasted no time jumping up and starting the song, *May I Have This Dance*, a great Waltz by Anne Murray.

Daniel got to his feet, pulled Beth to him and placed her in the dance position. He attempted to lead her around the room, but Beth stumbled almost causing both to fall. Starting from the beginning, she stumbled again, and again, and again.

Frustrated, Beth restarted the song and when in Daniel's arms, she struggled to get the straightforward three-beat measure. There seemed to be a block in her brain keeping her from flowing with this particular rhythm.

"You're concentrating too hard, just move to the beat." Placing her in waltz position again, Daniel counted to the waltz beat out loud, "One, two, three, one, two, three, one, two, three."

"I got it, I got it." Again, her foot got in the way, almost making her fall back. She laughed at her clumsiness, "I don't have it, I don't have it."

"I don't understand. You're such a good dancer. You danced all day at the house. I don't know why you can't get this?"

"It's the three-beat measure. I have to concentrate to dance to it. To most music, I feel the beat, and I just move."

"Do you want to give up on the waltz?"

"Me? Give up? Hell no."

"Do you have a different waltz song? I think we used this one up."

Beth went to her music player and picked the song *Waltz across Texas*, an oldie by Ernest Tubb.

When the song played, Daniel took Beth's arm and lined her up once again. Beth moved like she had two left feet. At one point, after almost breaking her ankle, she cracked up laughing.

"Are you ready to give up now? Daniel couldn't stop from laughing himself.

"No, if I don't get it, at least I think the laughing is therapeutic. Let's try again. I can't be that stupid."

"Okay, come here." Daniel put her back into position and counted. The song ended and the waltz *Are you Lonesome Tonight* by Al Martino started. He wrapped his arm tighter around Beth's waist and pulled her closer. He whispered into her ear, almost like he breathed the words rather than speaking them, "One, two, three, one, two, three..."

With each count, Daniel maneuvered her thigh between his. While keeping the pressure on her leg, he could guide her around the room like a rudder guiding a ship.

No man had ever done this before. She found it quite libidinous and instantly she could follow him. "I like this, why didn't you do this earlier?"

"Because it gets me too turned on, and I'm tired of thinking of horse names."

"What's with you and the horse?"

Daniel whispered in her ear. "Never mind, just dance."

Soon they were flowing around the room like pros. When the song changed to *You are so Beautiful*, by Joe Cocker, the traditional slow dancing took over. Now their dancing became foreplay. Daniel brushed his hands down Beth's waist to the small of her back. Getting brave, he moved them further until they settled on her buttocks. "Hmm, so this is what it feels like...nice."

"Why don't you unzip my dress? You can feel the real thing."

Daniel wasted no time. He unzipped the garment and slipped in both hands, caressing her skin with his fingertips. Her softness amazed him. She felt like smooth velvet. Running his hand down the curves of her waist, he went for her panties and was surprised to find how tiny they were. Desire swelled up in him *it's too soon. Change your thoughts. Dang horse name... Martha, Marie, nope.*

Beth slipped his vest off and tossed it onto a chair. Daniel knew it was a losing battle when she unbuttoned his shirt. His hands went back to her behind. This time he slipped his hands underneath the panties and pulled her against his erection. Bending over, he put his mouth full over hers and waited for the sensuous tongue moves. And then it happened. Beth slipped her tongue in and grazed his outer lips with the tip. For the first time, Daniel slid his tongue into her mouth and mimicked her moves. Soon their tongues entangled one another's as they learned a whole new way of making love.

He bent over and kissed her neck from one side to the other. Slipping the dress over her shoulder, Daniel let it fall to one side. He smothered her shoulder with kisses. When Beth pressed her body against him, Daniel let out a moan. *It's too soon. Concentrate, Ingrid? Mary?*

The music stopped, and so did Daniel's crazy horse name thoughts. However, the groans, fondling, and grinding didn't. Their heavy breathing and moans were the only sounds echoing throughout the house. The passion escalated to where

Daniel gave in to his desire because the erection he had wasn't going anywhere. And if that wasn't enough, Beth began to unzip his pants.

Beth whispered, "Let's continue this in the bedroom, I'll grab the wine and glasses and meet you in there.

Daniel's eyes got huge as he watched Beth step out of her dress. She wore some bad-ass underwear and those sexy heels that drove him crazy.

He raced to the bedroom removing his shirt on the way. He yanked off his pants, jumped into bed, and pulled the blankets up to his waist. Under the covers, Daniel wiggled out of his undergarment and threw it on the floor. He propped himself up against the headboard and waited. He pulled the blankets out and peered underneath, and once again. His manhood stood straight up. *That didn't take long.* He shook his head at his lack of control.

Beth emerged through the door wearing the white lace bra, the soft nylon panties, and those high-heels. Several seconds went by before he realized he was gawking.

Beth raised her brows and said, "You better be naked under those blankets."

"You come over here and find out. Do me a favor and keep those shoes on for a while."

Beth purred, "Oh, so you are kinky."

Daniel couldn't take his eyes off of her. The glow from the lamps made her hair look like long strands of liquid gold flowing down around her shoulders. Her blue topaz eyes seemed to ignite with a "glow in the dark," kind of glow. The dark bronze hue of her arms and shoulder made her skin glistened in the dim light making every muscle stand out.

Daniel leaned up on his elbow watching her. As soon she got to the bed he grabbed her by the hip, pulled her up and put her flat on her back. He propped himself up again and ravished her with his eyes.

"Whoa, such a wild man, I love it."

"You haven't seen anything yet, woman." Daniel brushed his lips back and forth on hers as if he were painting them with a brush. He whispered with his mouth on top of hers, "You make me a wild man." Teasing her with his tongue, he did moves he learned from her.

That's all it took for Beth. There was a fire in her belly. She was eager to teach him all kinds of sexual moves. But since they were all new to him, she took it slow. After all, they had the rest of their lives to experiment with one another. Their traditional lovemaking session was short, yet extremely satisfying for both.

Once Daniel's beating heart died down, he turned onto his side. All he could say was, "Wow."

"You weren't so bad yourself." But inside Beth was thinking *you have no idea of how much you will love what I have to teach you.*

Out of the blue, Daniel sat up and declared, "I have a name for our horse."

"A name for the horse? What brought that to your mind?"

"I've been contemplating on it for some time now."

"So, what's our horse's name going to be?"

"Her name will be *Desire.*"

"I like it. I don't know how you came up with it, but I like it."

"Good, then it's settled. Now, what'd you say we take a glass of wine and observe the full moon?"

"Good idea. At least we can tell the kids we saw it."

Daniel sat up at the edge of the bed and turned to Beth, "What are we supposed to wear since we have no bedclothes?"

"You grab the blanket, and I'll grab the sheet." Beth pulled the spread off the bed and handed it to Daniel. She wrapped herself in the sheet and they wobbled in their makeshift robes to the outdoors.

A flashlight wasn't needed. It was a clear star-filled night and the full moon's light was sufficient.

Daniel led Beth to the log bench overlooking the creek. He

wrapped his arm around her and focused on the silk maroon covering wrapping her body. He couldn't keep from grinning, "Have I ever told you how beautiful you look in a sheet? It kind of shimmers with the moon's light. Kind of makes you look like Royalty."

Beth held up her arm and demanded, "Where's my scepter?" Shifting her weight, she checked out Daniel's bulky bedspread and cracked up, "We both could've fit in your blanket."

Daniel unwrapped his covering, "Drop your sheet and come on in."

"I just might do th…"

They jumped when between them and the house, the sky lit up from the familiar flash of the Scorpion. Daniel and Beth hopped to their feet wrapping their blankets tighter.

The door to the machine opened, and a person stepped out.

The light from the moon was enough for Beth to see something wasn't right. She groaned, "Oh shit, that's not Russ."

"This would be a good time to be wearing bedclothes," Daniel groaned.

A young male stepped out of the Scorpion, held up his hand and shouted, "Don't be afraid. My name is Henry Knutson."

Beth and Daniel's mouths dropped open and they turned to one another, "Henry? Mrs. Knutson's, Henry?"

Chapter 51

Daniel and Beth must have appeared to be suspicious of Henry, but they weren't. They were, however, surprised about the young Henry showing up outside of the barn. About anything could happen these days. So they knew they should get used to the Scorpion showing up at any given moment in any given place.

Henry stayed next to the machine. Still holding his hand up, he asked, "Are you Daniel and Beth?"

Beth rolled her eyes, "Of course he's here to see us. Can things get any weirder?"

Daniel stepped forward, "I'm Daniel, and this is my wife, Beth."

"Beth, I know your brother Russ and his girlfriend, Zena. They came to me for help. Look…" Henry dug into his pocket and pulled out Mrs. Knutson's pocket-watch and held it up. "This is the watch my future wife gave to Russ."

Beth's heart skipped a beat. She wasn't expecting anything to happen so soon. "Were you able to help Russ?"

"Yes, we may have the aging issue solved. You'll see him and Zena soon. Since you just got married, they wanted to give you some time before bombarding you."

Daniel walked over to Henry and shook his hand. "Please come inside. Give us a minute to get dressed, and we'll sit and talk."

Beth and Daniel threw on the clothes Beth had packed for the following day. Afterward, Beth went into the other room and grabbed the wine and an extra cup.

Daniel found Henry roaming around the private living area, and Henry asked if they could talk in there. Daniel told him it would be okay and got a fire started.

Beth came in with the wine and poured them each a glass. She carried Henry's to him, but he was preoccupied with admiring his future wife's décor.

Daniel took his glass and sat down on the couch while Henry strolled around the chamber, observing everything.

Beth sat next to Daniel watching Henry. He looked young, *maybe in his mid-twenties.* The man appeared fit even though he was on the thin side, but his broad shoulders made up for it.

A mop of dark, almost black hair parted down the middle and was tucked behind his ears. It wasn't quite long enough for a ponytail. Some haphazard strands of straying hairs fell over his thick, defined eyebrows which brought attention to his dark auburn eyes.

A drawing on the mantel caught Henry's eye and he zoomed in on it. He took it off the shelf and concentrated on it. Facing Beth, he said, "This is me and Anita."

Beth raised her brows, "You and who?"

Daniel answered her, "That's Mrs. Knutson's first name."

Henry, grinning now, handed the picture to Beth, "This is my future wife. Isn't she beautiful?"

Beth and Daniel examined the drawing - it resembled the image of the man standing there now. And Henry proved to be right. Mrs. Knutson, Anita, was a real knockout.

Beth handed the picture to Henry along with the glass of wine, "So, why are you here now? You said you helped Russ and Zena?"

Henry took the picture and the glass and sat on the worn-out chair, "Russ and I worked together for ten months. We worked on the aging issue, plus we figured out how to make traveling to precise dates and times possible."

"That's awesome. Where did they stay for ten months?" Beth moved to the edge of her chair.

"They stayed with me. We kept the time machine locked up in a vehicle on my property. We can take the Scorpion anywhere now which is how I ended up here at Anita's. Russ will give you all the details when you see him."

This whole scenario felt weird - Beth had seen Russ earlier that day and yet - he had already lived another ten months or more. It was like when she traveled to the future the last time. She spent over ten hours at Russ' home, but to the girls, it had been not even fifteen minutes.

"Zena and Russ also acquired a plentiful supply of nanorobots, so Russ' in good shape, no more cancer." Henry took a sip of his wine.

Beth let out a sigh of relief, "Henry, can I ask you a personal question?"

Henry gave Beth his attention.

"Since you have proven time travel is safe, are you going to stay on with Russ and Zena? I mean, you know if you go into the wormhole, you'll be trapped in the past for the rest of your life?"

"Kind of like you, Beth?"

"I'm not stuck in the past. I chose to stay."

"Exactly, I don't want to sound like some lovesick poet, but you found true love, as Zena and Russ did. I haven't found mine yet. Russ told me according to Anita, we had a magical marriage. I don't want to change a thing. I'm going through the wormhole, and I'm going to meet and marry this fantastic woman." Henry's looked back down at the picture.

"You won't regret your decision," said Daniel.

"Thank you, I have an important matter to bring up. Russ

informed me of the two up-coming wars and how you're preparing for them. Anita's brother lives in St. Paul, did she ever speak of him?"

Daniel's brows furrowed, "No, I didn't know she had a brother."

Henry reached into his jacket pocket and pulled out a paper. "Her brother, John and his two grandsons are well-known carpenters. They're famous for building Victorian style homes. They've designed and built many beautiful houses for the elite."

"What does any of this have to do with Anita?" Daniel asked.

"The boys are fifteen and sixteen. They're as renowned as their grandfather for their carpenter skills.

Beth cut in, "Where's the boy's father?"

"He passed away years ago. John took in the boys and raised them. Unfortunately, John's going to die in a few months of a heart attack and his life's savings will get depleted.

All I can find on those two boys is the obituary of one of them, the sixteen-year-old. He faked his age and died in the Civil War. Apparently, no one took in the boys because the money was gone."

Beth put up her hand, "What does this have to do with us?"

"According to my research, these boys were hard workers and took pride in everything they did. It's a shame there was no one to catch them when their world fell out beneath them."

Henry stood up and gave the paper to Daniel. "Here is John's name and address. Maybe you can get Anita to look into this. It'll give you a chance to get to know them. When the time comes, you'd be wise to take these two into your household.

From everything Russ told me, you'll need manpower for cutting down a forest. I've been to Russ' house, Beth. It looks like many of the homes they built. That's how good they are. Even if you don't want them to help build you a house, they'll be a big help with clearing land and shearing sheep. Plus, you'll give two young men a new chance at life."

You've been to Russ' house?" asked Beth.

"Yes, we did quite a bit of experimenting. Although we're more cautious about mingling with the inhabitants then we were in the beginning. It causes quite a commotion when people get two memories."

Beth laughed and looked at Daniel saying, "Yeah, we know all about that."

Daniel stood up and ran his hand through his hair, "We'll speak to Anita about it tomorrow. If she's willing, we'll go and meet the boys."

"That's all I ask." Henry stood and the frame holding the drawing slipped off his lap. The glass broke as it hit the floor. "Oh no, I'm so sorry."

Beth picked the frame up and plucked out the broken glass. "I'm sure your future wife won't be mad at you." Beth pulled the paper out of the frame and gasped, "What is this? Oh, my goodness, under the drawing is a real photograph of you and Anita. It looks like a Polaroid."

Henry took it from her, stared at it and grinned. Anita was more beautiful in the actual image. Henry looked closer and what he noticed now, more than anything else, was the look of satisfaction on his own face. Beaming he said, "This was taken with my camera. I guess I better pack it for my travels. By the way, why don't you two keep one of the time machines here? You can use it to travel."

Beth wasted no time responding, "No, we want to keep our lives as normal as possible."

Henry laughed, "The way I see it, there won't be anything normal about your lives."

Daniel stood up, "You can say that again."

"Oh, one more thing before I leave, Beth. Russ cashed in your portion of the inheritance. It became his at your supposed death. He's getting it converted to money you can use here. You two are going to be quite wealthy."

Henry drank the rest of his wine and set the glass down, "Well, I best get going so you two can continue on your honeymoon."

Henry shook Daniel's hand, "I won't be back. Tomorrow I'm due at the Time Travel Research Facility. I'll be there until they send me through the wormhole."

Henry reached into his pocket and pulled out the pocket-watch and handed it to Daniel, "Will you give this back to Anita? Tell her I'll meet her soon, and I can't wait. You two stay strong. You have a very challenging road ahead of you."

After Henry left, Daniel grinned and slipped his hand around Beth's waist, "What'd you say we work on making a baby?"

Beth giggled, "You men are all the same. It doesn't matter what century it is."

"And don't you forget it, woman." Daniel laughed, and scooping up his bride he headed for the threshold.

Beth locked her arms around her husband's neck. She glanced back, one last time, to the spot where the Scorpion disappeared. With a sly, half smile on her face, she shook her head and thought *so... the Saga continues.*

Lightning Source UK Ltd.
Milton Keynes UK
UKOW01f0653060218
317434UK00001B/1/P